His shoulders are s   is temples. He picks u know what Monday is,

"I've been dreading … turns away. She has the glint of fear etched in her eyes. The blue has turned to mud.

I wait for somebody to say something.

Nobody does.

I wait a couple of minutes more.

It seems longer. Nothing but silence.

Rebecca and Mister Holland are lost in their own little worlds.

"What's Monday?" I finally ask.

"May Twenty Third."

"God, help us," whispers Rebecca.

I barely hear her. "What happens on May Twenty Third?

Mister Holland turns slowly around. His face is pale. His eyes are pools of water. His hands are trembling. He drops the calendar on the floor.

"Somebody dies every May Twenty Third," he says.

"Somebody dies somewhere every day."

"The last one was Judge Amos Fitzsimmons. Drowned in the baptismal tank down at the First Baptist Church," Rebecca says. "And the one before the judge was caught on the fifty-yard line of the high school football field and shot point blank with a shotgun in the back of the head. Hardly found enough of his skull to bury."

"Here in Magnolia Bluff?"

"Every year for the last eight years." Rebecca has a tear in her voice.

Mister Holland stands and walks slowly to the front door. He watches the rain a moment, then says. "We know there's a funeral coming," he says. "We just don't know who'll be lying in the casket."

ISBN 978-1-63789-784-3

For information address Crossroad Press at 141 Brayden Dr., Hertford, NC 27944
A Gordian Knot Book. Gordian Knot is an imprint of Crossroad Press.
www.crossroadpress.com

First Edition

# EULOGY IN BLACK AND WHITE

THE MAGNOLIA BLUFF CRIME NOVELS BOOK 2

BY CALEB PIRTLE III

# DEDICATED

To the most talented group of authors and mystery writers I've ever known: Linda Pirtle, Roxanne Burkey, Charles Breakfield, CW Hawes, James R. Callan, Kelly Marshall, Cindy Davis, Richard Schwindt, and Jinx Schwartz. Once upon a time, they all took a chance on living for a while in a mythical little Texas town known as Magnolia Bluff. You'll be surprised to find out what deadly secrets are hidden away in places where you'd never expect them to be. Magnolia Bluff is a wonderful Hill Country town to visit for a spell. But I don't think you'd want to stay around for very long. Strange things go on in Magnolia Bluff.

# 1

**Wednesday**
**7:14 a.m.**

It has been eighteen years, six months, and fourteen days since Harley Spooner died. Just fell dead not six feet away from me. Boots up. Eyes open. A look of curiosity etched on his face. Gone, and I could tell by the look in his eyes he knew he was going. Couldn't stop it. Like falling off a cliff. Once you fall, you can't go back.

There he was, walking down a narrow trail in the mountains on a foggy morning much like the one that lies as if it's a gray cotton shawl just above the downtown streetlights of Magnolia Bluff. Clear in the South. Clear in the West. Rain dripping from a dark cloud that sits perched atop the gold plaster crest of the courthouse.

I wait for the thunder. I hear only the rain rattling against the dark red tin awning that reaches out over the front door of the First National Bank.

The thunder has taken another road to another town and left us with a chilled drizzle on an uncomfortable May morning, and the bitter sting of a harsh wind whipping across the San Saba River works its way into my bones. I know immediately it will take the taste of a long, hot, summer and a tall, skinny glass of Texas Blue Corn bourbon to chase away the frostbite in my blood.

Harley had been laughing softly and whispering to himself that morning. He was in front of me, so I couldn't hear what he was saying, but I saw his shoulders shaking, and I knew Harley was telling himself another one of those jokes he made up as he walked along because he couldn't remember any of those we told while sitting around in each other's shade, the sun a burnt orange, and the beer as hot as the hard rock candy mountains around us. He had a million of them. Most had to do with home, and, Lord, how he wanted to go home.

Small place, he said.

Mostly off the grid.

Might stop a while if you're driving through.

No stranger ever came on purpose.

Fishermen did.

But they weren't strangers, not after they bought bait and a cold Bud Light.

Quiet town, he said.

Not much ever happened.

But when it did, he said, God didn't have mercy on anybody's soul.

Harley had stopped at a trailhead beside a bluff where we could look down the mountain for a long way, and even then our eyes couldn't touch bottom. He looked over his shoulder and whispered, "I'm gonna be a millionaire."

"Another one of your crooked schemes?

Neither of us dared speak aloud.

"I've invented the perfect rabbit call," he said.

"How's it work?"

"It sounds like lettuce."

The laughter lodged in his throat.

He fell at my feet.

A bullet hole just below his larynx looked as big as a silver dollar.

I reached down to stop the flow of blood.

He was choking, clawing at his throat.

I heard Harley say, "I need him now."

"Who?"

"Jesus."

Tears had paled the blue in his eyes.

He left me before Jesus arrived.

And all hell broke loose.

Gunsmoke was as thick as the fog.

Thunder.

Lightning.

The sounds of war.

The ground shook beneath my feet.

Eighteen years, six months, and fourteen days ago, Harley Spooner died.

It seems like yesterday.

I walk across the street to Flo's Flower Shop, wedged crookedly between a back alley and Barron Schiff's Funeral Home and Wedding Chapel. The glazed white jar is waiting for me. I knew it would be. Florence never forgets. I pick up the wildflowers – a handful of pink, yellow, and purple blooms – and leave the jar lying in a window box overflowing with some kind of ivy and sweet potato vine. I know about the ivy and vine because Florence told me about them. I have no idea what the flowers are that she left this morning. But they are bright and colorful and can light up a dreary day no matter how dark or gray it is or becomes. Florence never charges me for the flowers. Says she gets them free. Probably picks them out of her garden or on the side of the road coming into town. I roll up a dollar bill, just as I do every morning, and stuff it into the jar. Tip money. She never mentions it. Neither do I.

I almost bump into Ember Cole at the street corner. She's running, holding a black Saturno hat on her head with one hand and staring down at the pavement to keep the rain sprinkles out of her face. The fog has apparently decided to drip all over Magnolia Bluff. Nobody minds. We had a long dry winter, cold but dry, and if the sky wants to spit on us for a day or two, we appreciate the moisture or anything else that knocks the dust out of the air.

I've tripped over her smile more than once. Ember is long and lean and would look like a tabletop dancer if you took off her full black skirt, but nobody tries, or at least nobody has bragged about it around the back table at the Silver Spoon Café. Everybody's sinning in their own little way, but nobody's confessing. Texas is hot enough, and the rumor is hell's even worse.

Ember is the card-carrying preacher lady who presides over the congregation down at St. Luke's Methodist Church, or maybe it's Saint Andrews or Saint George. Can't remember which one, but I know it's one of those saints. She's been chased but remains chaste as far as I know. She's sweet and perky and cute as a button. But she and I don't see eye to eye on a lot of things, most notably religion. She thinks I may be a sinner. I think she may be right. But she hasn't caught me doing anything dastardly yet.

I hurriedly step back.

She almost stumbles.

I would grab her arm and help her regain her balance.

But she's a preacher lady.

I'm not sure that's allowed.

Her eyes open wide.

I've been told they're green, the color of burnished jade.

But I'm color blind.

Her eyes could be the color of molten asphalt for all I know.

"Sorry," I tell her.

It sounds lame.

It is.

She drops her umbrella and waits like a lady for me to pick it up.

I don't disappoint her.

She's laughing now. "That's all right." Ember looks down at the flowers I'm clutching. They're still fresh. They won't wilt until tomorrow. "On your way to see your friend again?" she asks.

I nod.

"Even in the rain?"

"Especially in the rain."

"He's lucky," she says.

"Why would you say that?"

"Not everyone has such a loyal friend."

"Don't have many," I say. I force a smile. I know it's crooked, but she doesn't seem to notice. "Don't want to lose the ones I have."

"You have a lot of friends in town." The rain is a steady drizzle in our faces.

"A lot of people know my name." I shrug. "I know most of their names. That's all."

Ember folds her arms across her chest and blinks the rain out of her eyes. "Then what would you call a friend?"

I think about her question a moment, then answer slowly and methodically, "If I had a bad heart and was stuck up in the hospital waiting to die. And if you had a perfectly good heart and knew I needed a heart transplant, would you give me your heart?"

I pause.

She stares at me blankly.

"But that means I would die," she says.

"But you would give life."

"That's not a fair question," she says.

"A friend doesn't hesitate." I'm hoarse now, my voice as soft as a whisper. "A friend values someone else's life more than his own." I wait a moment while she mulls over my words. "And if I was a real friend," I say, carefully choosing my words, "I would refuse the heart. Your life is far more important than mine."

"So who wins?" she wants to know.

"We both lose." I wipe the rain out of my eyes. "I die and you feel guilty for the rest of your life. If you forget me, you were never a friend in the first place."

"Were you a philosophy major?" she asks.

"I had a real friend once."

Ember pulls her umbrella down a little closer to her face. Her eyes are hidden now. "I think you're skating on the thin edge of insanity," she says.

"You're kind." I wink. "Most think I've already fallen off on the wrong side."

She studies my face.

I wink again.

I wait for her to raise the umbrella slightly and wink back.

She doesn't.

Instead, Ember gestures across the street toward the Really Good Wood-Fired Coffee Shop. She knows she can't reason with a fool. She stops trying. She moves on to pity instead. "Chilly morning," she says. "Wet morning. Cup of good coffee might warm you up."

I shake my head. "Thanks," I tell her, "but Harry's coffee is a little rich for my blood."

"I'm buying."

"Not today you aren't."

"It's the best coffee anywhere in fourteen counties." She shrugs. "Especially the Chocolate Mint Frappuccino with whipped cream and a cherry on top."

Such a comment from most women would sound downright seductive. Ember makes it sound like coffee. Nothing more.

"My daddy wouldn't let me do a thing like that," I say.

She raises her eyebrows. "Let me buy your coffee?"

"Said it's a mortal sin to pay four dollars and thirty-two cents for two bits worth of second-hand coffee beans."

Her laughter is musical. On key, but I don't know which key. I'm as tone deaf as I am color blind.

I stand and watch her run across the street. I've been out in the rain since sunup, so the chilled drizzle no longer bothers me. Shirt merely feels like I've been working up a good sweat. I know she won't turn around and look back at me, but I give her the chance anyway. She's through the door. It closes. And I can't prove she exists either in or out of the rain.

# 2

**Wednesday**
**7:38 a.m.**

At the corner of Main and East Third, the two-year-old Dodge Charger Pursuit of Sheriff Buck Blanton makes a sudden U-turn, its headlights splintered by the rain. I pull my denim jacket collar tighter around my throat and watch him ease slowly to the curb beside me and stop. The only sounds Magnolia Bluff can manage at four minutes past eight on a soggy morning are distant rumbles of thunder and Buck's windshield wipers slapping back and forth in a lackadaisical effort to shove the spatter of raindrops aside.

The sheriff rolls down his window and pushes his blue-tinted Shady Rays sunglasses up above his thickening gray eyebrows. Buck fits the job description of a country sheriff perfectly. Sunglasses, rain or shine. A thick neck. Broad shoulders. Barrel chest. Sagging jowls. Broad nose, probably broken more than once. Hands big enough to grab a grown man by the throat, jerk him off the floor, and shake him into submission. A gray felt Stetson hat lies in the seat beside him. I can't see his feet, but I know he's wearing his full quill Justin cowboy boots as black as his skin. Wouldn't be caught dead without them. Says he was born in them. Says he will die in them. I don't doubt it for a minute.

"On your way up to see Freddy?" He asks, glancing at the flowers in my hand. The rain has beaten them up pretty good. His voice is deep and mellow, a full octave lower than the thunder.

I nod.

Buck has one facial expression. He grins when he sees you. He grins if he is about to hit you with the hickory club that hangs from his belt. He grins if he's praying over your lost soul at the First Baptist Church. He's grinning when he throws you in jail. He's grinning if he has to shoot you first. I suspect he grins in his sleep.

"Need a lift?"

I shake my head.

"It's a bad day for walking," he says. "You still got a mile or so to go before you reach Freddy."

I shrug. "It's fine," I say. "I'm already wet."

Buck opens the car door. "Get in before I arrest your sorry ass," he says.

I look closely.

His grin has reached his eyes.

I climb into the front passenger seat. "Hate to mess up your upholstery," I tell him.

"Don't matter." The sheriff wheels back down an empty street. "I'll have a couple of drunks in here before the day's out, and they'll be a damn sight wetter than you are." He leans forward and studies the rolling black clouds closing in from the west end of Burnet Reservoir. "That's the trouble with the weather," Buck says. "It rains on the just and the unjust alike."

"Sound like a preacher," I say.

"Tried it once." Buck shrugs. "Didn't like it. Found it's easier to drag the bad guys to jail than drag them to the altar."

His laughter fills the car.

His windshield wipers are working just fine.

His heater isn't.

I don't think he's noticed.

"You and Freddy pretty close?" he asks softly.

I know he's prying for information.

I have it.

He wants it.

I throw him a bone.

"We both went to war."

"Where were you, Huston?"

"Places where I wasn't supposed to be."

"Special forces?"

"Nothing special about it."

"Have any idea what you were fighting for?"

"Thought I did at the time," I say. "Found out I didn't."

Buck nods. "They sent me to Iraq," he says. "Early days. I never figured it out either. Lost a lot of good friends over in those sandhills."

The rain turns the road white. Can't see the ditches on either side. But I know they're running high with rushing water.

"Rain much in Afghanistan?' Buck asks.

"Never saw a drop."

"Freddy never liked the rain." Buck squints through his sunglasses. "Boy never liked to swim. Couldn't stand water in his eyes. I guess he would have liked Afghanistan. Vietnam was a wet place to die."

I think about Freddy. I try to put his name to a face. It doesn't fit. No matter how hard I try, it never does.

The rain has slacked off by the time Buck brakes to a stop beside the front gate. It's big. It's old. It's the color of rust. And it's never locked. The wrought iron gate looks as if it should be standing at the front entrance of a grand manor filled with valuable possessions, and maybe it is.

I step out on the loose gravel driveway. "Thanks, sheriff. Appreciate the lift."

Buck casts his eyes up at the sky again. "I'll be back around in about ten minutes or so," he says. "I can pick you up and carry you back downtown if that gives you enough time."

"Thanks." I am as sincere as I can be. "But I may sit for a while," I tell him. "I can make it back just fine whether it rains or if it doesn't."

The sheriff gives me a two-finger salute, pulls away, and grins his way into the fog. I wait until his taillights fade into the gray mist, then open the gate and walk into the massive live oaks and clustered mesquite thickets of the Magnolia Bluff Cemetery. I'm glad the quiet solemnity of the place has not been ruined by some name like Garden of Rest or Rose Lawn of the Redeemed, although I admit that the Magnolia Bluff Burying

Ground might have been a better choice. It is what it is. Show up. Find a hole. Crawl in. Don't think about leaving.

As always, I wander across mounds of wet leaves that during dry weather would crunch beneath my footsteps. The gnarled oaks are starting to hide their mistletoe with the greenery of a late spring, and the mesquites have been covered with beans all winter. Cattle eat them. Tree huggers say they may be the next gluten-free superfood, but, frankly, I've never been quite that hungry. The same folks eat prickly pear cactus, too, as soon as they burn the thorns off. My throat gets scratchy just thinking about it.

My eyes scan across the names of old friends chiseled in slate or stone.

Don't know any of them.

Never met them.

Never danced with the ladies.

Never drank bourbon with the men.

Never gone with them to marry off a daughter or tree a possum.

Wish I had.

Their whole lives have been pared down to three lines.

Name.

Date of birth.

Date of death.

It's not much of a biography.

I always wonder about them, but I never think about them as children, only aging and weary and hanging on for as long as they can until the sands of time spill their last grain. They lay in the darkness and wait for the next breath and wonder for a moment, but only a moment, why it doesn't bother to come.

Did they live beside the creeks that were dammed up to form Burnet Reservoir?

Did they farm?

Raise cattle?

Run horses?

Who did they love, what did they fear, when did their childhoods fade, and why did they choose to battle the hard times of a hard-scrabble land that tempted them and taunted them and tried but never really tamed them.

One thought always strikes me.

We only carry one thing with us when we go.

Our secrets.

I am walking upon a sacred ground of secrets.

One name is lodged in the back of my mind.

Harley Spooner.

Not old enough to vote.

Not old enough to drink.

Old enough to die.

Harley Spooner.

Born February 16, 1985.

Died November 25, 2004.

Who could fill in the blanks?

Nobody.

I tried.

I tried to recall every word, every story he had ever told me.

Had a momma.

Had a home.

Had a sweetheart.

Had a broken heart.

Had a dream.

Wanted to run horses.

Wanted to run fast horses.

Wanted to be a high-dollar man.

*But there he was, walking down a narrow trail in the mountains on a foggy morning much like the one that lies like a gray cotton shawl just above the downtown streetlights of Magnolia Bluff. stopped at a trailhead beside a bluff where we could look down the mountain for a long way, and even then our eyes couldn't touch bottom. He looked over his shoulder and whispered, "I'm gonna be a millionaire." The laughter lodged in his throat. He fell at my feet. A bullet hole in his larynx looked as big as a silver dollar.*

I never heard the sound that killed him.

I only heard the sound of him dying.

Crying for Jesus. That's what he was doing.

I held his hand and waited with Harley for Jesus.

Didn't see him.

But I'm pretty sure Jesus came.

Harley was smiling when he felt the last beat of his heart.

I didn't know Harley long. But I would remember him forever.

I walk to the back of the cemetery on the far side of the hill. One grave is a lonely grave. No one else around. The headstone is smaller. White with a cross. The rain has washed the dirt away from the cross.

When the days are dry and crisp, just beyond the fence, I can see a world peaceful and quiet with reverence. A whisper of wind ruffles in my ears. Gentle waves follow the wind to the banks of the reservoir.

Sometimes, sails are reaching for the winds as small boats wander lost between one cove and the next. It's a world in miniature. It could fit in the palm of my hand. And from where I stand, nothing can dim the beauty nor disrupt the grace and dignity of a valley where chaos is a stranger and madness has gone elsewhere.

I kneel down beside the headstone where the Army has carved the name of PFC Freddy Millstone. He's been there a while. Mostly alone. Soldier went to Vietnam. Casket came home.

I place the flowers on the grave.

I say a prayer for Freddy.

He's not Harley Spooner.

But, on an unusually cold and foggy morning in May – eighteen years, six months, and fourteen days later – with rain on my face and the sound of thunder beating like a broken drum across the river, Freddy's as close as I can get.

# 3

**Wednesday**
**9:22 a.m.**

The newsroom of the *Magnolia Bluff Chronicle* smells like ink and paper. This morning's ink. Last week's paper. Some swear all news smells, and I won't argue with them. Everybody wants the truth. Very few are willing to tell it. And those who do are generally run out of town. Let's all live a lie, and none of us will get stung. Let a poor boy go to jail, and it's front-page news. Let an advertiser have a closed-door meeting with the judge, and the report of his indiscretions wind up in the trash, burned and the ashes scattered somewhere in the next county. A man may bury his conscience, but it will always come back to haunt him. I know. I live with the ghosts.

Nobody, with the exception of Rebecca Wilson, bothers to look up when I walk through the door. She's tall. She's a brunette. She could have walked in from the cover of some magazine, wearing a deep blue dress that looks like silk or satin. Rebecca was probably a cheerleader and quite possibly the Homecoming Queen a few years back. She was definitely a heartbreaker but stayed around while most of her classmates left town for college or better-paying jobs, and then she looked up one morning and realized there were no hearts left in Magnolia Bluff to break. I'd be willing to let her break mine, but I'm not sure my heart made the trip back from Afghanistan when I did. I'd at least appreciate Rebecca looking for it, but what would either one of us do if she found it? She wouldn't want it, and I'd just throw it away again.

Rebecca is the receptionist, the society editor, and the head of advertising sales. Want your daughter's wedding picture on the front page? Buy an ad. Want a photograph of your grandchild's graduation tucked prominently in the newspaper and above the fold? Buy an ad. Want Rebecca to throw away the cell phone shots of you dancing naked at a biker's bar in Austin? Buy an ad. Rebecca Wilson is a top-of-the-line sales lady. She makes more money than the publisher and deserves every cent she can stuff into the bank. She knows who's having a shotgun wedding, who's getting divorced, who's involved in which extracurricular activity at the high school, which preacher has given up booze for smack, who's pregnant, and who the real father is.

Rebecca winks, and her smile can light up a dismal room. She's not flirting. It's her way of saying hello without breaking the cold, deadly, morning silence of a newspaper office that has all the personality of a funeral parlor.

"Lose your umbrella?" she asks quietly.

"Didn't think it was supposed to rain."

Her laughter sounds like the black keys on a piano. "Where'd you get that idea?"

"Read it in the newspaper somewhere."

Neal Holland grunts loudly. He's the owner, publisher, editor, and guiding genius behind the *Chronicle.* He's bent over the twenty-four-inch screen of his ink-stained iMac Pro, either writing the news or making it up as he goes. I'm told he's good at both.

"Sounds like insubordination to me," he says without looking toward me.

"That's what my Colonel said."

"He shoot you?"

"He tried."

"Close range?"

"From one side of the room to the other."

"That's the reason," Neal says.

"Reason for what?"

"Reason we can't win a damn war." He stops typing long enough to straighten the ragged end of his white mustache. "Damn brass can't shoot straight."

Neal Holland is as close to being a legend as anyone who has ever walked the town square of Magnolia Bluff. He must be in his sixties, but maybe he's older. His very presence can strike fear into the self-appointed power brokers of Burnet County. Mister Holland is a little too short, a little too round, and his face looks like a rock boulder after sparring with a stick of dynamite. His white hair is always in need of a good trim. His white mustache is a little too shaggy. His eyesight is failing. His dark-rimmed glasses are coke bottle thick. But nobody wants to get on the bad side of a small-town editor who loves nothing better than a good fight.

He's dug up dirt on politicians who have wallowed in a lot of dirt, had the chief of police arrested, the district attorney disbarred, and I know at least three members of the city council who always find out before the meeting which way Neal Holland wants them to vote. They may get out-voted from time to time, but none of them is ever crucified in front-page headlines or skinned alive in print. They have learned the golden rule of small-town journalism. Don't ever pick a fight with a man who buys ink by the barrel and will use as much as he needs to soundly whip you as often as he needs on page one.

I'm standing there with floodwaters dripping off my denim jacket. My jeans are soaked. And the toes of my boots are smeared with mud and charcoal. My hair is plastered dark like shoe polish against my head. A puddle is forming around my feet. And nobody cares. I was hired to sweep the floor, mop it when it's wet, push a button on the old Web-Offset Press every Thursday afternoon and Saturday morning to print six thousand, four hundred, and twenty-two newspapers, then clean the presses before I go home each day. Doesn't pay much. But I only work as hard as I want, and Mister Holland pays me enough to eat twice a day at the Silver Spoon Café and rent a place to stay in Nell Walker's three-room boarding house over behind the football field. On most nights, it's quiet. In May, it's so quiet you can hear the mosquitoes mating. But on Friday nights in the autumn, when football is as holy and sanctified as a ladies' prayer meeting at the First Baptist Church, it sounds like an Assembly of God Revival meeting: music, madness, and mayhem.

"You know where the mop is," Mister Holland tells me.

"Pressroom closet."

"Might as well put it to work."

The rain grows louder as it peppers against the building's tin roof. Sounds like a snare drum. I know. I live behind the football field.

The newsroom is about as spare as a room can get. Big plate glass window across the front, looking out on the stone columns of the old rock courthouse, has the name of the newspaper printed in bold white letters with a tagline that says: "The Truth, The Whole Truth, And All The Truth That's Fit To Print, So Help Me God," which is a glorified way of saying: "In this newspaper, you'll find all the news that Neal Holland and his ad-selling assassin believe is fit to print."

The office is no larger than a good-sized bedroom, just big enough for Mister Holland and Rebecca to each have a desk with a third computer perched atop a World War II surplus table in the back corner. It's only used by Thomas Hedrick, owner of the Firestone Tire Store, who writes the game stories about the Magnolia Bluff Bulldog football team on Friday nights. They have not lost a game during the last five years, although time did run out on them twenty-two times.

Hedrick is given forty-two column inches for each game, not counting the statistics, of which there are legion. The Kennedy Assassination had a total of twenty-six column inches, and the 9/11 attack on the Twin Towers scratched out thirty-four column inches. Magnolia Bluff's heart lies in football, not politics, and any story that takes place as far away as twelve miles outside the city limits is considered political and probably a conspiracy theory, not worthy of Neal Holland's trouble.

As I run the mop beside his desk, I can tell the day did not start well, nor will it be ending well. Mister Holland has broken two yellow pencils with his hands and is chewing on a third as if it were a toothpick. His face is red, his eyes narrowed to a stare as sharp as the pointed end of a scalpel. He leans back in his chair, and his gaze moves across the ceiling from one spider web to the next. I offered to sweep the webs away the first week I was on the job, but Mister Holland said no. He likes the spiders. They may be, he says, the only ones in town who truly understand him. Perhaps he's right. He sleeps in the newsroom as often as they do.

Rebecca shoots a frayed rubber band that slaps Mister Holland upside the face. His head jerks around. He's scowling.

"What's wrong, boss," she says.

He waits to see if she is laughing at him.

She isn't.

A deep concern has worked its way into the crystal blue of her eyes.

"Trying to decide the lead article for Thursday's paper," he says, sitting up straight, his elbows on his desk. "We've got the running horse auction out at the barn, and Luis Salas swears he bought himself a Kentucky Derby winner for less than twenty-five thousand dollars. And the city council voted to build a new marina out at the reservoir but looks like we may have to raise property taxes to fund it." He pauses and rubs his eyes. "Can't figure out in my mind which story is the most important to our little town."

"If that's all you got," Rebecca says, crossing her legs as the lace hem of a tight red dress slides up her thighs, "then we might as well forget the newspaper and roll out toilet paper Thursday afternoon. "You know Luis won't ever win the Kentucky Derby. I hear he's selling shares to raise enough money to pay for the horse, and he's only twenty-two thousand dollars short as of yesterday about noon. And this is the fourth time in five years the city council has voted to build a new marina, and none of the little twerps has balls big enough to raise property taxes. They're just spinning loose thread in their yo-yo's."

She waits for Mister Holland to respond.

He doesn't.

His shoulders are sagging. The veins are pulsating in his temples.

He picks up a calendar and turns the page. "You know what Monday is," he says.

"I've been dreading it for months." Rebecca turns away. She has the glint of fear etched in her eyes. The blue has turned to mud.

I wait for somebody to say something.

Nobody does.

I wait a couple of minutes more.

It seems longer.

Nothing but silence.

Rebecca and Mister Holland are lost in their own little worlds.

"What's Monday?" I finally ask.

"May Twenty Third."

"God, help us," whispers Rebecca.

I barely hear her.

"What happens on May Twenty Third?

Mister Holland turns slowly around.

His face is pale.

His eyes are pools of water.

His hands are trembling.

He drops the calendar on the floor.

"Somebody dies every May Twenty Third," he says.

"Somebody dies somewhere every day."

"The last one was Judge Amos Fitzsimmons. Drowned in the baptismal tank down at the First Baptist Church," Rebecca says.

"And the one before the judge was caught on the fifty-yard line of the high school football field and shot point blank with a shotgun in the back of the head. Hardly found enough of his skull to bury."

"Here in Magnolia Bluff?"

"Every year for the last eight years." Rebecca has a tear in her voice.

Mister Holland stands and walks slowly to the front door. He watches the rain a moment, then says. "We know there's a funeral coming," he says. "We just don't know who'll be lying in the casket."

# 4

**Wednesday**
**Noon**

The lunch crowd jams the front of the Silver Spoon Café about the same time the bells atop the courthouse begin chiming straight up noon. The bells are seven minutes late and have been, I'm told, since the storm of 2012 rolled down Main Street, took a sharp left turn at the end of Maple Avenue, and tore into the boats moored out at the reservoir. If the newspaper was correct, the town had experienced an F-2 tornado, but the farmers simply call it the day of the big wind.

Usually, there is a line of customers as far down the street as the Bluff Bakery, but the rain has washed everyone inside, and I walk in behind Rebecca to the sound of plastic raincoats bustling and umbrellas snapping shut. The men, as a rule, wear their umbrellas – straw hats with wide brims – stomping the rain off their boots as soon as they fight their way through the front door.

Rebecca doesn't hesitate. She brushes the hair out of her eyes, waves at Lorraine Dillard, and we are immediately seated in a back booth behind the jukebox, the only corner of the Silver Spoon where the sun has never shone. Lorraine pitches the menus on the table. She's thin, and the wrinkles are deepening under her eyes. Her blonde hair is beginning to show touches of gray. Her crooked smile is infectious. And in the fading light, she's still a right pretty lady.

"Need a minute?" she asks.

"I'll take the special," Rebecca says.

Lorraine raises an eyebrow and points at me. "You want the same?"

"Gravy on the side," I say.

Lorraine winks. "You'll get the gravy the way I bring it," she says.

She shuffles a handful of menus back in place as deftly as a blackjack dealer, shoves them under her arm, and heads toward the kitchen, stopping long enough to touch the arm of every man at every table on her way toward the batwing doors that lead to the grill where Dudley Ray Sanders is flipping burgers and soaking chicken fried steaks in yesterday's grease and this morning's batter.

I look across the table at Rebecca. "You're a magician," I tell her.

"Thanks, I think, but what makes you say that?"

"It's a fifteen-minute wait to get a table in here this time of day," I say, "and you snap your fingers, and a table suddenly appears. We're in here sitting down while everyone else is crammed shoulder to shoulder in a lobby no bigger than a piano bar."

"Lorraine and I have a deal worked out," she says.

"You blackmailing her?"

Rebecca laughs out loud. She's not offended. She likes her reputation.

"Where'd you get that idea?"

I grin. "I hear rumors about the *Chronicle's* society assassin."

Her laugh is throaty and genuine. "You make me sound like I run with the mafia," she says.

"No." I shake my head. "I think you run the mafia."

Rebecca grows serious in a casual, nonchalant kind of way. "My deal with Lorraine is quite simple," she tells me. "She buys a fourteen-column-inch ad every week. I give her twenty column inches to advertise the Silver Spoon. I never wait for a table."

"What does Mister Holland say about that?"

"That's six column inches he doesn't have to fill up with stories about Toby Davidson catching an eighty-six-pound catfish in Shoal Creek, or Agnes Nettles winning first place in the Dahlia Society's weekly flower show, or Betty Bodine heading back to the wedding chapel for the third time in the past five years, this time with the man she broke up with to marry husband number two." She pauses. She winks again. It's a million-dollar wink on a million-dollar woman. "Besides, Neal eats here free every Saturday night."

"Mr. Holland part of your deal with Lorraine?"

"Neal wrote a very touching obituary about Lorraine's husband when he passed."

"So she owns the Silver Spoon."

"Now she does."

"What happened to her husband?"

"Died suddenly."

"Heart attack?"

Rebecca closes her eyes.

The smile fades.

She doesn't look like she'll ever wink again.

The smile may have left town with the wink.

Silence.

George Strait finishes singing "Amarillo by Morning" on the jukebox.

The music stops.

It seems as if everything in the Silver Spoon has stopped.

"Hank Dillard," Rebecca says, "was victim number four."

"On May twenty-third?"

"In the year of our Lord twenty-seventeen."

"I'm somewhat confused." I notice the elbow of my shirt is dripping rainwater on the table. I pick up my napkin and rub the spot dry.

"Others are merely curious," Rebecca says. "And the rest don't know what to think."

I lean heavily on the table. "It appears to me," I say, "that you are upset about these May Twenty Third murders. Neal is worried sick. But Lorraine, what about her? She lost her husband, and she's as bright and flighty as a spring butterfly at a summer garden party."

"See the sign out front?"

"Which sign?"

"The one on the door."

"Missed it."

"Silver Spoon's closed Monday." Rebecca sighs. "It's closed every May Twenty Third."

"Back open the next day?"

"Last year, it didn't re-open until Thanksgiving."

"Lorraine go out of town?"

"She took a cot to the cemetery and slept every night until it turned hot, and Magnolia Bluff, on a still night, can be hot enough to scald a running lizard's tail."

"What about the rain?"

The smile reappears on Rebecca's face. "It never rains in Magnolia Bluff."

I glance toward the front glass window. The water rushing alongside the gutter is up to the lug nuts on the mail truck. "Could have fooled me."

Lorraine slides two plates on the table. Chicken-fried chicken. Green beans cooked with ham. Slaw. And mashed potatoes.

Gravy on the side.

She places an iced sweet tea beside each plate.

"I didn't order tea," I say.

"It comes with the Special."

"I wanted Coke."

"Can't help you."

"Why not?"

"Coke doesn't come with the Special."

She winks and walks away. I'm beginning to think that winking is a lost art found only in the innards of Magnolia Bluff and only practiced by the eyes of tall, attractive women who make winking as sophisticated as the Blue Danube waltz. Like the rest of us, winking so far hasn't found a good reason to leave.

I take a sip of tea.

It has a hint of mint.

It has a hint of powdered sugar.

It has a jolt of bourbon.

A bolt of lightning crackles in my throat.

I look at Rebecca.

She places a finger to her lips.

"We don't ask what's in the tea," she says. "We pay five dollars a glass and drink it."

"What about the Baptist preacher?"

"Usually orders two glasses."

"Then repents before Sunday?"

Rebecca's face has no expression. "Why would you repent for drinking iced tea," she says.

I don't have an answer.

But I do ask her, "What happened to Lorraine's husband?"

She drops her fork beside the chicken fried chicken. "Hank worked late Saturday night," she begins. "Always did. Usually left the café around eleven o'clock. He would walk around the corner to Phineas Henry's pharmacy and meet a half dozen of his running buddies. They would play a few hands of penny-ante poker in the back room to calm their nerves after a hard week of work, then along about two o'clock, Hank would head on home. It was his Saturday night ritual. Had been for at least twenty years, maybe longer. About two-thirty, Lorraine called Phineas. She was looking for Hank. Phineas was worried, too. It wasn't like Hank to skip out on a poker game. Buck found him two days later in an abandoned feed store between here and Holland Springs. Hank was sitting in a rocking chair on the front porch, hands folded in his lap, his head leaning back against a pillow. His feet were missing."

Rebecca shivers.

"They never did find his feet," she says.

"Any clues?"

"Have you met Buck?"

"Seems like a good guy."

"He is a good guy." Rebecca's words falter for a moment, then she continues, "But Buck wouldn't know what a clue was if you sent it in a special delivery letter marked C-L-U-E."

"What's so special about May Twenty Third?"

Rebecca shakes her head. "Nobody knows."

"Are any of the victims connected with each other?

"They're only guilty of one thing," Rebecca says.

"What's that?"

"They live in Magnolia Bluff."

I finish the chicken fried chicken and sop the last of the gravy with a buttered roll. I'm tempted to order an iced tea to go but think better of it.

"And police still don't have a suspect."

"That's where you're wrong."

My ears perk up. "What do you mean?"

Rebecca stands and drops a five-dollar tip on the table. "This is Magnolia Bluff," she says.

I wait.

She winks.

"Everybody in town is a suspect."

"Even you?"

There was the sound of that magical laugh again. "Only two people didn't make it to the poker game that night." Rebecca shrugs. "I was the other one," she says.

I follow her through the crowd and outside while I hear the faint sounds of Willie Nelson on a jukebox singing "Blue Eyes Crying in the Rain."

He has no idea how blue the rain can be.

# 5

**Wednesday**
**11: 32 p.m.**

The telephone rings too soon, too late, and always at the wrong time. Should be asleep. I'm not. Can't get May Twenty Third off my mind. Mister Holland was worried. He knew he was four days away from losing another member of his family. Everybody in Magnolia Bluff was family, except those irreverent hypocrites who don't read the *Chronicle.* Rebecca Wilson had tried to laugh it off with her coy little comments, but it was easy to see that down deep inside, she was nervous and probably a little frightened. One day a year is easy to forget until you look up and here it comes. Nobody else in town seems to give a damn. Maybe they have just learned to bury their fears and go about their business as though nothing has ever happened and might never happen again.

I yawn and pick up the phone on the fourth ring. I recognize Mister Holland's laconic voice immediately.

"Glad I caught you," he says.

He knew he would catch me.

Where else could I go after eleven o'clock in Magnolia Bluff? Maybe LouEllen's Lounge. But I've lost most of my friends, don't have a lot of interest in making new ones, although Rebecca might have an outside chance of making me change my mind, don't know LouEllen, doubt if she's as pretty as the lady in the neon sign out by the highway, don't dance, hate loud music, and refuse to drink alone when I'm the only stranger in the place. Besides, the dance hall is in the next county, on the other side of the river, and I forgot to bring a car to Magnolia Bluff.

"What's going on?" I ask.

"I have a problem." I can hear the concern scratching his throat like poison ivy.

"What's wrong?"

"Just received a call from Buck." Mister Holland is breathing harder than usual. "He says we got ourselves a two-bit killing down at the motel."

"Cozy Corners?"

"That's the one." He pauses. There's nothing more irritating than a long period of dead air on the telephone. "I wonder if you could run down there and get the story for us."

"I thought murder was your beat." I saw a movie once that had pretty much the same title.

"Nothing like a good crime story," Mister Holland says. "But this damn rain has my rheumatism acting up pretty fierce. Not for sure I can straighten both legs at the same time."

"I'm not a reporter," I blurt into the phone.

"You're not a floor sweep either, but the man who runs the place tells me you do a pretty damn good job." He chuckles.

"I've never written a thing in my life."

"Hell, Huston," he says, "I don't need Hemingway to go down there and win a Pulitzer Prize for *The New York Times*. Just ask a few questions and find out what's going on. Get the facts, nothing but the facts. That's what we do anyway at the *Chronicle*. We just print the facts."

"The fact is," I say, "I'm about to go to sleep."

"The newspaper never sleeps," he barks.

I'm trying to think of something off-the-wall to say.

And he hangs up.

Nothing in the room at eleven-thirty-eight but me and the dial tone.

Rain hasn't quit, but it's slacked off to a slight drizzle, just enough to make the streetlights look as if they've cracked and the glass shattered in a kaleidoscope. The Cozy Corners Motel is only eight blocks away. I throw my denim jacket around my shoulders and start walking. Could call a cab. But the city fathers, in their infinite wisdom, canceled the license of the only taxi business in town. Seems like Tennessee Lovejoy the Third was running hard whiskey when he wasn't running passengers, and he made house calls. Leave a twenty-dollar bill in the mailbox, and there would be a bottle waiting for you when the sun came up. He's still running whiskey as far as I know, mostly to the pious and pecksniffians who believe it's not a sin to drink as long as you don't get caught drinking in public or with somebody else's wife.

I see a splinter of moonlight curving through a crack in the clouds, and a flash of lightning dances across the roof of the Cozy Corners, an old tourist court that once opened its doors to businessmen and politicians traveling between Austin and Dallas. But that was long before interstate highways laced together the small towns of Texas and made out-of-the-way tourist courts stale, moldy, and unfashionable. Its good days ended long ago. Its better days never existed.

The Cozy Corners has eight wooden cabins, painted a dull brown to blend in with the prairie when the grasses died and the rocks cracked. It had been built alongside two blocks of Wintergreen Street. The office at the far end is closed, but a light in the window keeps blinking to let me know that the motel does have a vacancy. At least it does in cabin number six. The light is on. The door is open. Buck Blanton's cruiser sits parked out front. No red and blue lights flashing. But Blind Lemon Jefferson is singing the "Matchbox Blues" on his car radio. Must have an old CD. The rhythm of the guitar and the angst of the song match the night.

I walk inside without knocking.

Don't know what's legal at a crime scene.

Don't know what's not.

If Buck doesn't throw me out, I'll stay.

He's leaning on the far wall, his right hand resting on the butt of a Glock 19 still in its dark leather holster. He's chewing on a toothpick. His eyes are tired. He's working overtime. Doesn't get paid for working overtime. He looks at me warily and asks, "What are you doing here?"

"Mister Holland couldn't make it."

"Not like him to miss a good wife shooting story."

"Says his rheumatism's acting up."

"Must be the rain."

"That's what he thinks."

Buck folds his big arms across his chest. His eyes cut back to the bed.

It's not a pretty scene.

An old man who's probably not as old as he looks sits on the foot of the bed, making curious noises as if he's been crying for a while. He sounds like he doesn't have any tears left. His naked shoulders are wrapped with a frayed, flannel bedspread. His hands are cuffed to a bedpost. He's wearing a pair of twill trousers Goodwill threw away, and his feet are knotted inside a pair of cheap white running sneakers. I bet he doesn't even remember the last time he shaved. His hair is all curls and axle grease.

Behind him, a woman lies sprawled on the bed. Her blood has left the wall looking like an abstract painting created by Jackson Pollock on one of his worst days. The day has certainly not been a good one for her. I have no idea if she was pretty or not. Blood has smeared where the lipstick had been. Red is red, and sometimes red is shotgun ugly. A 12-gauge lies across a dresser beside Buck. Don't know how many times it was fired. Don't know how many shells it holds. But the shotgun sure did some damage at close range to a hundred-pound woman wearing a strapless dancing dress.

She's is barefoot. Her shoes are nowhere in sight.

Buck rolls the Tootsie Roll Pop from one side of his mouth to the other. He smells like cherry cough syrup and chocolate. He asks me, "You working as a reporter now?"

"Just gathering the facts."

"There's not a lot of them."

"I'll collect what I can."

Buck stifles a yawn. "Wish you'd brought coffee."

"Didn't think about it."

"Your boss always brings coffee."

"He didn't mention it."

"You want to stay here with the perpetrator while I go get coffee?"

"I'd rather not."

"Afraid you wouldn't."

The room smells like drug store cologne, the kind of perfume you give a lady if you never expect to see her again, rye whiskey, vomit, and shag carpet soaked with rainwater and blood.

"What happened?" I ask Buck.

"Don't know," he says. "I wasn't here when the shooting started."

His face has no expression.

I know he's laughing at me.

Buck nods toward the man perched on the edge of a dirty mattress. "Ask him." He shrugs. "Near as I can tell, the little man saw the whole damn thing."

I'm at a loss. No one has ever told me what to say to a man who has just killed a woman in a cheap motel.

I look at him.

He's not much to look at.

He stares at the wall.

I stare at the dead woman.

It is already nearing midnight, and time is ticking away.

Buck grins. He likes to see me squirm. He already knows what it doesn't take me long to figure out. Newspapermen are only playing games in a real world where men actually do put a shotgun to a woman's chest and pull the trigger.

Crime of passion.

Crime of pity.

Crime of jealousy.

A crime, nevertheless.

The man looks as if he is ready to start crying again.

Too late to bargain with God.

Too late to repent.

I look for a place to sit down. There isn't any.

I simply say, as politely and respectfully as I can under the circumstances, "Sir, what did the lady do to make you mad?"

He looks from me to the shotgun and back at me again.

I glance at Buck. "Don't worry," he says. "It's unloaded." His grin is wider this time.

"I wasn't mad," the man with two-day's worth of whiskers on his face whispers.

"An accident?" I ask.

"She was gonna walk out on me," he says.

"You didn't want to lose her?"

He shrugs. "She had my wallet," he says.

I wait.

He laughs softly. "But I had her shoes," he says.

I keep waiting.

"And somehow," he says. "between her trying to leave me and me trying to keep her from leaving, and me begging her to stay, and her calling me every name she could think of, a shotgun went off."

"You shoot her?" I ask.

He glances over his shoulder, lets his gaze drift down and across the dancing dress. He shrugs again. "Somebody sure as hell did," he says.

The hundred-pound woman in bare feet did not make it past the door.

She didn't even make it out of bed.

One shot.

One final breath.

Two lives had come to an end, one for good.

"Why didn't you run?" I ask.

He scratches the whiskers on his chin. I think for a minute he's going to laugh. I think for a minute he's going to cry. "No reason to run," he says. "The room is already paid for."

I walk to the door, then turn around. "What's the color of the room?" I ask Buck.

He frowns. He squints. "I'd call it mustard," he says.

"How about the dress?"

"It's short."

"The color?"

Buck grins. "I'd call it the color of ketchup," he says.

I nod.

"You color blind?" he asks me.

"I see colors," I say. "I just don't know if I see the same colors you do."

"You got what you want?" Bucks asks.

I nod.

I'm one foot out the door when I suddenly stop and look back over my shoulder. "You think this killing has anything to do with May Twenty Third?"

"Not a chance."

"Why not?"

"The perp's not a serial killer. He's Wayne Barlow's son. Been knowing him all my life. Runs a tattoo parlor over near San Saba. I knew he would wind up bad someday. I just didn't figure it would be this bad." Buck shakes his head sadly. "I'm glad his daddy died two years ago in a car wreck. Finding out that his son shot a woman would have killed him. No. Tater Barlow doesn't have nothing to do with the May Twenty Third murders. I doubt if Tater can even read a calendar."

"And the girl?"

"She's a party girl. I've seen her around from time to time. Comes into LouEllen's Lounge alone. Never leaves alone. Charges by the hour. I guess Tater's fifteen minutes were up." Buck takes a long, deep breath. "Her fifteen minutes certainly were."

"She have a name?"

"Driver's license says it's Miranda Hawthorne." Buck's eyes darken. He's deep in thought. "But I knew Miranda Hawthorne. She left Magnolia Bluff three years ago. Headed West. Headed to California. A pretty good singer. Wanted to be an actress. Nobody ever saw her again." Buck slumps against the wall, his shoulders sagging. "I knew Miranda Hawthorne," he says. "This is not Miranda Hawthorne."

"Maybe it's just a coincidence."

Buck picks up the shotgun and walks to the door as the headlights from a Ford SUV bounce into the parking lot.

"Maybe frogs can fly," he says.

Wylie Garrison pulls his car up alongside us. He's the justice of the peace. He rolls down his window. His sandy hair is thinning. Narrow face. Wire-framed spectacles hanging crookedly and desperately on a snub nose. Nearing fifty. Rebecca says he loves the pay but hates the job. Looks like he just crawled out of bed. He's wearing his striped pajamas beneath his raincoat.

"What do we have, Buck?" Wylie makes no attempt to open the door.

"Got ourselves a shooting."

"Anybody dead?"

"Woman."

"Anybody we know?"

"Party girl."

"Stranger?"

"I certainly don't know her."

"Murder?"

"Be hard to prove."

"An accident?"

"Looks like it to me."

Garrison shakes his head. "If that's what you think, Buck, then it's good enough for me. Load her up and take her to the morgue."

He drives out of the parking lot and back toward the far side of town where dark rain clouds are slowly rising above the streetlights like the opening curtain at a community theater. The stars are out. The moon is full. A woman's dead. And Tater's probably going home come morning.

Wrong man.

Wrong place.

Wrong time.

Wrong woman.

I left her lying where I found her.

A stranger in a Ketchup-colored dancing dress.

Never saw her again.

Didn't need to.

Strangers don't stand a chance in a small town.

# 6

**Thursday**
**5:26 a.m.**

I give up on daylight. It's a long time coming on a night where a life has flown away without any good reason to leave or stay. Miranda Hawthorne, or whoever she was, had danced her way into the promised land.

A last song.

A last dance.

A last shot.

Sudden darkness.

I'm not troubled or haunted by a nightmare. I've seen death before. I've walked across deserts suffocating with the stench of death. I've left behind friends. Dust in the dust.

Drank together the night before.

A laugh for breakfast.

Tonight one of us dies.

It's not me this time.

It could have been.

Maybe it should have been.

But as my old grandfather told me, "Death rides a tired horse. Don't always catch you when he has the chance. But he's coming. Don't ever slow down. He's coming. Bet on it. The horse is tired. But he don't ever stop and won't ever stop until the day or the night you're too tired to run any longer and can't run any faster. As death rattles in your throat, you can hear the hoofprints, and chances are, you won't hear anything else."

I lie in the night.

I wait to hear the hoofprints.

Any day now.

Any night now.

But not tonight.

Death has come and already ridden the horse out of Magnolia Bluff.

One stranger tonight is enough.

Thursday
7:44 a.m.

I've already swept the newspaper office and have moved into the press room by the time Mister Holland limps through the front door. Wet weather. Chilly weather. The ache runs deep. Rheumatism holds a cruel hammer in its gnarled hand. Outside, Rebecca eases her new Mini-Cooper into her a designated parking spot on West Main. The sky still looks like rain. Black clouds rolling back and forth in the wind. But the streets are mostly dry.

Mister Holland appears startled when he sees me. He hangs his raincoat on a nail beside his desk and pitches his plaid newsboy cap on top of a dictionary. Its pages have been worn smooth and yellowed by his fingerprints.

"Don't expect to see you 'til nine o'clock or later," he says.

He glances up at his clock on the wall.

It's twelve minutes past six.

I figure it's closer to seven.

Clock hasn't been right a day since I've been here.

The clock's like me.

It loses time.

"You wanted a story," I say. "I got you a story."

"Make it down to the shooting?"

"Wasn't much to it."

"Never is." Mister Holland shakes his head sadly. "Motel shootings usually have to work hard to make the back page."

"Didn't amount to much unless you were the girl," I say, leaning on the broom.

"Man kill his wife?"

"Didn't say she was his wife."

"He confess?"

"Not while I was there."

Mister Holland reaches down and picks up a piece of copy paper beside his desk calendar. "This what you wrote?'

I nod.

He scans the page, reading out loud to himself as Rebecca dashes into the office. She's carrying a tall cup of Real Good Wood-Fired Coffee.

He reads:

*One man.*

*One woman.*

*One shotgun.*

*One shot.*

*One crying.*

*One dying.*

*One hell of a mess.*

Mister Holland looks up. He is frowning, his eyes as black as his inkwell. "You call this a news story?"

"You said get the facts, nothing but the facts," I tell him. "Those are the facts."

"Man have a name?" he wants to know.

I nod.

"The woman?"

I nod again.

He pitches the page toward me. It flutters to the floor. "Fill in the blanks," he says.

Rebecca is aghast. "You're not planning to print that, are you?" she asks.

"Might," Mr. Holland says.

"That's a travesty of journalism."

Mister Holland tilts his head and looks through the front glass window, watching a cloud do its best to squeeze out another raindrop. "Near as I can figure," he says, "journalism died years ago and nobody noticed and nobody cared. This story's not written right. It's all wrong. It breaks all of the rules. Copy editors from one end of the world to the other will be turning in their graves. You can hear Funk and Wagnall crying themselves to sleep tonight. Webster will resign from his dictionary. But I kind of like the way it sounds. Might get us a few more readers."

"Might get you run out of town on a rail," Rebecca snaps.

"Can't."

"Why not."

Mister Holland grins. "I bought the rails at the last chamber of commerce auction."

Rebecca drops into her chair and rolls her eyes.

I reach down and pick up the paper. "Can I use your computer?" I ask him.

"You type?"

"Two fingers."

"So do I," he says. "I use the first two fingers when I type a news story. I use the ring fingers when I type an editorial. And I use the middle fingers when I type a city council story."

"Don't like the city council?"

"Love the council." Mister Holland shrugs. "Don't like the members."

He grabs his raincoat and heads for the door. "I'll be back as soon as Harry brews up a fresh cup of his Wood Fired Coffee."

"The Mocha's good," Rebecca says.

"So's the Kahlua." Mister Holland closes the door.

I sit down and begin again.

*One man.*

*Tater Barlow.*

*He's local.*

*One woman.*

*Miranda Hawthorne.*

*She's not.*

*One motel room.*

*Number eight.*

*Cozy Corners.*

*Four walls.*

*The color of mustard.*

*That's what the sheriff said.*

*One dancing dress.*
*The color of ketchup.*
*Sheriff said that, too.*
*One shotgun.*
*Twelve-gauge.*
*One shot.*
*Up close.*
*And personal.*
*One crying.*
*That's Tater.*
*One dying.*
*That's Miranda.*
*Didn't take her long.*
*Two feet.*
*Hers.*
*Bare.*
*Two shoes.*
*Missing.*
*Murder?*
*Can't prove it.*
*Not there.*
*Neither was the sheriff.*
*No one saw what happened.*
*Only one knows what happened.*
*Tater's not confessing.*
*Miranda's not accusing.*
*Must be an accident.*
*That's what the justice of the peace is ruling.*
*One dead.*
*One guilty.*
*One buried.*
*One back on the street.*
*One trial.*
*Avoided.*
*One verdict.*

*Silenced.*

*One travesty of justice.*

*One easy way out.*

*One hell of a mess.*

*Don't pray for Miranda.*

*Too late.*

*Pray for Tater.*

*I hear she has a boyfriend.*

Mister Holland prints it.

Front page.

Above the fold.

A forty-eight-point headline.

We're off the press at four o'clock. We're back on at five.

"Need another two thousand copies," Mister Holland says.

"Why?"

"Everybody in town's talking about your story."

"I don't write stories," I tell him.

"It's beautiful," he says.

"What makes you say that?"

"Sheriff's mad. Justice of the Peace is mad. The judge is mad. The chief of police is mad. City council's called a special session. Jobs are on the line. Heads may be rolling." Mister Holland laughs out loud. "It's a great day for the *Chronicle,*" he says.

"How's that?"

"We've got what I always like to have."

"What's that?"

"One hell of a mess."

# 7

**Friday**
**6:04 a.m.**

The Friday morning circle of scalawags, reprobates, misfits, and the great unwashed are sitting around the back table of the Silver Spoon Café when I walk in and grab a chair beneath an image of Elvis printed on black velvet. Everybody's thinking. Nobody's talking. They're wading through shallow water with deep thoughts.

These are the official, card-carrying sweaters of a town that sweats a lot. They are farmers, ranchers, hunters, fishermen, politicians, merchants, bankers, lawmen, and an occasional member of the Fourth Estate.

They sweat about the price of cotton, the price of wool, the price of gasoline, the sale price of cattle down at the auction barn, the rumor that a big box store is coming in to close downtown Magnolia Bluff, the war in the Middle East, rampant immigration that's a little too close for comfort, killer hornets, drought, flash floods, lightning strikes, the new blonde divorcee who's giving facials and makeup tips down at the pharmacy, and things that go bump in the night.

Two pairs of eyes cut through me like a hot butter knife dropped in a bucket of hog lard when I sit down. One pair belongs to the jovial Buck Blanton. He's grinning, but it's a surly grin, the same kind you see on a bear just before he takes the top of your head off with a single swipe of his paw. Buck's grinning like he just found a new lawbreaker that needs a good shooting.

The other pair has been known to slice up smart aleck,

out of town, big-city lawyers who believe they can swagger into the Burnet County Courthouse and run roughshod over a soft-voiced, mellow-faced, over-the-hill district judge who's too thin to cast a decent shadow but earned a silver star flying a helicopter across the Mekong Delta in Vietnam. Won't talk about it. I asked him.

Judge Abner J. "Peashooter" Peacock would rather talk fishing. The only thing he likes better than hauling big mouth bass out of Burnet Reservoir is throwing two-bit criminals in jail and sending six-bit criminals to prison. Never sent anybody to the death house, but he says he's hanging on until he gets the chance. He tilts his wire spectacles down on the end of his nose and looks at me like his long wait is about to pay off.

Buck breaks the silence. "What are you trying to do?" he says. "Get me fired?"

"What are you talking about?" I'm not about to offer a defense until I know exactly what I'm defending.

"That damn news story."

"Don't write news stories." Lorraine taps my arm, reaches over my shoulder, and pours me a cup of coffee. Black. No cream. No sugar. At the sacred circle of scalawags, reprobates, misfits, and the great unwashed, neither cream nor sugar is allowed. Drink it the way God invented it or go somewhere else and see how tough you feel with Mocha or Frappuccino on your breath.

"What you write is a bunch of unmitigated crap." Buck is chewing on coffee grounds.

"Won't argue that point," I tell him.

"Has no business in the newspaper."

"All I wrote were the unmitigated facts, Sheriff," I remind him. "The only thing I left out was you chewing on a lollipop and the justice of the peace roaring into a crime scene wearing his striped pajamas."

Barron Schiff snickers. He presides with a certain amount of dignity and solemnity over the downtown funeral home and wedding chapel. He gets you coming and going, and you can buy both at a serious discount if you pay upfront and pay for both at the same time.

Phineas Henry laughs out loud. He sells a wide assortment

of cheap perfumes, colognes, vitamins, hand sanitizers, and body lotions, along with your usual assortment of under-the-counter and over-the-counter pills, erection stimulators, and condoms down at his pharmacy, next door to the First National Bank. Nothing illicit or illegal but a few personal items you'd rather not be seen carrying in anything other than an unmarked brown paper bag. You need plausible deniability if you're caught, and you almost always are.

"My Lord, Buck, what in hell were you doing at a motel shooting with a lollipop in your mouth?" Xander Littleton wants to know. He's barely thirty with curly hair and eyes the color of burnt cocoa. Denim jeans a little too tight. Khaki shirt tucked in behind a leather belt held together with a World Championship Rodeo belt buckle. Probably bought it in a pawn shop. His alligator skin boots have pointed toes, the kind that are good only for going after water bug in the corner of the room. Xander thinks more highly of himself than the rest of us do, but he doesn't mind. He wears a badge and keeps it shined with bath rag saturated in Orange Glow. Xander works for the fish and game department and spends most of his days running a power boat from one end of Burnet Reservoir to the other. Keeps it safe. Keeps the fish under control. We haven't had a fight amongst the largemouth bass since he got here. He came in feeling his oats this morning. Took a couple of shots at a couple of poachers. Didn't hit anybody, but, Lord, he loves to hear the noise when that pistol of his goes off.

"It was a Tootsie Roll Pop," Buck spits out. He's breathing hard. Sounds a lot like a boar hog snorting when he's in a chain-link cage and can't figure a way out.

"Well, hell, Buck," Dr. Michael Kurelek says, "that makes all the difference in the world. We just didn't know if you were sucking or licking." He's a big man, tall and strong, likes to kill things if they're four-legged and wearing antlers, and he teaches psychology over within the liberal confines of the Burnet College of the Arts. Dressed the way he always is: tie loose, top button on his white shirt unfastened, sleeves rolled up. Not a hair is out of place.

The laughter is genuine but nervous.

The forever grinning Buck Blanton has a low boiling point.

And I guess I lit the fire.

He's not boiling yet.

But his eyes are smoldering.

Buck's fists are clenched and tattooed with scars from stitches as crooked as blue lines on a West Virginia state map. His fingers, I'm told, have been broken twenty-seven times by drunks, domestic disturbers, hijackers, deer poachers, whiskey runners, and a misplaced beer bottle or two thrown by a jealous husband or two.

If you're in a fight with Buck, only let him hit you once. Go down and lie there. Don't whimper or wail. If he hits you a second time, he may well kill you. Won't mean to. Just can't help himself.

Judge Peacock leans across the table and places a small, wrinkled hand on top of Buck's knotted fist. "Gentlemen," he says, "let's cut Buck a little slack." His voice is so low we have to strain to hear him above the sound of the ceiling fan. "Long night. Hard night. You might think the sheriff is a little upset. He's not. Not really. Buck doesn't have a short temper. He just has a quick and a potent reaction to bullshit."

Nobody laughs.

The laughter is churning inside us.

We're simply too ill-at-ease to turn it loose or let it out.

The judge is not finished yet. He turns his head toward me. "And, Mister Huston," he says, "you know, and I know, and everyone here knows that the piece you wrote in last night's *Chronicle* was pure sanctified, justified, and glorified bullshit." He pauses, and the faint wrinkles of a smile quiver as they touch the corners of his mouth. "What you wrote was wrong. It sheds a bad light on our community, on our law enforcement officers who, by the way, do an awfully good job of keeping our little town safe. It even casts shadows of suspicion and doubt on our justice system, and, sir, when you tamper with our justice system, you are working your way onto my bad side, and that is not a place you want to be. I am not too different from our esteemed sheriff. Like Buck, I have a quick and a potent reaction to bullshit, and neither one of us is known to forgive or forget in a man's lifetime. It may take us months. It may take us years. But one of these days, we will get even. However, Mister Huston, let me be the first to say out loud and in public that what you wrote was damn good bullshit."

We hear Jack coming down the hallway long before he steers his wheelchair through the door and into the back room Lorraine reserves us for us promptly at five o'clock every morning.

Jack Rice is big and burly, yet he's only the ghost of the man he once was. His face is hard as granite, yet he looks every bit of his seventy-two years. Jack lost one leg in a Viet Cong minefield, and diabetes took the other one a couple of years ago.

He's blunt.

He's irascible.

He fought a war.

He lost a war.

He tells me he loses it again and again when the nightmares come, and they sit on his shoulder and taunt him whether he's sleeping or not. He's rigged up his old Ford pickup so he can drive it, and nobody wants to occupy the same highway with Jack if it's raining or he's been drinking, and you can smell hard liquor on his breath anytime day or night.

*Whiskey's gonna kill you, I once told him.*

*It's about time, he says.*

*Death would have caught him years ago.*

*But death is still riding that tired old horse.*

Jack's wearing his old St. Louis Cardinal baseball cap and has his faded combat jacket thrown over his shoulders.

Didn't keep out the rain.

Kept out the chill.

Lorraine has his cup of coffee waiting on him by the time he rolls to the table.

"Tell me what it was, Buck." Jack's voice is loud, his words brittle. He takes a sip of coffee and wipes his mouth with the back of his hand.

Buck shakes his head.

He knows what's coming.

"Was it murder?" Jack asks. "Or was it an accidental shooting?"

Buck drains his cup and leans back in his chair. His grin is as wide and as crooked as the San Saba River. "Looked to me like an accident."

"Sounds to me like murder." Jack's smile is more of a smirk.

I know Jack. He doesn't give a tinker's damn if it was an accident.

Or murder.

He just likes to jangle Buck's nerves. And he's one of the few people in Magnolia Bluff who can get away with it. Buck lost a daddy in Vietnam.

*Jack can't take my daddy's place, he once told me.*

*But he was there.*

*He saw what daddy saw.*

*He crawled through the same jungles where my daddy crawled.*

*He fought in the rice paddies where my daddy fought.*

*He drank the same cheap Saki my daddy drank.*

*He felt the pain daddy felt.*

*He's bitter.*

*I'm bitter.*

*Jack's not family.*

*But he's damn close.*

# 8

**Friday**
**6:34 a.m.**

Jack Rice Puts three drops of Four Roses into his coffee cup from a small stainless steel flask he carries in his pocket. There was a time when he only drank Wild Turkey, but his army pension doesn't go quite as far as it once did. He can either buy shells for his Winchester Model 94 deer rifle or sip expensive bourbon. He's opted for Four Roses. We all look away and pretend not to notice, hoping the whiskey can deaden the kind of pain that prescription drugs only numb for a while.

Jack squeezes his eyes shut and waits for the first drop of bourbon to slide down his throat and jam up against his heart. The muscles in his shoulders relax. "Buck, I read where old Tater took the lady out with a shotgun blast."

Buck shrugs. "Twelve gauge. One shell fired."

"You know," Jack says, warming up, "you don't see many accidental shootings when a shotgun's involved. A pistol? Now, that makes all of the sense in the world. Probably half of the shootings that happen in this country are the result of a pistol that somebody thought was unloaded." He pauses, glances around, and rubs the back of his hand across a face that's been abandoned by the razor. "Usually, when you decide to pull the trigger on a shotgun, you damn sure mean it."

"Not sure who pulled the trigger." Buck leans back in his chair and rests his right hand on the butt of his pistol. His words are as calm, as matter-of-fact as if he were talking about the weather. "Tater says they were squirming on the bed at the time."

"You sending the body down to Austin for an autopsy?" Jacks asks.

"No reason to." Buck's feet are planted on solid ground now. "An autopsy would only show what we already know."

"What's that?"

"A shotgun can do a lot of damage."

"Was she pretty?" Phineas asks.

Buck pushes his chair away from the table and stands up. He walks slowly to the window and watches the rain splatter against the pane, leaving tiny trails through the dust that had collected on the glass.

"She had black hair," he says.

Thunder dances across the top of the Silver Spoon.

"Dyed," he says.

"Have any idea who she is?" Kurelek asks.

"Phony driver's license." Buck shakes his head. "Phony name. Probably just passing through."

"Probably needed a room for the night." Kurelek folds his arms across his chest. "Tater was an easy mark."

"Maybe he was in love," Phineas says.

"Maybe she wasn't," Xander says.

"Still, he shouldn't have killed her." I stare at the bottom of an empty cup. Can't read the coffee grounds like tea leaves. Can't read tea leaves either.

"I still think it's murder." Jack's voice is raspy.

"You know Tater?" Buck asks. He turns and wanders back to the table.

"I've seen him," Jack says. "Don't believe we've ever drunk from the same bottle."

"Well, then," the sheriff says, sitting back down, "You know that the good Lord didn't see fit to give Tater the good looks, the personality, or pocket change heavy enough to make him attractive to many women."

"Never saw Tater with anybody wearing a skirt," Xander says, frowning as if he's trying to remember.

Buck nods. "This is the way I figure it," he says. "If Tater was finally lucky enough to wind up in a motel room with a woman,

I don't think he would have killed her on purpose before he got his pants off."

"Won't argue with that." Phineas is motioning for Lorraine to bring him a refill.

Silence.

It lasts too long.

Jack finally breaks it.

"What if she made fun of him?" he asks.

I feel a chill.

It has nothing to do with the rain.

Judge Peacock leans forward as if he were perched behind the bench and presiding over a trial.

"If she did," he says, "then it's not an accident."

He pauses.

He looks around.

"And it's not murder," he says.

The judge waits for a moment.

We wait for the verdict.

"It's justified," he says.

A few nods.

A few shrugs.

Nobody questions him.

The jury of scalawags, reprobates, misfits, and the great unwashed has voted to acquit, and as near as I can tell the verdict is unanimous with Jack Rice abstaining.

Xander glances around to make sure Lorraine has left the room. His voice softens. "Do you think this killing has anything to do with what happens every May Twenty Third?"

I can see a flicker of fear darken his eyes.

No one answers him.

A sudden and unsettling apprehension hangs heavy in the air around us.

A sense of dread.

The air has been sucked out of the backroom.

How do you escape a nightmare?

Can't.

It's real.

It's foreboding.

It's not a nightmare.

"I doubt it," Judge Peacock says after a long silence.

"Why not?" Phineas is rubbing his hands together, a nervous habit.

"We're four days away from May Twenty Third," the judge answers. "The killings that have our nerves endings raw may be all random. Nobody knows for sure. But they are damn well premeditated. The lady down at the Cozy Corners? The lady bunking with Tater? She was an accident."

"You sure?"

"Tater's a simple-minded little man." The judge removes his spectacles and wipes the smudges away with his napkin. "Never had much. Never needed much. Never wanted much. He loves everybody and just about everybody I know loves him. He gets into mischief from time to time. But nothing malicious. Not until last night. I doubt Tater even remembers being with a woman last night, much less shooting her. I had Tater put away at the state hospital a few years ago. The doctors turned him loose, saying he was nothing more than a little man who had bad dreams. As far as Tater knows, last night was a bad dream. That's all. He is just not smart enough or conniving enough to kill eight of our fine citizens for no reason."

"I'm guessing the May Twenty Third killer has a reason." I throw the comment out because the thought happened to cross my mind.

"Don't know what it is," Buck says.

"Any witnesses?"

"Nary a one."

"Any clues you're hiding in that thick head of yours?" I ask him.

"Got more witnesses than clues," Buck says, shaking his head, "and I haven't found anybody who's seen a damn thing."

"Any connection that ties the victims together?"

"One," Buck says.

My eyes light up.

"Can you say what it is?'

"I can."

"So tell us."

"They're all dead."

Buck chuckles as if he's told a joke.

A bad joke.

Nobody's laughing.

"Think you'll know anymore come Monday?" I ask.

"Maybe the killer's moved on." The big grin wavers on Buck's face. "Maybe he was only mad at eight people, and they're gone, and he's not mad anymore. Maybe Monday will be like any other day in Magnolia Bluff. We all wake up and at the end of the day, we're all still breathing, and the only thing we have to dread is going back to work the next day."

Buck's last sentence hangs in the air like a falling leaf on a calm day.

Some are nodding.

Some are shrugging.

Jack removes his St. Louis Cardinal baseball cap and lays it on the table beside his coffee cup. His face is sweating profusely. "I wonder who number nine will be," he says.

# 9

**Friday**
**10:54 a.m.**

Mister Holland drops his aging frame into the aging mahogany swivel chair behind his aging desk and stares through the plate glass window at the rain pounding the streets and pouring like a raging river into the storm drains. He's looking glum, as miserable as the weather outside. I can see that his mind is in a winner-take-all wrestling match with itself. His lips are moving, and he hasn't said a word. Not out loud, anyway. He looks up as I push my broom past him.

"Huston," he says. It's almost a shout.

"Yes, sir."

"We lost four subscribers yesterday."

"Didn't like my story?"

"Didn't pay their bill." He leans his head back and watches a spider dangling from a web hanging onto the ceiling fan. Isn't working, the fan that is. Hasn't worked in years. The spider is working like her life depends on it, and her existence probably does.

His shoulders shake as he laughs to himself. "I did have two advertisers ask me what kind of journalism we were practicing down here."

"What'd you tell them?'

"Told them it was a brand-new style taught by the finest journalism schools in the country."

"Did they buy it?"

"Asked what it was."

"What'd you tell them?'

Mister Holland bursts out laughing. "Told them it was what we in the know call *scattershot journalism*. Said they liked it. Said it was easy to read. Said it was quick to read. Said I should have been writing that way years ago." Mister Holland shrugs his thick shoulders. "Told them I would have, but it hadn't been invented then."

He pauses and waves at Rebecca as she comes running in the front door with rain dripping off her bright yellow, or maybe it's a tarnished gold, umbrella and puddling on the floor. It's suddenly as wet inside as it is outside. Her hair is plastered against her head, and her cheeks are tattooed with fresh smudges of running mascara.

"That's the problem," Mister Holland says. "We only have two news stories a year worth writing about."

"What are they?" I ask him.

"May when it rains, and the rest of the year when it doesn't."

"How about the third story?" I ask him.

He looks at me with a blank stare.

"Monday," I say. "It's May Twenty Third."

The blank stare turns as fragile as glass. His face grows ashen. It's drained of all color. His shoulders sag. I can almost see his skin start to shrivel.

"What do you know about May Twenty Third?" Mister Holland asks.

"I know everybody in town is afraid of it."

"You a smart fella, Mister Huston?" he asks.

"Some days are better than others."

"Monday's not one of the good days," Mister Holland says." Don't say that date aloud."

"Why not?"

"Maybe nobody will remember."

"They'll remember."

"How do you know?"

"They're already talking about it."

I glance at Rebecca.

Her face is flushed. Her hands are trembling. She drops the umbrella. It's too wet to make a sound.

I feel as if the world has stopped.

The merry-go-round quits spinning.

It has no place to go.

The lights are on.

The room goes dark.

Nobody's moving.

Breathing is shallow.

I hope the phone rings.

At least someone will answer it.

I cut my eyes around to the phone.

And wait.

It doesn't ring.

Finally, Mister Holland finds his voice again. He's clenching and unclenching his fists. "That's what kept me awake all night," he says.

"Are you like everybody else in town?" Rebecca's voice has been whittled down to a hoarse whisper. "Afraid he's coming after you this time?"

"Why would he?"

"Why wouldn't he?"

"No reason for me to be worried," Mister Holland says. "I only print the news. I don't make the news."

"Then what has you concerned?" Rebecca places a gentle hand on his shoulder.

"The *Chronicle* prints on Thursday afternoon and Saturday morning," the publisher says. "That's tradition. That's the way we've always done it. I began back thirty some odd years ago so we could get the football stories out and on the streets by the time the boys had showered and driven the cheerleaders out to some lover's lane hideaway. But, hell, we don't play football in May. I've decided that we won't go to the trouble of printing a newspaper on Saturday this week. We'll publish next Tuesday instead."

"In case something happens on Monday?" I sit down on the edge of his desk.

"In case the bastard gets up, checks the calendar, and strikes again." Mister Holland's words have a hard edge to them.

"Oh, my God." Rebecca has turned pale.

I reach out and take her hand. "What's wrong?'

She looks straight at me with mesmerizing eyes rinsed with fresh tears. "What if he kills an advertiser? Only the good Lord knows how hard it is to sell advertising in this town. There's no way I can lose another store that's closing down."

I look at Mister Holland.

He looks at me.

He reaches over and pats Rebecca's hand. "We'll just print seven pages instead of eight," he says. He looks up at me and winks. "We'll leave the last page blank."

"What about my paycheck?"

"Don't worry about it."

"Why not?"

"It's never enough anyway."

"But what'll I do?"

"I know what I'll do," Mister Holland says.

"What's that?" Rebecca walks to her desk and sits down, her knuckles white from holding her purse so tightly.

"I've got a bottle of James Beam that's just begging me to finish it off."

"But what about me?"

"I'd start praying if I was you."

"For my life?"

"No. For enough ads to fill up eight pages."

Rebecca curls her lips into a mischievous snarl. "You're laughing at me," she snaps.

"I'm not now," Mister Holland says. "But I probably will be by the time the day ends."

He stands, picks his London Fog raincoat off the floor, throws it around his shoulders, and ambles toward the front door.

I think he's whistling.

Maybe "Love Sick Blues."

Perhaps "Amazing Grace."

It's hard to tell where one ends and the other begins.

"Where are you off to?" Rebecca calls after him.

"I have a lunch date with Mister Beam," he says.

"You be here tomorrow morning?" There is a tremor in her voice.

"Sleeping in."

"What if somebody comes looking for his Saturday paper?"

"Give him Thursday's paper."

"What good will that do?"

"Not a lot's changed since yesterday."

Mister Holland waves without turning around.

And the door shuts quietly behind him.

# 10

**Friday**
**7:16 p.m.**

The rain comes and it goes, and it washes away everything in Magnolia Bluff but the blues. Rain cleanses the streets but not the soul. Guilt walks along beside me, but guilt found me years ago crawling across a rocky ledge the color of blood and has been hanging around ever since.

The Army sent me to a shrink.

I didn't say much.

I just answered questions.

*"Name?"*

*"Graham Huston."*

*"Rank?"*

*"Captain."*

*"Serial Number?"*

*"None of your damn business."*

*"Did you kill anyone in combat?"*

*"What do you think? I was in combat."*

*"Still see their faces?"*

*"I see their eyes."*

*"When you're asleep?"*

*"When I'm awake."*

*"How do their eyes make you feel?"*

*"Guilty."*

*"Well," he said, "it was a time of war, and you had merely answered*

*the call. You should never feel guilty." He smiled. "You are not guilty."*

Then it was my turn.

I looked hard at him.

I saw the corner of his mouth quiver.

*"You ever in combat?" I asked.*

*He shook his head.*

*"Then how do I know?" I asked.*

*"Know what?"*

*"If I'm guilty or not."*

*He swallowed hard.*

*"We'll get you through this," he said.*

I never went back.

A year passed.

Maybe five.

Another road.

Too many roads.

Another town.

Another night.

Guilt had a partner now.

But by now, misery and I were old friends as well.

Friday
7:43 p.m.

The neighborhood bar had been small, smelled like liniment and spilled beer, and on the wrong side of town.

I felt like I belonged on the wrong side of town.

Atlanta, I think it was.

Dark.

Depressing.

A single light bulb hung from the ceiling.

It had probably been yellow before age smeared it with streaks of black and gray.

Neon flashed blue and red on the jukebox.

Johnny Horton was singing.

He sang like a man who had been dead for years.

He had been.

The bartender was a little too old but looked tough enough to serve as his own bouncer in case there was trouble. Bald head. Scar angled across his forehead. Nose broken one too many times. Broad shoulders. Thick arms. The hint of a mustache. So red it was black, or maybe it was the other way around.

I could feel the waves of heat rising off the floor.

Air conditioner was rattling.

It no longer cooled anything.

Sweat crawled down my back and formed a ring around my throat.

Tight.

Wet.

Felt like a noose soaked in brine.

I blinked back the darkness and looked around me.

A man sat alone.

He was worn.

A woman sat alone.

She looked as if she were waiting for someone.

She had waited a long time.

She might wait forever.

She sat dangling her bare legs off the frazzled end of a misspent life.

She kept reaching into a ceramic bowl for pretzels, and the pretzels were gone.

If she had a name, it would be Rita.

I didn't ask.

I was afraid it wasn't.

He sipped whiskey.

She had a gin fizz.

He was lost somewhere between light and dark, between yesterday and morning.

She was waiting to be found.

They would pass each other like shadows in the night.

There would be no trouble.

*"You a veteran?" I asked the bartender.*

*"I did my time."*

*"Vietnam?"*

*"Korea."*

*"Tough war."*

*"They're all tough."*

*"You kill anybody?"*

*"What do you think?" he answered. "I'm still among the living."*

*"You ever feel guilty?" I asked him.*

He poured me two fingers of Maker's Mark.

The good stuff.

*"Which war did you get trapped in?" he asked.*

*"Afghanistan."*

*"War causing you problems?" he wanted to know.*

*"I can't make sense of it," I answered.*

*"Politicians do. Soldiers don't."*

*"You ever have nightmares?" I asked him.*

*"I drank 'til they felt ashamed of themselves and left me." He began wiping the bar down with a wet rag. "What causes yours?"*

*"My best friend died," I said. The bourbon slid down my throat as smooth as raw honey. "I didn't."*

*"So you feel guilty," he said.*

*I nodded.*

*"See that woman at the end of the bar?" he asked.*

*I nodded again.*

*"She left her husband last Wednesday. Took his Cadillac. Sold it. Moved to Atlanta. Rode a Greyhound from Mobile."*

*I stared at her.*

*Tall.*

*Slender.*

*Hair the color of sunrise.*

*She must have been beautiful.*

*But that was a long time ago.*

*He pointed to the other end of the bar.*

*"See the gentleman with the busted knuckles nursing his whiskey?"*

*Third nod.*

*"He got out of prison last Sunday."*

*"What was he in for?"*

*"Jury said he killed a guy."*

*"Did he?"*

*"Never asked him."*

*I frowned.*

*I emptied the glass.*

*"What are you trying to tell me?" I asked.*

*He shrugged his broad shoulders.*

*"We're all guilty of something," he said.*

*"How about you?"*

*"You a priest?" he asked.*

*"No."*

*"Then you won't get a confession from me."*

*He grinned.*

*He had one gold tooth and another one missing.*

The bourbon had turned sour by the time I walked back out on the street, and the night was as dark as my conscience.

So why the hell did I wind up in Magnolia Bluff?

It was the one place I never wanted to be.

But I came anyway.

I had no choice.

Blame it on the Greyhound bus.

Blame it on the road.

Blame it on guilt.

I had one thing left to do.

Then it didn't matter anymore.

# 11

**Friday**
**11:48 p.m.**

The sharp knock on the door should have awakened me. But I never fall asleep until after midnight, usually the witching hour. I had cleansed the scattered thoughts from my mind just as I had been taught in intelligence school at Fort Holabird in Baltimore. Stare at the darkness until a door opens, then throw your thoughts inside, and lock them up tight. Don't let one thought get out. Seal them all inside. The thought that gets away is the one that can get you killed. I glanced at the clock on the table beside the bed. It was four minutes after eleven. Too late for anyone to be knocking, I thought. I cringed. There was the thought. It was loose. Perhaps it was deadly.

I was still wearing my jeans. Another wrinkle wouldn't hurt them. I pulled on a cotton tee-shirt, walked barefoot across the floor, pulled the drape aside, and looked into the wide-eyed face of Rebecca Wilson. No raincoat. No umbrella. Soaking wet. The fabric of her cotton dress clung tightly around her body as though it was part of her skin. I could almost see the chill bumps. Her white sneakers had been walking through mud.

I unlocked the door and opened it. Rebecca fell inside the room, grabbing my arm to keep from losing her balance. Her breath came in short bursts. I saw it in her eyes, sharp pinpoints of black obsidian searching for small pinpoints of crystal in the darkness. I know what fear looks like. I have seen it in the eyes of the living and the dying. It never changes. Hope in white. Doubt in black. No reason for them to clash. It doesn't matter which one wins. Hope doesn't save you. Doubt doesn't kill you. The game is decided by a bullet. Or a blast. Don't see it coming. Know it's coming. One blink. Maybe two. A last moment. Reach for it. Hold it. Why is it slipping away like quicksilver? Then it's over. Hope and doubt die hand in hand.

Rebecca presses her face against my chest.

I can think of nothing better to do.

So I hold her.

I know there's something I'm supposed to do next.

I have no idea what it is.

"What's wrong?" I ask.

"I don't want to be alone."

"What were you doing in the rain?" I ask.

Dumb question.

I know them all.

"Walking," she says.

"Without an umbrella?'

"It wasn't raining when I started," she says.

I take Rebecca's hand and lead her to the bathroom door. "You need to dry off," I tell her. "Don't want you drowning on my bedroom floor. Clean towels. Never been used. Hang your dress in the shower until it sheds the rain."

"But what'll I wear?"

I walk over, pick my denim shirt off the back of a chair, and toss it to her. "Wore it twice. It's been rained on once." My smile turns into a grin. "Shirt's long enough to cover the parts you don't want seen by a leering public."

She doesn't see my smile.

Or my grin.

Too dark.

Both are wasted.

She slams the door shut.

I wait beside the window that looks out toward a small park across the street. Dark clouds, little more than lumps in the sky, hide the moon. The lumps have spent the last of their rain. Not a drop is falling. I may as well unlock the door to the darkness. The thoughts are leaking out anyway. Why did Rebecca come to my room? How did she even know where I lived. Then again,

Rebecca knows everything about everybody in Magnolia Bluff. But now, she looks frightened. She acts nervous. She reminds me of a broken doll thrown away, no longer wanted, lost in an alley and left too long in the rain.

She doesn't look like the Rebecca I have worked with for the last seven months and sixteen days. She looks fragile, and no one in town has ever called her fragile. The society editor and advertising guru of the *Chronicle* is strong, defiant, sure of herself, and wouldn't dare give the impression that she needed a man for any particular reason unless, of course, she wanted to rip his Adam's apple from his throat.

She walks back into the room, a silhouette against the pale light of a small lamp on the bathroom counter. Her hair is straight and still wet. The towel didn't have a chance. She's dressed in my denim shirt. I'm surprised. It doesn't cover nearly as much as I had imagined. Then again, my imagination often sees things that aren't there. To me, there's not a lot of difference between wishful thinking and a meddlesome imagination.

She sits on the bed and fluffs up a pillow to lean against.

"There's room for you, too," she says.

She pats the bed beside her.

I sit down, my hands folded, my arms on my knees.

"Do I make you uncomfortable?"

"It's my lease," I say. "You know what a stickler for decorum Nell Walker is. She has a stiff list of rules, and I think *No Women Allowed* is probably at the top."

"Don't worry about Nell."

"Why shouldn't I?"

"She won't throw you out."

"How do you know?"

"Nell's closer to forty than sixty, and she's dating a married man in Fredericksburg and sleeping with a beautician in Boerne."

I look at her with a new sense of curiosity. "How do you know these things?"

She laughs. "I have pictures."

"How did you get pictures."

"I have ways." She shrugs. "Fred Bonnet who owns the

photography studio has a few secrets he wants kept secret. All it cost him was an eight-dollar stem card for his Nikon."

"I could ask you about Fred."

"But you won't."

"Why not?"

"You know I won't tell you."

I smile. "Who knows your secrets, Rebecca?"

"I don't have any."

"I find that hard to believe."

"I'm an open book," she says. "Born here. Raised here. Poor little rich girl. Daddy owned the bank before Gunter Fight bought it. Parents divorced when I was twelve. I went to live with Daddy. He built a sizable fortune and left it all to me when cancer stopped his wheeling and dealing. I live here. I like it here. Don't date."

"That surprises me."

"I don't think men like being around me."

"I find that hard to believe."

"I think they're afraid of me."

Rebecca unfastens the top button of the denim shirt but folds her arms across her chest. "That's why I'm intrigued with you," she says.

"No reason to be."

"You're not afraid of me."

"I don't know you well enough to be afraid of you."

She raises an inquisitive eyebrow. "How can you say that? We've worked in the same office for the last eight months."

"You're high society," I tell her. "I'm just the broom man."

It's nothing more than a passing thought.

She lets it pass.

She lies motionless, eyes open, staring at a dark ceiling as if it was a Rothko painting. He believed his art could free the unconscious energies previously liberated by mythological images, symbols, and rituals. The ceiling at night is dark and foreboding, not unlike the strange work he left behind when he slashed his wrists and took flight, maybe to someplace where there is no light, and there is no dark, and he has no other images to hide in shadow and gloom. Was there substance and a sense of meaning in his work? Or did old Rothko fool us all?

Silence.

That's all I hear.

Silence.

The steady rhythm of Rebecca's breathing.

And the rain.

"What's your story?" Rebecca asks at last.

"I don't have one."

"Everybody has a story."

"Mine's a blank page."

She turns and stares at me.

Her eyes are like flint.

Maybe I'm the Rothko painting.

Dense.

Senseless.

"Why are you running?" she asks.

I've heard the question before.

Didn't have an answer.

Still don't.

"Maybe I'm looking for the end of the road," I say, "and I haven't found it yet."

"What will you do when you find it?" Rebecca's voice softens.

"Don't think it has an end." I mull her question over in my mind for a moment, then add, "I think that when you come to the end, you simply take one more step and drop off."

"You think the earth is flat?"

I shrug. "Mine is," I say.

She touches my arm gently with her fingertips. "I've often wondered what kind of man you are," she says.

"Any conclusions?"

She smiles. In the soft, thin layer of light that comes through the window and spreads atop the darkness, she looks like a schoolgirl, young and vulnerable and innocent. "You're a man of mystery," she whispers. "You're our mystery man."

"Not to me."

"To everybody else in town, you are."

"They don't count."

"I do."

"What are you going to do about it?" I ask.

"Solve the mystery," she says.

We lie together, hand in hand, and stare at the ceiling until Rothko takes his painting and leaves for the night.

The rain peppers the street outside.

It's as steady, as muted as a heartbeat.

"The storm's gone," I say.

"Maybe not."

She places her head on my shoulder.

"I can make the lightning," she says, "if you can make the thunder."

I frown.

I have no idea what she's talking about.

By daylight, I have it pretty well figured out.

She leaves me somewhere between one kiss and the next.

# 12

**Saturday**
**9:32 a.m.**

From a block away, it appears that I am the last to arrive. But that's all right. Freddy has his morning flowers. He and I have talked for a while. That's not quite right. I've talked. Freddy has listened, provided the dead are still connected to the human voice. I'm not so sure they aren't. Then again, I'm not so sure if they are.

A small crowd has gathered outside the *Chronicle* office, wandering around aimlessly on the sidewalk, pressing their noses against the front window, looking into the dimly lit confines where Mister Neal Holland prints the biography of a small town's daily life. They are trying to turn a doorknob that's been locked for the past fourteen hours. There they are: the concerned, the confused, the curious, a collection of busybodies who comprise the lifeblood of a town whose heart always beats to the tune of a different drummer.

Some frustrated.

Some flustered.

Some out of sorts.

Some look as though they might be contemplating an orchestrated break-in to find their newspaper like they do every Saturday morning before the ink dries. Have no idea why they want it. The only thing going on in town, as far as I know, are a wedding, two funerals, and Billy Bob Baskin who left the parsonage of the First Presbyterian Church long enough to catch an eight-pound bass down at Russell's Bend on the far side of the reservoir. Says being a fisher of bass is a lot easier than being a fisher of men, and he never gets his photograph in the newspaper when he signs up a new member. Catches more bass than new members anyway. His mother named him William Robert, which is a good, solid name for a Scotsman. But after he had wandered into town for a day or two, Neal referred to him as Billy Bob, and, after a while, so did pretty much everybody else in Magnolia Bluff.

The Right Reverend Billy Bob Baskin sees me first. He's a runner. Not tall but tall enough. Beat cancer. Lost weight. I say he's thin. The preacher says he's slender. I don't argue with any man or woman who talks regularly to God. Just as soon they don't mention me at all. He enters a 10K race somewhere almost every Saturday morning but not this one. His hair doesn't slow him down. Must have run out from under it. Says he's training for a marathon. The last time I went twenty-six miles, it was on a bus.

"Where's Neal?" he wants to know.

Broad smile.

Soft voice.

"No paper today," I tell him.

The smile fades.

"Said he was going to run the picture of me and the big boy bass on the front page," Baskin says, working hard not to show any disappointment.

"He'll run it."

"When?"

"We're coming out with the Saturday paper on Tuesday," I answer.

The small crowd has caught up to us. I'm surrounded now by downcast eyes, loose tongues, nervous fidgeting, and a measure of dismay that's one or two words away from outrage. The good folks of Magnolia Bluff look as if depriving them of their Saturday newspaper ranks right up there with stealing a man's first child or running off with his last wife. They would miss their wife and child but not until Sunday.

"Neal's never done that before." Caroline McCluskey wears a concerned frown, nervously rubbing her fingers together across the clasp of the briefcase she's holding. She's fairly tall, probably carrying a pound or two more than she did when she was in college, wears her long blonde hair in a ponytail, and meets most of her friends in books. She fell in love with Mister Darcy until Rhett Butler arrived. Changed her mind. Caroline serves as the city librarian. The *Chronicle* prints the daily news. Caroline archives it until the news is history, then she puts it on microfilm so no one will ever forget it.

"First time for everything, I guess."

Comes out of my mouth before I realize it.

A dumb answer.

I have them cataloged.

I know them all.

"Is Neal all right?" she asks cautiously.

"Neal's fine as far as I know."

"I was afraid he might be sick."

"Neal's as healthy as a horse."

I cringe.

Clichés?

I have a pocketful.

I've heard that cliches are the verbal crutches of the ignorant.

We ignorant need all of the crutches we can get.

Caroline has worry lines tucked under her eyes like footnotes on a research paper. On her, they're as cute as a handful of dimples. "He's worried, isn't he?"

I think of a couple of dumb answers, but this time I keep them to myself.

I shove both hands in my pockets and glance up at the sky. Clouds still black, but they have silver linings. A streak of sunlight cuts through the hemline of a thunderhead. Looks to me like the rain may not be gone, but it appears to be drying up and blowing its way out of town.

"Neal took a day off," I tell her.

"Neal doesn't take days off," Xander Littleton barks, a well-chewed toothpick dangling from between his lips. "I've seen him sit in there by himself all day Saturday and all day Sunday and into the night, afraid something big might happen and we would know about it before he did."

"He's not waiting for some news story to happen," Lorraine Dillard snaps. The sun touches her dangling earrings, and they glisten like new crystal trying to pass for diamonds. Her mint green sundress was designed to catch a lot of sun. "He's in there waiting for some lazy ass advertiser to come in and pay his bill so he can eat before Monday."

"Neal's not hurting for money." Xander cuts each word short.

"Maybe not," Lorraine says, "but he's hurting."

"Something wrong with him?" Caroline wants to know.

"Something's wrong with all of us," I say.

"How would you know?" Xander bites off the end of his toothpick and spits it on the ground.

"We all have our secrets. Some just happen to be more painful than others." I turn and wink at Caroline.

She looks at me as if I don't have a clue about what I'm talking about.

She's right.

"The only secrets I know are in the mystery section of the library," she says.

"How about that long weekend in Galveston?" Phineas asks.

"It was a vacation, that's all."

"Didn't tell anybody you were leaving."

"Didn't think anybody cared."

Phineas laughs. "The postcard was for you," he says. "For some reason known only to the gods who run the post office, it came to my store. It was signed Fred Sawyer."

"You shouldn't read other people's mail," Lorraine tells him. She's not mad, but she's beginning to fume a little.

"Wasn't mail. Just a little writing on a postcard."

"Keep it yourself." Lorraine is angry now. If I were Phineas, I wouldn't order anything down at the Silver Spoon. Mashed potatoes might be spiced with razor blades.

Caroline looks as if she is torn between two emotions.

Crying.

Or murder.

My money's on the razor blades.

"Mysteries, secrets, and life make for an uncomfortable

trinity," I say as I lean back against the light pole. Suddenly, I feel very tired. I can't afford to bear the emotional burdens of a small town. I can't even bear my own. The morning has lost its chill. Behind the courthouse, I can see the distant fog rising off the reservoir.

Stanton Lauderbach, the best legal mouthpiece in Magnolia Bluff, has been watching us from afar, seated on a bench alongside the village green leading toward the courthouse. He looks like the lawyer he is, dressed in a three-piece charcoal gray suit, his dark hair combed straight back. His face is hard, his eyes piercing. He stands, straightens his tie, and wanders toward us. I've seen him walking the same way when Stanton is pacing back and forth in front of the jury box, doing his dead-level best to send the judge, the district attorney, the court clerk, the shoeshine boy, and the bailiff to jail. When Stanton delivers his final sermon to the jury, everybody in the courtroom is on trial and guilty except his client.

A wry smile cracks his lips. "I wonder what mysteries are following you around," Stanton tells me. "We have a killer running loose, and nobody knows who he is, and it strikes me that you, sir, are the one man in town that nobody knows."

"Just a wayfaring stranger," I say.

"What are you hiding from?"

"I'm just passing through."

"Where are you headed?"

"I'll know when I find the road."

"Which road?"

I grin. "The road out of town."

Stanton steps closer to me. "Of all the two-bit, run-down, worn-out towns on the road from here to yonder," he says, "what made you happen to stop in Magnolia Bluff?"

I look him dead square in the eyes.

I feel my fists clench.

My eyes shift from face to face.

Good people.

Decent people.

Hard-working people.

Frightened people.

The strain on their faces shows it.

"Lorraine's chicken fried steak," I tell him.

She snickers.

Stanton's eyes harden, but his smile cracks a little wider.

I know he's lying. But I don't know which expression is the lie.

The eyes?

Or the smile?

"You're a man who sure does move around a lot," he says.

"You been checking up on me?"

He nods. "I have," Stanton says. "Just curious. It's a lawyer thing." His eyes narrow. "You leave quite a crooked trail behind you. Lots of towns. Lots of miles. Most remember you spending time in their nice little town for a while. Nobody remembers you leaving. Nobody knows why you came or why you left. You're kind of like the night. When morning comes, you're gone."

"Find anything nefarious?"

Stanton shakes his head. "All the Army has is your name and serial number. Says you fought in Afghanistan early in the war. Left with an honorable discharge."

The lawyer kicks at the ground for a moment.

He's thinking.

He's buying time.

Finally, he looks up. "Anything else about you that's honorable?" he wants to know.

"I'm pretty good at pushing a broom," I tell him.

Stanton's frown deepens. "Army taught you to kill."

I wink. "It's not habit forming."

His eyes are searching mine.

Mine are fairly blank.

As Stanton Lauderbach turns and saunters away, Caroline grips my arm with her fingertips. "I know why Neal's not here," she says.

"You know more than I do," I tell her.

"It's about Monday, isn't it?"

She tightens her grip.

"Neal's worried about Monday, isn't he?"

When in doubt, tell the truth. That's what mama told me too many years ago.

Some can survive the truth.

Some can't.

Caroline has that strained and anxious look you see in a jackrabbit's eyes when a coyote is waiting on the other side of a barbed-wire fence.

Where can you go?

What can you do?

Can I run fast enough?

Can I run far enough?

Or if I stay real quiet, will he even see me?

The coyote always does.

I look to see if Rebecca may be coming to rescue me. She should be here by now. But maybe she took the day off, too. I left her sleeping. She's nowhere in sight.

We're not standing in complete silence. But if the train wasn't passing through town on its way to Marble Falls, there would be no sound at all.

Our thoughts are like tumblers in a lock, and nobody has the key.

"We all fear what Monday may bring," I tell Caroline. "But nobody knows for sure until it gets here."

"If you're smart," she says, "you'll be gone."

I think it over.

I glance down one street and up another.

The Greyhound headed east runs at four-fifteen.

The Greyhound headed the other way runs two hours later.

Catch either one.

It doesn't matter.

I could grab a seat and see where it takes me next.

But I won't.

I'm not that smart.

# 13

**Saturday**
**10:03 a.m.**

The door to the newspaper office is thrown open and Mister Neal Holland steps out onto the sidewalk. He squints when his eyes touch daylight. He must have slept in his chair all night. His khaki pants are wrinkled, and his blue and white striped dress shirt is falling loose around his substantial waistline. His shock of white hair is blowing in the wind. His eyes are red veins floating in a sea of pale light. On second thought, he may have sat in his chair all night. Doubt if he slept.

He forces a tired smile. "Sorry for the confusion," he says.

"Where's my damn paper?" Xander wants to know.

"Be on the street Tuesday morning."

"Neal." It's Caroline. She whispers as if she were in the front row of a funeral. "Are you thinking he'll strike again?"

Mister Holland's shoulders tighten.

He pats his shirt pocket as if he's looking for a package of cigarettes.

Maybe matches.

Mister Holland doesn't smoke.

"Why is he stalking us?" She raises her voice. It has a nervous inflection.

"No way of knowing, Miss Caroline." I detect a slight quiver in Mister Holland's voice. "He comes. He goes. He leaves no trace he was here. And the boys who wear the badges are no closer to figuring out why he does what he does or why he did what he did when he hit us the first time. I think that was about ten years ago."

"Eight," Caroline says. "Eight of the most important people who live in Magnolia Bluff. Their lives snuffed out on May Twenty Third for no reason."

"Miss Caroline." Mister Holland puts his arm around her shoulders. "He has a reason. We just don't know what it is."

She looks around at the crowd. "It could be one of us," she says.

"Not me," Mister Holland tells her.

"Why not?" Xander asks.

"Robert Baker was buried behind his barn with a backhoe." Mister Holland shrugs. "I don't own a backhoe, I'm too old to steal one, and I couldn't drive one if I did."

"You could hire it out."

"I could," Mister Holland says. "But I hear tell that the only folks around here who have a backhoe stuffed back in a storage are the game and fish boys. Don't know if it's legal to rent one out. Don't know if it isn't."

Xander's face turns red. The muscles in his jaws are clenched tight. "Are you accusing me of something?" he says loudly.

"All I'm saying, Xander, is that you have access to a backhoe, and I don't."

Reverend Billy Bob Baskin steps between the two men. "Let's settle down, gentleman," he says softly. "We're all friends here. We're all neighbors. We're almost family. Some of you have been living in Magnolia Bluff since your birth. I pray that nothing happens on May Twenty Third. I pray that we are saved from another tragic and untimely death this year. But it is not a time to let fear reach down and threaten us. It's a time to pray for deliverance in our time of need."

He bows his head.

He closes his eyes.

He begins to pray softly.

He prays for the town.

He prays for each of us.

He calls us all by name.

He chooses his words carefully.

They are beautiful words.

I hear something about faith, salvation, and the inner sanctum of God.

When Billy Bob Baskin looks up, he's alone with me on the sidewalk.

**Saturday**
**6:27 p.m.**

Mister Holland drives us out into the hills that line each side of the road like great cathedrals created by granite boulders stacked on top of each other. Indian paintbrush and blankets of bluebonnets lay thick in the broad meadows where Herefords and horses and longhorn steers graze on centipede and Bermuda grasses that grow between thick patches of crimson clover. The sun is hanging low in the sky and casting tall shadows down the hillsides and across the fields. We have driven through an empty land for at least an hour and have seen no other cars. We are as close as we can get to the backside of beyond.

Mister Holland pulls his old Dodge Ram off the highway, rolls down the window, and cuts off the engine. We sit for a while in the quiet that comes with the end of day. He hasn't spoken. I would not dare break the silence or the solace of a fading afternoon.

"Ever see anything as pretty as this?" he finally says. His voice is as gentle as the wind on the clover.

I shake my head.

"Lived here all my life," he says, "if you don't count the days I took off to go to college or go turkey hunting in Vietnam."

"Which college?"

"The University of Texas. Damn good journalism school back then." He laughs, and I can detect a taste of bitterness.

"How long in Vietnam?"

"Three days." He chuckles. "Never saw the jungle. Never saw a rice paddy. I saw a twelve-year-old kid in the street in Saigon, gave him a chocolate bar, and the sorry little bastard shot me three times."

"I'm surprised he didn't kill you."

"Could have," he says. "Wasn't much of a shot."

I nod.

"So you came home with a Purple Heart," I say.

"I came home." Mister Holland takes a heavy breath. "Gave the Purple Heart to a little girl waiting for her daddy to come home."

"Did he earn one?"

"He wasn't coming home."

We sat and watched the long shadows slide down the back side of the hills and turn the crimson clover black. A doe and her fawn amble between the longhorns, wandering down to the banks of a river so far back no one ever gave it a name. That's what Mister Holland says anyway.

"That's why I like you, Huston."

I arch an eyebrow.

"You were an Army man," he says.

"Afghanistan."

"And you take flowers up to Freddy every day in the cemetery."

"He deserves them."

"Why?"

"Nobody else takes him flowers."

"You were in different wars," Mister Holland says.

"Separated by thirty years."

"How do you know Freddy?"

"Don't."

Mister holland looks surprised.

"He's a name on a piece of marble," I say.

"What makes him so important to you?"

I feel the pain cut through me. It's anger heated to a slow boil.

"Because he's not important to anyone else," I say.

"I knew Freddy." Mister Holland sits low in his seat, his hands resting idly on the steering wheel. "I was quite a bit older than he was. I'd gone to Nam and come back by the time the Army finally got around to drafting him."

"Good kid?"

"Hired him to throw papers for me." Mr. Holland grins.

"Had us a daily newspaper back then, and I was full of piss and vinegar. Finally decided it was easier being broke once a week than six times a week."

"Freddy have any family?"

"Mama died when Freddy came home in a box." Mister Holland is silent. Memories must be wandering the caverns of his mind. He has a lot of them. Memories and caverns both. "Sister ran off with a railroad man. I guess baby brother's still down in the state pen. If he got out, he didn't come back here."

"So Freddy's alone."

"Always was." Mister Holland frowns and starts the engine again. "Wished I could have paid him more. Mama never had much. If Freddy hadn't thrown my newspapers, doubt if they would have had much to eat."

"Poor side of town?"

"Didn't have enough money to move to the poor side of town."

Mister Holland drives out under a stand of oaks, makes a sharp U-turn, spins a little gravel behind his tires, and heads back toward Magnolia Bluff.

"You're a strange man, Huston," he says.

We ride in silence for a mile or two. Finally, he says, "You should consider settling down in our little town."

"Why me?"

"Because there's nobody else in town quite like you."

# 14

**Sunday**
**5:44 a.m.**

I throw on my jeans and grey sweatshirt shortly after one o'clock. Couldn't sleep. Some kid in a rigged-out jeep kept racing up and down the street outside my window, grinding gears, and, I guess, blowing his Saturday night frustrations out the tailpipe. I could smell exhaust fumes seeping into the room. Stood and watched him for a while. Couldn't quite tell if he was celebrating or doing penance. His ride would be stripped down and in the hands of some shade-tree mechanic by early next week. He would be afoot again unless, of course, he was dismantling a stolen car and trying to leave every spare bolt bouncing on the pavement.

Thought I could sleep by the time he left town and headed southeast toward Austin.

I was wrong.

Counted sheep.

Sheared sheep.

Sold sheep.

Nothing helped.

I hike a mile or two until I come to that long narrow path that leads me to Freddy's grave. A quiet place. A peaceful place. They say the ground collects bones, and the spirits dance with the winds, and the winds are always blowing. The birds are nesting, and even the crickets have nothing to chirp about.

I spend most of the night sitting with Freddy, leaning back against the trunk of a Sabinal Maple tree. I ask him a lot of questions.

Did you want to fight?
Or were you glad to find a way out of town?
Where were you when that last bullet came?
Were you scared?
Were you in a firefight?
Did you feel the bullet?
Did you know you were dying before you died?"
Did you leave a sweetheart behind?
Did you kiss your mama goodbye?
I always ask the same questions.
Freddy always gives me the same answers.
Nothing.

Freddy keeps his little secrets close to a heart that no longer beats. No one will ever know his final thoughts, provided he had any, and maybe he was gone before he ever knew he left. I like to think that's what happened.

No pain.

No trepidation.

Death is terrible.

Fear is worse.

I leave Freddy behind when I see the first hint of daylight leak through a cut in Hazzard Hawk mesa and crawl fitfully across a valley of scrub oak and mesquite as it snakes its way toward the burying ground. It's a long walk back to town. It's less than a mile, but this morning, it's a walk I've been dreading to make for eighteen years, six months, and seventeen days. It should be over by now. That's what I tell myself every morning. But it's not. And it's my fault. God didn't make me a coward. It's a trait I was able to pick up on my own.

I have someone in town I need to see.

She doesn't know I'm coming today.

She doesn't know I'm coming at all.

She doesn't know who I am.

She doesn't know I exist, and I'm afraid to confront her.

I have a secret.

It's been mine for a long time.

It's been festering for a long time.

It's time I gave it away.

Let someone else detest me as much as I dislike myself.

I hear the chimes in the courthouse tower ring six times.

Morning has officially broken.

I guess I could wait a little while longer.

Give her time to awaken.

Then again, I wonder if she ever sleeps.

I don't.

I haven't slept all night for eighteen years, six months, and seventeen days.

I try.

I can't.

Nights are filled with the aroma of death.

My footsteps lead me to the front door of the Silver Spoon. I can almost smell the coffee brewing, hot and fresh and warm in my throat.

I turn the knob.

The door is locked.

A closed sign hangs in the window.

It's Sunday.

It's Lorraine's busiest day.

How in the world can she be closed?

On Sundays, the cash register rings like a slot machine in Vegas.

I hear the quick squeal of breaks and glance back over my shoulder. Sheriff Buck Blanton has come to a sudden stop, and he's rolling down his window. The black Dodge Charger Pursuit is rocking, and I can feel the heat rising from the hood.

"If you're looking for coffee, you best be looking somewhere else." His grin doesn't match his cold, gray eyes.

"Where's Lorraine?"

"Gone."

"Bad time to be gone." I walk to the edge of the curb and look down at him.

"Bad time to be in Magnolia Bluff," Buck says. "We got ourselves a madman hanging around close, and chances are he's gonna be in town sometime tomorrow, and somebody amongst us won't be here anymore. Lorraine always leaves early on the eve of May Twenty Third. Losing her husband has been hard on her. Hell, it's been hard on all of us."

I nod. "Tomorrow must have painful scars for her," I tell him.

"We all have a few scars." Buck shuts off his engine and stares for a moment down an empty street. "We all know we're gonna die one of these days," he says. "Don't like it. But we know that we start moving toward our final day on earth the moment we're born. Most everybody is just like me. We want to take our final breath in our own bed with a member or two of the family at our side to cry when we make that journey to the other side, wherever the hell that might be. But none of us expect to have life ripped away from us by somebody sneaking into town with a machete or hangman's noose or some other contraption of death. Lorraine's husband, he was buried alive." Buck shuddered.

"Who do you think it is, Sheriff?"

"No idea."

"You're bound to have a list of possible suspects."

"Not this time."

"Clues?"

"Nary a one."

"What'd the FBI find?"

There is no humor in Buck's laugh. It's as dry as his grin. "They left and didn't know as much as I did, and I didn't know a damn thing."

"Think he'll come back tomorrow?"

"Don't know why he would," Buck says, "and don't know why he wouldn't. What's his motive? Your guess is as good as mine. If he was just mad at eight people, he's got them all, and we'll never see the likes of him again. But maybe there's a ninth person. Maybe there's a tenth. Maybe we never get rid of him. Maybe he just likes to kill people. There are some twisted minds running loose out there." Buck sighs heavily. "I wish the whole damn town would take Lorraine's example and get the hell out of Dodge. I'd sleep a whole lot better."

"Would you leave?" I want to know.

His grin brightens up as his car roars to life. "If there was nobody in town, I'd pull out, too, and I'd turn out the lights when I left."

It's a bad day to be in Magnolia Bluff.

The streets are devoid of people.

Downtown is as quiet as Freddy's grave.

Somebody is waiting to die.

Don't know who.

But the stalker does.

Right now, I'd kill for a cup of good coffee.

Maybe the stalker kills for less.

I walk past the Wood-Fired Coffee shop.

Harry Thurgood has wonderful coffee.

Everybody in town says so.

But I see Harry Thurgood sitting at a front table and feeding the Reverend Ember Cole a muffin one bite at a time. Looks like cinnamon. Looks damn good. Can't preach a sermon with hunger pains gnawing at your gullet. She may be thinking about scripture. I bet Harry's not.

I see him laughing.

The Reverend Ember Cole is laughing with him, her face as bright as dew on a morning meadow. Wonder what they think is funny? Must have something on their minds other than death.

I'm not laughing.

I keep on walking.

The aroma of rich coffee lingers long after I have crossed the street on my way to 3215 Robinson Avenue. Don't particularly like or dislike either Harry or the preacher lady. They are simply annoying in their own individual ways. Harry is mister charm with the girls, wives, and single women of Magnolia Bluff. Even grandmothers wait at street crossings, hoping he will come along, gently take them by the arm and escort them through the traffic, provided any trucks or cars happen to be cruising through town. Harry Thurgood is also brash. He will tell you what he thinks even if he knows it will make you mad. Maybe he just wants to make you mad. Maybe he just wants to kill you. Don't know why he brought his coffee shop to our little hamlet. Don't know what secrets lie behind those dark eyes. There is something not quite right about Harry Thurgood. He's a true enigma and works hard to remain that way.

Ember, on the other hand, looks as if she might be a lingerie model in an old Sears and Roebuck catalog. She walks to the pulpit as if she's walking the runway at a fashion show. I don't personally think she's wearing anything beneath her black robe on Sunday morning. Bet it's lined with silk or satin. She will flirt with almost every man she meets but keeps the Holy Bible between them. She treats it like her shield of morality. Might as well be a barbed-wire fence. You might get through, but you would come out scratched and scarred on the other side. Her words are filled with *thou shalt nots.* Her eyes often seem to be pleading *come on and get it.* If anyone has, it's old Harry Thurgood. Strange bedfellows. Then again, maybe they deserve each other.

I glance at the sky.

Gray.

The color of wet cement.

I turn down Robinson Avenue.

Near as I can tell, I'm only a block, maybe two, away.

I feel like a condemned man on his way to the death chamber.

One step in front of the other.

One meeting.

One confession.

But no redemption.

I can taste the dread in my throat.

I'm in.

No way out.

Then again, maybe I'll be struck by lightning.

I'm looking for a storm. But the rains are gone. The thunder is silenced.

I have to force my legs to keep moving.

*My heart is pounding.*

*My heart is breaking.*

*I feel the sweat.*

*I smell the gunpowder and the blood that splashes against my face.*

*I'm screaming for help.*

*And nobody comes.*

*Nobody ever comes.*

# 15

**Sunday**
**10:46 a.m.**

The house is small and sits back off the street behind a massive live oak tree, its decrepit limbs hanging low to the ground. No grass. Just scattered weeds. But they have been mowed and neatly trimmed around a flower bed where roses have already begun to bloom pink and red. Once, the house had been painted white, but hard years of bad weather and neglect have colored it a pale shade of yellow. The porch creaks like the bad joints in my knees when I step on boards that are no doubt one more good rain away from mildew and rot.

I take a big breath and knock on the front door.

I feel my hand trembling.

I wait.

No one opens the door.

I knock again.

And wait.

I've finally talked myself into coming this far.

I'm not about to walk away now.

I'll sit in the rocking chair all day if I have to.

I don't have to.

The door cracks open, and I see the black, swollen eyes of a lady staring up at me. I figure she is in her sixties, although she looks older. Her dark hair is cropped short around an oval face and streaked with gray. No makeup. No lipstick. Nothing to hide the wrinkles and sunspots. She has a faded maroon chenille robe wrapped tightly around her, and she is barefoot.

I break the silence. "Are you Sylvia Spooner?"

"That's me." She stiffens. "Who wants to know?"

"I've come a long way to see you."

"What about?" She looks through me. No offense. A lot of people do.

"I knew your son."

"Harley?"

I nod.

"Harley's not here."

"I know." It's barely a whisper.

"He's dead."

"I was with him when he died."

Her knees weaken, and she catches the door to keep from falling. Her eyes glaze over like cracked marble. A tear hangs on an eyelash.

"That was a long time ago," she says.

"Eighteen years, six months, and seventeen days."

"Nobody ever told me what happened to Harley," she says softly.

"That's why I'm here."

Her stare cuts through to my heart. "What took you so long?"

My shoulders slump. I can feel my blood rushing through my veins, searching for a way out. "For a long time, I couldn't tell you."

"Why not?"

"We were where we weren't supposed to be."

"Were you lost?"

"There were seven of us," I answer quietly. "Some army brass with stars on their shoulders sent us into the mountains. Wrong time. Wrong place. Wrong country. We knew if something went wrong, and it always goes wrong, they would pretend we didn't exist."

She shakes her head as if trying to grasp the remnants of what I'm telling her. "But that doesn't make any sense."

"War never does."

"The letter said my son died in a jeep accident."

"It was all a big lie."

"You mean Harley died for a lie?"

Sylvia Spooner's knees can no longer support her. She begins sliding down the door. I catch her before she falls to the floor, carry her inside the house, and place her gently into an old overstuffed easy chair. The lights aren't burning. The room is dark. It suits us just fine.

Her emotions break like a dam that has blocked too many floodwaters for too many years. Now it is fractured, and the tears she has buried deep inside her for such a long time are spilling as if they may never stop.

She sits on the edge of the easy chair, her face in her hands, her hands in her lap, and I wait silently in the cool darkness around us and let her cry. Her sobs are deep and filled with anguish, a woman hurt, a woman angry, a woman who wants to hold her baby boy and touch his face one last time no matter how old he may be, and Harley Spooner hasn't aged in eighteen years, six months, and seventeen days.

# 16

**Sunday**
**11:12 a.m.**

Sylvia Spooner composes herself long enough to brew me a cup of instant coffee, then leaves me alone in her living room for a good hour while she showers and dresses to hear about the last dark day her son walked upon the earth. She returns wearing a simple black dress, the hem around her ankles, with a single strand pearl necklace and matching black shoes. Her hair is neatly brushed, and a new shade of facial powder has taken a good ten years off her age. She tries to smile as she walks into the room and fails miserably. She walks slowly, her hands moving from one piece of furniture to the next. She looks as if she will fall without something solid to grasp. Age has trapped her before her time, age and grief have made an old woman out of her. Sylvia Spooner appears for all the world as though she has dressed for a funeral.

She turns on a lamp, sits down across from me on a brown leatherette sofa, and says calmly, "Tell me about my son."

"He was a good man," I say, "a good soldier and a good friend."

She holds up her hand and stops me. "No," she says, "tell me about the day he died."

"We were on patrol," I begin.

"Where?"

"Still can't tell you."

"Why not?'

"Still classified."

"Why would the Army keep a secret from a mother?" she wants to know.

"You have to understand the Army and how it operates."

"Explain it to me."

"The Army tells various and assorted lies until it gets caught." I shrug. "Then someone from the top changes the lies, and the game begins all over again."

"And our boys? My son?"

"Pawns on a chessboard." I taste the bitterness on my tongue. "We lose one soldier. We put another in his place. And the fighting goes on."

"And another mother cries herself to sleep at night."

"Everyone cries but the general."

"Why doesn't he cry?"

"He's the chess master." I smile a sad smile. "He never dies."

"It's not fair."

"We know how to go to war. We just don't know when to pack up and come home." I place my empty coffee cup on the small end table beside me.

"Another cup?" Sylvia asks.

"I'm fine."

"What happened on the patrol?" she asks.

"It was sometime in the shank of the day," I tell her. "We were in the high country. Rough. Rugged. Hot. Wind coming up from the valley floor felt like the inside of a furnace. Don't know how many miles we had marched along a narrow little trail. Nobody talking. Sweat in our eyes. Shirts plastered on our backs. Another hour, maybe two, and we would camp for the night. We never saw the enemy. We never heard anyone at all. Out of nowhere, a bullet hit Harley, and he fell at my feet. Must have been a sniper from a long distance away. Before I could say a word, machinegun fire was cutting across the mountainside like a heavy rain."

"And you survived."

I nodded.

"And Harley didn't."

I feel guilt squeeze my heart as if someone had tied a leather belt tightly around my chest.

"He didn't." The words sounded as if they had been spoken by a stranger.

"Tell me one thing," she said.

"I'll try."

"Where did the bullet hit him?"

"In the throat, just above his Adam's apple."

Sylvia is nervously rubbing the palms of her hands together. "Did Harley suffer? Did it take him a long time to die? Was he in a lot of pain?"

I stare at the floor.

I shudder.

In my mind, I am back on the mountain.

I see it all.

Every moment seems to last a year.

I remember it all.

*A bullet hole in his throat looked as big as a silver dollar.*

*I reached down to stop the flow of blood.*

*He was choking, clawing at his throat.*

*I heard Harley say, "I need him now."*

*"Who?"*

*"Jesus."*

*Tears had paled the blue in his eyes.*

*I yelled for a medic.*

*I held Harley's hand.*

*I saw the medic running.*

*But not toward me.*

*Not toward Harley.*

*I yelled his name.*

*For God's sake, a man is shot.*

*He's dying.*

*The medic kept running.*

*Harley's jaws were clenched in pain.*

*He screamed once, so loud I could no longer hear the bullets hammering into the rock face of the mountain.*

*Blood dripped out of the corner of his mouth.*

*All he wanted was Jesus.*

*He left before Jesus came.*

*Then again, maybe Jesus was already there to take him home.*

I look up at Harley's mother. She's small and fragile, and her faded dress hangs loosely from her shoulders. Her face is tense, her fingers nervously rubbing the strand of pearls around her neck as though they are rosary beads.

"His death was quick and sudden" It's a lie, and I know it. "I don't think Harley was ever aware he died."

"Is that the truth, Mister …?" Her voice trails away.

"Huston," I say. "Graham Huston."

"Is that the truth, Mister Huston?"

"Between one breath and the next, he was gone."

I feel dirty.

I am choking on guilt.

And remorse.

And shame.

Sylvia lets out a deep breath. "At least, I can thank Jesus for that," she says.

"You can."

For a good ten minutes, neither of us speak.

"When did you learn about Harley's death?" I ask, finally cutting through the silence.

"A soldier came to see me," she says. "A nice young man. An officer I believe he was."

I nod. "He would have been an officer."

"He told me Harley was missing in action."

"He was."

Sylvia stares into the darkness as if she is looking into a well that has no bottom. "A year or two later," she says, "I received a telegram from the Office of the President telling me Harley was a prisoner of war. I wasn't able to sleep at night, I lay in bed until the wee hours of the morning wondering where he was and how he was doing and if he was hurt and were they feeding him enough or were they feeding him at all. I could see him in a little concrete cell, no window, no light, all alone, and I feared he would never be free again." She wipes the angry tears from her eyes with a man's handkerchief. "I thought the days would get easier. They didn't. Not once did I ever give him up for dead. Then about nine years ago, a letter came informing me that Harley had been killed in a jeep accident. There was no mention of him being MIA or a POW. Two sentences was all it said. *We regret to inform you that PFC Harley Spooner has been killed in a jeep accident. We will be unable to return his body home for burial.* I had an attorney write letters for me. Nobody ever wrote me back. I made telephone calls. I was always told the same thing. We will get back to you, Mrs. Spooner. No one ever did. That's all I've ever known until you came to see me today."

Sylvia stands and walks to the kitchen table, holding on to the backs of furniture to keep from falling. She looks frail, uneasy and unsteady. Behind her, through the window, I can see a little garden of roses, mixed with weeds and geraniums and hydrangeas. The rains have given them new life.

"There was no jeep accident, was there?" she asks. Her voice is hollow.

"No, ma'am."

"They knew all along, didn't they?"

"Yes, ma'am."

"For more than nine years, they let me fret and wonder and hope for a miracle, praying every night that he would come home again someday."

I let her sentence hang in the air.

She wasn't talking to me.

She wasn't talking to anyone.

"There's one more thing I need to tell you," I say quietly.

She slowly turns around, her arms folded across her chest.

She waits.

"Your son should not have died that day."

She frowns. The wrinkles in her forehead are cut deeper.

She's still waiting.

"I was supposed to die, not Harley."

The light in the lamp flickers.

The cool air is sucked out of the room.

But the chill remains.

"Why would you say that?" she wants to know.

"We had a seven-man patrol," I say slowly to make sure she understands. "The point was out front. I was the second man behind him. Harley was the third. I slipped on some loose rocks coming through a narrow cut in the mountain and fell. By the time I stood up again, Harley had passed me, said I was too unbalanced to be in the army anyway. Too slow and with two left feet. He was laughing at me. Harley was always making jokes. The bullet hit the second man on patrol. I should have been the second man. That was my position. It should have killed me, not Harley. You see, Harley died in my place."

A strange thing happens.

Sylvia Spooner's face softens.

It's the first time I've seen her smile.

"Harley saved your life, didn't he?"

"He should be sitting here with you today, not me."

Sylvia sits back down on the sofa.

The smile has not moved from her face.

The tension is gone.

No tears.

No anger.

She picks up a framed picture of Harley that has been sitting on the coffee table. She brushes the dust off the glass. He must be about twelve in the old polaroid snapshot. He's standing beside a creek, holding up a line with two catfish and a perch. His grin is a mile wide.

Sylvia looks up at me. "Thank you," she says.

"For what?"

"You gave me back my son today."

I walk out the front door.

I leave her holding the photograph against her face.

She's smiling.

He's smiling back at her.

*Her son is only twelve.*

*In her eyes, he will always be twelve.*

There are no goodbyes.

Neither one of us has anything left to say.

# 17

**Monday**
**8:46 a.m.**

The front door of the *Chronicle* office is open. I'm not surprised. Mister Holland is always the first to arrive and generally the last to leave. He says he loves the smell of paper and ink in the early morning, and he generally spends most of his days sitting beside the phone, waiting for it to ring, waiting for it to dump the remains of another page-one article in his lap. He lives for the big stories. He tells me that someday he'll have a news flash so important he'll have to set the headline in 128-point type. Doesn't know what it could be. But he'll recognize the story when it happens. That's what he says anyway. Most newspapers are saving their 128-point type for the Second Coming. Of course, the revelation of Revelations will be old news by the time any of us hear about it. I glance toward his chair. It's empty.

Rebecca's not at her desk either. Didn't expect her to be. Mondays are always a slow day. Nobody makes news on a Monday. Nobody prints the news on a Monday. Nobody wants to buy advertising on a Monday. Down at the back table in the Silver Spoon, the scalawags, reprobates, misfits, and the great unwashed have presented the city council with more than one petition calling for the abolition of Monday. Nobody works. Nobody shops. Nobody comes to town. And no business is open unless the owner happens to be peddling fresh, rich, hot coffee. The Silver Spoon wasn't even open today. Lorraine's still out of town and always saying she won't be coming back, but she always does. Folks tend to hunker down on days like this.

Then again, there's only one day a year like this one.

I guess they're all staying home.

I guess they're all staying inside.

I guess they're all hiding from the bogeyman.

Don't blame them.

*It's morning.*

*May Twenty Third.*

*Will it happen again?*

*Who's waiting to die?*

*Who's waiting to kill?*

*Or has death ridden a tired horse somewhere else?*

I'm only showing up at the *Chronicle* office for the obvious reason.

*Don't work.*

*Don't get paid.*

*Don't get paid.*

*Don't eat.*

Dedication has nothing to do with it.

It had been so quiet outside when I came to work, I thought that, perhaps, I was walking through a ghost town.

Maybe I was.

No one on the streets. No scattered tidbits of chatter. No dogs barking. No truck gears grinding. No doors slamming. No train rattling its way through town. No car horns honking. Not a car in sight. Not even Buck Blanton's black Charger Pursuit. May Twenty Third is a morbid kind of holiday in Magnolia Bluff.

I go straight to the press room.

Clean it up.

Ink it up.

Get it ready to run on all cylinders if Mister Holland wants to print a special edition today instead of waiting until tomorrow.

*It all depends on who dies.*

*When he dies.*

*And how he dies.*

You can tell how important a person is by the size of the type above his or her obituary.

I pick up a bucket of ink.

I drop it.

My breath catches in my throat.

My heart forgets to beat.

I'm not certain it will ever beat again.

A knot forms in my stomach.

That's when I see him.

*Mister Holland.*

He lies across the printing press, his arms outstretched, his eyes staring at the ceiling fan as it chases away the flies above him.

He is pale.

His face is waxen.

His eyes are the color of milk left too long in the sun.

His mouth is gaped open.

He looks as if he wants to say something and just can't get the words out.

Maybe it's a scream cut short.

A pair of nickel-plated scissors have been thrust into his chest.

A puddle of blood has dried beneath his shoulders.

*The lights flicker.*

*That's odd.*

*The lights aren't on.*

The lights are like flashbulbs in the deep recesses of my mind, and I fear they are about to short out.

A piece of paper has been pinned to his shirt.

It's the page of a calendar. Two things have been circled in red ink.

*May.*

*Twenty-third.*

Three words, written in ink, have been scrawled on the page.

*Lest we forget.*

But what is it?

*A message?*

*A reminder?*

*Or a threat.*

# 18

**Monday**
**8:52 a.m.**

Mister Holland is dead, and the morning has lost its luster. The voice of Magnolia Bluff is silent. The conscience of Magnolia Bluff has taken a journey we all must take, but no one wants to go today. His was always a balancing act on the wrong side of curiosity. As he once told me, "I want to find out the truth behind the story if it kills me." It has. Now he has been granted a look beyond the veil of time. He knows what none of us suspect. He's got it figured out. He's in the middle of the biggest story in his lifetime, and he can't do a damn thing about it.

I can hear him barking orders now.

*What's the lead?*

*Got a headline?*

*Make it larger.*

*What do the police say?*

*They have a motive?*

*They have a theory?*

*Hell, they couldn't catch the killer if he came in and confessed.*

A siren wails in the distance. Must be the ambulance from Barron Schiff's funeral home.

Police wouldn't use a siren.

Nobody's in trouble.

Nobody's a threat.

Come in.

Clean up the mess.

And tell the press, although I'm the only one around, "We are not yet ready to call it murder just yet. An autopsy will determine that. The medical examiner will be here this afternoon and take the body of Mister Holland back to Austin. The matter is presently under investigation. We'll know more when the forensics team has finished with the crime scene."

I smile.

It's a sick smile.

The May Twenty Third murders have been under investigation for nine years.

No arrests.

No suspects.

No speculation.

No charges filed.

One dead end chases after another.

I look up when I hear the door open. Reece Sovern bolts inside the office, his gaze cutting sharply from one end of the room to the other. His snub-nosed belly gun still resides in its holster, but his hand is holding firmly to the butt of the revolver. He's all business. Reece looks more dour than usual. I called before he had a chance to shave. His brown gabardine trousers are baggy, the sleeves on his white dress shirt rolled up to the elbows. His hair is still wet from the shower. His face is stern, his square jaw set. He's a man in a hurry. He's a city detective but prefers to call himself the police investigator. I think he simply fills out reports, files them away, and either forgets or loses them.

His gaze settles on me. "You make the call?"

I nod.

"You're new here, aren't you?"

"Eight months and counting."

"I've seen you around."

"I've been around."

Sovern squares his shoulders and loosens his grip on the revolver. "Where is the deceased?" he barks.

"Back room."

"Where in the back room?"

"On the press?"

"What's he doing on the press?"

"You'll see."

"You sure he's dead?" The bark is not so vicious this time.

I nod.

"How do you know?"

"I was in Afghanistan," I say with irritation crawling into my voice. "I know what dead looks like."

I stand and motion for him to follow me.

"You find the body?"

"I did."

"When?"

"A little before nine."

"You have a key?"

"Door was unlocked."

"What were you doing here?"

"I work here."

I lead him into the press room, and even a hard-nosed detective like Reece Sovern seems stunned at the sight of Mister Holland. He grabs onto the end of the press to keep from losing his balance. His face has a strange, green tint.

"Jesus," he whispers.

If it's not a prayer, it should be.

"You touch him?" he asks.

"I left him alone."

"You touch anything?"

"The phone to call you."

"Which phone?"

"Rebecca's. I didn't figure you'd want anybody contaminating Mister Holland's phone."

He grins. "You're smarter than you look," he says.

"I'm smarter than any of us look," I say.

His grin fades.

He's back to business.

We both turn when Barron Schiff strides into the room. He plays the part of the perfect mortician. A thousand-dollar black suit with tiny white stripes. White shirt. Gold cuff links. Clean shaven. And not a hair out of place. Nobody's dresses that well on a Monday morning. But I figure Barron has been pacing the floor down at his funeral home since before daylight. He knows what day it is. He no doubt woke up expecting a new client before dark. Just didn't know who it would be. Now he does. It will be the funeral of the year. Mister Neal Holland may not be the richest of men. But he's the best-known commodity in Magnolia Bluff. Barron may need to schedule two funerals to pack everyone into his chapel. Let the drum rolls begin. Shoot the fireworks and shoot them high. It's showtime.

Barron looks across the room at Mister Holland.

His face turns white.

The blood has gone elsewhere.

He's visibly shaken for someone who cavorts with the dead on a regular basis.

I'm sure Barron was made aware that Mister Holland had departed Magnolia Bluff when the police called him. He probably figured it was a heart attack. Maybe a stroke. After all, Mister Holland had turned eighty-six eleven months ago. But, obviously, nobody had told Barron it was the coldest of a cold-blooded murder. He looks back at Sovern, swallows hard, and says softly, "You think it's him?"

"Who?"

"The May Twenty Third killer."

"At the moment, Barron, I can't say if it was or if it wasn't. I just walked in two minutes ahead of you. Right now, it doesn't do any of us any good for me to speculate on who murdered Neal or why he was murdered. It may just be a robbery that blew up and got out of hand. Who knows? Somebody may have killed Neal in self-defense, then staged it look like the attack was something it wasn't."

"I doubt if it was robbery," I say.

Sovern looks as if he wished I would go away. "What makes you say that?"

"Mister Holland didn't keep any cash money around the office. Said it was bad luck. His diamond and gold Masonic ring was the only valuable thing he owned, and he's still wearing it." I suddenly feel as if my legs might collapse. It's as if I've run a marathon and still have miles to go. "I imagine if you check his wallet, you'll find a five-dollar bill autographed by

Ronald Reagan. It's not worth anything. But it meant the world to Mister Holland."

Sovern frowns. "How do you know all of this?"

"Like I told you, I work here, and Mister Holland talks a lot, and for reasons even I don't understand, I'm a pretty good listener."

"We'll check the wallet," the detective says.

"You'll also find a magazine photograph of Marilyn Monroe," I tell him.

"She autograph it, too?"

"No, but she sat on it at the Diamond Horseshoe out in Vegas." I grin. "That was good enough for Neal."

"Be good enough for any of us."

Barron Schiff straightens his red and blue striped tie, and tells Sovern, "I don't guess you'll be needing us for a while."

"Not until we finish with forensics."

Barron starts to leave, then hesitates.

He looks troubled.

He is troubled.

I can see confusion written all over his face.

"If it wasn't the May Twenty Third killer, then why would anyone else want to kill Neal?" Barron wonders aloud. "He could certainly be irascible from time to time, and he'd sometimes stir the pot a little with his editorials just to see who boiled, but as far as I know everybody in town loved him."

"Somebody sure as hell didn't."

We hear the front door slam and the sound of high heels running across the floor. "What's going on?" It is Rebecca. She's shouting. "What's a police car and ambulance doing out front?"

I run to meet her.

I'm not fast enough.

She bursts into the pressroom, the light bouncing dim on her colorful pink and yellow sundress and sees Mister Holland stretched across the press before I can turn her away.

"Oh, My God." It's the sound of pure agony, a frantic and tormented wail coming from somewhere deep inside her heart. I see her eyes begin to roll back into her head and catch her when Rebecca faints. I gently carry her away from the crime scene.

It is the saddest of days, the saddest I've experienced in eighteen years, six months, and eighteen days.

My friend is dead.

The *Chronicle* has died with him.

# 19

**Monday**
**10:18**

Rebecca has a chokehold on her Real Good Wood Fired mug of coffee. Black. Strong. Hot. Nothing fancy today. Her knuckles are white, the muscles in her jaws tight and bulging with tension. The wind has blown her hair every which way but loose. Her sleeveless sundress is awash with colors too bright for such a somber and disconsolate day. The coffee has melted her red lipstick, and she has wiped it away with a cloth napkin. Rebecca tosses her head back and drains the last of the robust blend down her throat. Her hand is trembling.

Harry brings her another mug and sits down beside her. "This one's on the house," he says softly. "You've had quite a shock."

Rebecca nods her thanks. She looks at me across the table and asks, "Did Neal go home last night?"

"Doubt it."

Harry interrupts. "Neal had a house over on Sixth Avenue, didn't he?"

"He preferred the office," I tell him. "Kept a cot in the back. Had a microwave, a coffee pot, and a stack of books. Said he didn't need anything else."

"I wonder if someone surprised him." Rebecca holds the hot mug against her forehead. The day isn't chilled, but she is. "Of if he was meeting someone."

"I think Neal knew his killer." Everybody has an opinion or will have one before the day is over. I have mine.

"What makes you say that?"

"Door wasn't forced open," I say. "Window wasn't broken. I guess the killer could have come down the chimney but the office doesn't have one."

Rebecca shudders. "Neal sees a friendly face. He unlocks the door and opens it. He smiles. He calls *come on in*. He turns his back. He's dead." Her eyes are bright as if they're reflecting the sparks from a bottle rocket.

"It's never that easy."

"The killing?"

"The dying."

For a moment, the smell of gunpowder burns my nostrils.

*The air is thick with smoke.*

*"Incoming."*

*A yell.*

*Then a scream.*

*He's down.*

*Laughing.*

*Joking.*

*Now he's looking for Jesus.*

*I don't see Jesus.*

*I hope Harley does.*

Rebecca is staring at me.

Harry's not quite sure what to do.

*No reason to smile.*

That's what I suspect he's thinking.

*No reason to quell their fears.*

*Haven't been around long enough to be that scared.*

"Was Neal worried about anything?" Harry asks.

"Today," I say. "He was worried about May Twenty Third."

"I guess most everyone in town was." Harry frowns. His coffee has grown cold.

"How about you?" I ask.

"I'm like you," Harry says.

I wait.

"I'm a stranger, too."

Rebecca narrows her eyes. She glances from me to Harry

and back to me again. "Maybe I should leave," she says.

Harry places his hand on top of hers. "Why?"

"Nine people in this town are dead," she says. "Nine times it's happened. I know everybody in Magnolia Bluff. I hear the Crimson Hats talking in the back of the coffee shop. It's not unusual for me to drop in and overhear the gossip tossed around in the tea room of The Flower Bed and Breakfast. I spend way too much time in the beauty shop. Everybody in town has a secret and I know just about all of them. But you two – Harry Thurgood and Graham Huston. You are a strange lot, the only new faces in this town or in this whole damn county. I don't know anything about either one of you and don't have the foggiest idea why either one of you chose to settle down in this godforsaken little hell hole."

"I needed a good cup of coffee," Harry says. He winks.

"I'm just passing through," I tell her.

Rebecca's eyes are accusing me, and they're probably accusing me of murder. "How many times have you passed through towns before?" she asks. Her voice has a stinger.

"I liked Mister Holland," I say.

"And why do you keep calling him Mister Holland." Her words are fired like bullets.

"Because he hired me. He was my boss. He paid me every week. He liked to have long, rambling conversations after everyone else had left for the day. He sometimes drove me up to the cemetery. He talked about Magnolia Bluff's past and present. I enjoyed his company. I respected him." I take a deep breath and feel my lungs burning. "It's an Army thing," I tell her. "I called my platoon leader *Sergeant* Bayfield. I called my commanding officer *Colonel* Halstead. To me, Neal was and always will be *Mister* Holland. It's a title he deserved."

Rebecca slumps in her chair. I can tell she's frightened. She's obviously weighted down by a lot of stress. She's no doubt sick with grief. She's lashing out at anyone who's closest to her. I happen to be sitting in the chair beside her.

I don't know how good the district attorney is in Magnolia Bluff. I don't know a lot about the judge.

But one thing's for certain.

If I'm on the docket for murder, I'm glad Rebecca Wilson isn't on the jury.

By the time Harry refills her mug with coffee, the anger seems to have melted away inside her. Her voice is suddenly much softer. She looks directly at me and asks, "How was Neal when you found him?"

"Just like he was when you saw him."

"That was such a cruel thing to do to a nice man like Neal."

"I believe it was a planned murder," I say.

"What makes you think that?"

"There's nobody in town who believes Neal was in the back room lying down on the press when somebody decided to end his life." I take a sip of hot Jasmine Green Tea. "He wasn't struck from behind. He didn't just fall across the press by accident. I think he died somewhere else, was dragged to the press, and draped across it. There was an irreverent madness behind the way his death was staged."

"Were there any other bloodstains in the office?" Rebecca asks, a touch of color returning to her face.

"Didn't see any." I shrug. "Of course, I didn't look."

"You should have."

"Why?"

"You're the reporter on the scene."

"I'm the broom pusher. That's all."

"Neal was a big man." Rebecca shudders. "It would take a lot of strength to move him across the office."

"Could have used a dolly," Harry suggests.

"The office doesn't have a dolly." I begin rolling up the sleeves of my shirt. It's suddenly very warm in the back of the coffee shop, almost as hot as my tea. "I believe Mister Holland was a dead man walking when he opened the door. He just didn't know it."

"Did the scissors come from my desk?" Rebecca asks.

"Not those scissors." I shake my head to try and drive the image from my mind. "Those were big scissors. You could have used them to shear sheep. The killer may have stabbed Mister Holland. But he used his fist to hammer the blades through the breastbone."

Rebecca cocks her head to one side. "You sure know a lot about killing."

"Join the Army," I reply.

"Why?"

"You learn a lot about killing."

Rebecca looks incredulous. "Even in an office?"

"That's where most wars are fought."

"How about the battlefield?"

"Men are sent to die on the battlefield." The sour taste of bile rises in my throat. "But the wars are fought in offices."

She blinks the moisture from her eyes and asks, "Do you think the scissors killed him?"

"They would certainly do the trick."

"But why would anybody go to that much trouble?"

"It looks to me like somebody had a real bad bone to pick with Neal."

Rebecca pushes a strand of dark hair out of her eyes. "But he was such a gentle soul."

"Nobody is who he seems."

She raises an eyebrow. "What is that supposed to mean?"

Harry blows the steam off a fresh mug of coffee. He leans forward with both elbows on the table and fills in the blanks. "We all think we know somebody," he says. "We hardly ever do. Each of us has a past that we want to keep a secret. It might be our undoing. It may be harmless, and then again, it might eventually lead to deadly consequences. We hurt someone. We don't realize it, but most times we do. We forget it. The victim doesn't. Our dastardly act may not be so dastardly, but it grows and festers, and the one we hurt waits to exact a measure of revenge. Sometimes they wait for years. Most times, nothing ever happens. Then suddenly it does and leaves the rest of us scratching our heads and looking for a motive when we have no idea what the motive could possibly be."

"You think that's what could have happened to Mister Holland?" I want to know.

"Wouldn't be surprised." Harry grins. "He's in the business of making people mad. He runs a newspaper. He skates on the narrow side of slander or libel in every issue."

"But what did Mister Holland have in common with the other eight victims struck down on May Twenty Third?" I want to know.

"That's the million-dollar question," Harry says. "Find the common denominator, and you'll find the killer."

Rebecca shakes her head. "How could anyone hate Neal that badly?"

"Maybe his past held a secret." I pour more hot water into my mug and douse the teabag once again. "Somebody else held a grudge."

Rebecca stares out the big front window of the coffee shop. A gray Chevy sedan and then a blue Ford F150 Pickup crawl down the street. Neither seems to be in a hurry. Drivers probably wondering why there are so many cop cruisers patrolling the downtown streets. Probably slowing down because the number of police officers with grim faces hurrying from one building to another have piqued their profane sense of curiosity. The city of Magnolia Bluff has four police cars, not counting Buck's Dodge Charger Pursuit, and not all of them ever show up at the same place at the same time. On this particular morning, they're parked at each corner of the square, their blue and red lights flashing.

Small town.

Quiet town.

Godly town.

The bars have a few drunks every now and then. A druggie sticks up a convenience store for two dollars and change. A thief sneaks a loaf of bread and a package of hotdog franks out of the Piggly Wiggly grocery store. State lawmakers speeding home from Austin. Going too fast. Cops just wave them on through. They have immunity in the eyes of the judge. Nothing bad ever happens except on May Twenty Third, and then everybody wants to get in on the act.

May not solve the crime.

May watch a hot case go cold.

But there's a killer on the loose and walking amongst us.

If you listen long enough to the rumor mongers or catch a veiled accusation or two from the queens of small-town gossip, the cloud of suspicion will touch us all by nightfall.

Secrets.

They are a wonderful commodity.

Find them.

Buy them.

Sell them.

Steal them.

And if you don't have one handy, make it up.

# 20

**Monday**
**11:16 a.m.**

Now what? They are the only two words that come to mind.
Now what?

I drop into the wrought-iron bench on the village green and find myself surrounded by those locations where the next scenes of our little drama, our little tragedy will play out.

To my right is the medieval stone cathedral that serves as our courthouse.

A murderer will face a judge within those walls.

He will hear a jury announce his fate.

He will walk a precariously thin tightrope between life and death.

Death has the better hand.

Down the street, Neal Holland – a rough and gruff and lovely man – will spend the night at Barron Schiff's funeral home.

It is the first long night's rest he has had in years.

Across the street is the *Chronicle* office.

Its presses will roll out headlines announcing all of the particulars that anyone in town wants to know.

Who died?

When's the funeral?

Who's the culprit?

When's the trial?

Guilty?

Or innocent?

All are questions none of us know.

All are questions that will keep me awake tonight.

Fergus ambles down the sidewalk and sits down beside me. I could smell him coming a block away.

Every little burg in Texas has a town drunk.

For better or worse, Fergus is ours.

His clothes haven't been washed or cleaned since whiskey started costing more than a dollar a bottle. His face could use a shave. But why waste seven dollars on razor blades when the same seven dollars can keep him in cheap whiskey for a week. He doesn't care about the brand, just the amount of alcohol it possesses.

Fergus nods at the flashing lights atop a police car. "What's the fuss all about?" he asks.

"We've had a murder in town."

"Who?"

"Neal Holland?"

"He publish the newspaper?"

I nod.

"That's tragic," he says.

"It is."

"If there's no newspaper, what the hell am I going to sleep under tonight."

He shakes his head and ambles away. I hear him muttering to himself. I have no idea what he's saying.

A big Cadillac pulls up alongside the curb. Mary Lou Fight sticks her head out the window. "Neal been killed?"

"He has."

"Who did it?"

"Don't know."

"Who do you think did it?"

"Don't have a clue."

"Who didn't like Neal?"

"Why?"

She brushes her hair out of her eyes. Mary Lou could be a pretty lady. But I know her too well. Rebecca Wilson may spread gossip. Mary Lou spreads dirt, and she likes it thick and black and as hard to wash as mud.

"The Crimson Hats are getting together in ten minutes," she says, "and they expect me to know the skinny on everything that's happening in town."

"We lost a good man," I tell her.

"What does that mean?"

"That's the skinny of everything happening in town."

"You making fun of me?" she says a little too loudly. "I think you're making fun of me."

I shrug.

"It's your grave," she says.

*Poor choice of words,* I think.

She frowns. She drives away.

I hear the tires squeal.

I look around.

He's long gone.

That's a shame.

I'd rather spend my time with Fergus.

# 21

**Monday**
**11:32 a.m.**

I watch a crowd begin to gather on the sidewalk, and I'm sure the line stretches around the corner and all the way to the *Chronicle* office. Death may ride a tired horse, but bad news rides a Kentucky Derby winner. Tongues are wagging all over town by the time a man strikes his wife, a wife shoots her husband, a banker is caught sleeping with the wrong woman, a gunshot breaks the silence of the night, a body hits the floor. The crowd paces back and forth up and down Main Street. Faces are drawn. Some have lost their color. Eyes are buried deep in a pit of uncertainty. Lips are moving either in prayer or with the latest rumor passed on by the latest piece of hearsay whispered by the latest member of the Crimson Hat Society. If a Crimson Hat says it, the rumor is true, or at least it will become the accepted truth by tomorrow. The good folks of Magnolia Bluff may not be on their way to a funeral just yet, but they're getting ready. The self-anointed mourners can cry on cue.

The lovely and reverent Ember Cole rushes into the coffee shop, her eyes darting in every direction at the same time. Her face has reddened. She's out of breath as if her clerical collar may be pinching a little too tight. She's carrying her saturno hat under her arm. She heads straight for our table.

"Is it true?" she asks.

I cock my head to one side. "Depends on what you've heard."

"Somebody was found dead inside the *Chronicle* office."

She steps back.

She points at me.

She swings her arm around to point at Rebecca.

She grabs the edge of the table with both hands. "You and Rebecca are both here." Emma's voice softens. "It must be Neal."

She slumps into the chair beside Harry and brushes the wrinkles out of her black skirt.

I wait for her to genuflect.

She doesn't.

I guess that's just a Catholic thing.

"What happened?" she wants to know.

"Have to ask the police."

"Heart attack?" The reverend is hoping.

I shake my head.

"Neal was murdered," Rebecca says, staring at the bottom of her coffee cup.

"God, help us," Ember says.

I think she's sincere.

I hope she included me.

I hope I've been stuffed into the circle she referred to as *us*.

"May Twenty Third," she whispers.

Nobody responds.

"Another victim."

"That appears to be the case," Harry says. "Nobody knows for sure, but it's a pretty good guess." He takes her hand in his and squeezes it.

Ember blushes.

"Huston found Neal when he came to work this morning," Harry continues. "Don't know how long he'd been dead. But it had to be after midnight."

"What makes you say that?" Ember wants to know.

"The clock had to strike May Twenty Third."

Ember shudders.

Rebecca turns pale.

"But you know it's murder?" Ember says.

"Scissors."

Ember jerks her head around and stares at me.

"Mister Holland had been stabbed with a pair of scissors." The hot water has cooled. The tea in my mug has turned cold.

It has begun to taste like bitterweed. "Blades were long," I add. "They were deadly."

Harry goes to the counter and returns with two mugs of steaming coffee for Ember and Rebecca. He looks at me. "More tea?"

I shake my head. "I'm done."

We sit at the same table on a warm Monday morning – acquaintances, perhaps, but perfect strangers – thrown together by time and circumstance, assembled by a good man's untimely death, the latest in a string of untimely deaths, and all of us are living in the midst of the worst nightmare of all, the one where we are confounded and confused and awake to contemplate the machinations of angry deeds in an angry world that has turned on itself and left us to wallow in the shallow depths of our own grief.

What does each of us feel? I don't know. I'm not even sure how I feel. Sadness of course. I will miss Mister Holland, but by this time next week I'll be back on the road and headed to somewhere, whether it's on the map or not, and Neal will be only a distant memory, living or dead.

Time doesn't erase our past.

Neither does distance.

But our minds are like the precision instrumentation of a fine Swiss clock that moves us forever forward, one second at a time, one day at a time until it's too late to look back and wonder what we missed. The chances we had. The games we played. The odds we defied. The loves we left. The fears we buried. They no longer exist.

We can run.

But our mortality runs with us.

We're always one step away from our last step.

Mortality stares at us with empathy, but its eyes are always taunting us.

*Don't know when?*

*I do.*

*Don't know where?*

*You'd be surprised.*

And on a warm Monday morning in a town where I don't

belong, I realize just how fragile life really is. The petals of a flower that blooms this morning may be lost in the wind by dark.

Today.

Tomorrow.

Then what?

Who knows?

A heart beats.

It doesn't.

I may be in the ground before Mister Holland.

Ember's eyes have been closed, her head bowed as if in silent prayer. Not surprising for a preacher lady when her town is again facing dire circumstances. She looks up and past the stand of plastic geraniums planted in a pot beside the door. Her eyes cut through the front window, and she frowns as she watches a growing crowd mill around on the sidewalk and spill out into the edge of the street.

A nod.

A brief hello.

Idle chatter.

Small talk.

I can't hear them.

I don't read lips.

But I know what they're saying.

*What happened?*

*Who died?*

*Has it happened again?*

*I thought we might get lucky this year.*

*Seen anybody new in town?*

*Seen a car you've never seen before?*

*When did it happen?*

*Lord, help us.*

*God, have mercy on our souls.*

*Too late.*

*Why?*

*God cut bait and left town.*

*We can deal with our own sins.*

*He's washed his hands of us.*

The Reverend Ember Cole's gaze darts from me to Rebecca. She leans across the table, her hands folded. "You've got to tell them what happened," she says.

"Who?" It's Rebecca.

"Those people on the streets."

"They'll find out soon enough," I say.

Ember slams a clenched fist on the table. "This town will run amok with lies and half-truths and inuendoes, and before you know it, names will be thrown in with the lies and innuendoes, and everybody in town will be suspicious of everyone else in town, and then we'll have crosses burning on our church lawns, and, likely as not, one of the fools will be shot in a crossfire or on purpose. Is that what you want to see happen?"

"I don't know what to tell them," I say.

"The truth. That's all they want."

"I don't know the truth."

"You know what you saw."

"Is that enough?"

"It's more than they know, and you can put a few lies and inuendoes to rest."

"I don't have a megaphone that big," I tell her.

"No." The preacher lady smiles. "But you have a newspaper."

"I'm not a writer," I argue. "I just push brooms."

Ember stands. Her mind is made up. "Tomorrow you'll push brooms," she says. "Today, you're a writer."

Rebecca stands with her. "We have to do it," she says. Her voice is adamant. "What Ember is saying makes a lot of sense. Those people out there, everybody in Magnolia Bluff, only know what they read in the *Chronicle.* They've been depending on the newspaper for a long time. We're smack dab in the middle of the biggest story this town has had since last year about this time. Neal never let them down. We're not going to let them down either."

She strides straight for the door.

Ember takes me by the arm. "Let's go," she says.

*There are two things in a life a man must understand. My platoon sergeant told me late one afternoon high in the desert of Afghanistan.*

*"A man has to know his own limitations," he said.*

*"Clint Eastwood said it best," I told him.*

*"He did."*

*Sergeant Bayfield put his arm around my shoulder. "Clint didn't say the second thing," he tells me. "And that's the most important thing."*

*"Then what's the second thing?"*

*"There are times in life when a man must know and understand and believe – truly believe – that he has no limitations. When you know you can't win and are facing the impossible, square your shoulders and spit in its face."*

We walk out the front door and I spit on the sidewalk.

"What's that for?" Ember asks.

I don't tell her.

She doesn't need to know.

# 22

**Monday**
**12:23 p.m.**

We thread our way through the crowd, Rebecca and I, saying nothing, trying not to make eye contact with anyone, looking straight ahead as we push closer to the *Chronicle's* front door. Not a stranger in sight. The faces are familiar even if I don't know the names. I've seen them around. No one is smiling, but they are drawn to the scene of a crime much like the hapless spider that can't resist the Black Widow's web. They all have questions. No one asks them. It's as if we are walking on one side of silence while they are standing on the other side. It is a wall that no one will dare breach.

Reece Sovern stands in the doorway, his arms folded across his chest. "That's far enough," he says as we move toward him.

"We have a paper to print," Rebecca tells him.

"Not today, you don't."

"It's our office," I say.

"It's my crime scene."

I mention something about the freedom of the press.

Sovern laughs.

"Our job is to tell those people out in the street what happened here today." It's Rebecca's closing argument.

It falls on deaf ears.

Reece does not budge. "My job is to keep the crime scene from being contaminated by people who have no business in the office," he says. "Haven't found a lot of evidence." He shrugs. "If we do, I don't want it corrupted with ink."

Our faces may be solemn.

His is stern.

I expect Rebecca will break out in tears at any minute.

Sovern's glare could melt glass.

I step toward him. "That's where you're wrong," I say.

"About what?"

"We have business in here."

"Don't make me arrest you," Sovern says, but his words have lost their bite.

"I won't let you arrest me," I tell him.

He removes his handcuffs from his belt.

I keep walking.

Sovern is running out of options.

He's running out of threats.

He has only one bluff left.

He knows it.

I know it.

He knows that I know it.

"Hey, Huston," the police investigator says loudly, "you keep walking and I'll have to shoot you."

His hand drops to the butt of his snub-nose belly gun.

"Shoot me," I say.

He hesitates.

In a fight, in an argument, in a confrontation of any kind, the one who hesitates has lost. I no longer wonder if Sovern will shoot me in the back. I no longer worry that the last sound I may ever hear is a gunshot.

He has three steps to make up his mind.

I'm three steps away from the press room.

Rebecca moves to my side.

*Who will he shoot first?*

*The odds say me.*

*The odds are not in my favor.*

*I suspect that Sovern has never shot a man in his life.*

*And he's too much of a gentleman to shoot a lady.*

I hear him muttering under his breath. Can't make out the words. But I suspect a few words of profanity are involved.

I hear the sound of heavy footsteps as Sovern begins walking toward us. "Don't touch anything," he says.

I pick up a bucket of ink.

"Jesus," I hear him say, "weren't you listening to me?"

Sovern is no longer talking to me.

He's just talking.

Deputy Detective Phil West is wearing a grin as crooked as the creek that runs from the Sixth Avenue bridge out to the west shoreline of Burnet Reservoir. He's a little pudgy, a little bald, and some think he might be a little slow. But Phil never says a word until he collects all the facts, sorts them out in his mind, and discards the obvious flaws in his investigation. He's usually a week late in deciding who's right and who's wrong, but he hardly ever makes a mistake. Once spent two years gathering evidence to send a child killer to death row, then spent another three years running down information that eventually proved the suspect was in Chicago the night the eight-year-old died. The man never had to eat his last meal. Phil West is that kind of cop.

"Finding anything?" I ask him.

"A few splatters of blood," he says. "Sort of expected that. Whole bunch of fingerprints on the press. I figure they belong to you and Neal." He chuckles. "Don't see none of Rebecca getting her pretty little hands dirty." He pauses a moment and glances over the press. "I'll need for you to come down and give me a set of your prints," he says.

"Tomorrow work for you?"

"Make it after ten o'clock."

"Morning or night?"

Phil shrugs. "Either one works for me. Got us a murder on our hands. Don't think any of us will sleep for a while. It's bad enough losing Neal. I'm just hoping we don't lose anybody else."

"How about Sovern?" I wink.

"Wouldn't be a great loss," Phil says under his breath.

"Then you could get his job."

"Don't want his job."

"What's Sovern do anyway?" I ask.

"Near as I can tell," Phil says, "he makes half the people mad and pisses off the rest of them."

The grin wraps around his face.

Phil West is a half dozen years away from retirement. He came from San Antonio. Said he could live longer working the streets of Magnolia Bluff. He is coasting. Likes the badge. Is an old acquaintance with murder. Knows it up close, personal, and generally bloody.

"Town's gonna miss Neal," he says, pulling the rubber gloves off his hands.

"Good newspaperman," I say.

"Better bridge player," he says. He pauses, then asks, "You play bridge?"

I shake my head.

"That's a shame," Phil says. "We need a fourth now."

"When will you be through in here?" I want to know.

"Why?"

"I have a newspaper to print," I tell him.

"Big story."

"Can't keep it a secret much longer."

"Give me thirty minutes. Tops."

I start to walk away, then turn and ask, "You think the scissors did him in?"

"No."

Short answer.

Stops me in my tracks.

"I think the bullet killed him," he says. "I figure Neal was lying on his cot when somebody shot him. We found traces of blood on the pillowcase. The killer simply jammed the scissions down the bullet hole."

"To make sure he's dead?"

"To make a point."

"What kind of point?"

"Only two people know what it is," Phil says.

"Who?"

"The killer." Phil West takes a deep breath. "The other one who knows is dead."

I reach for my pocket notebook.

Phil's words stop me. "Can't quote me," he says. "I'm just an old detective doing forensics work because there's no one else around here to do it. We'll send Neal down to Austin and let the medical examiner tell us for sure."

"What makes you think it was a bullet?"

"Never saw a knife or scissors make a round hole about the size of a .38 slug."

"Bullet kill him instantly?"

"Near as I can tell, old Neal never had a chance to fight back." I detect a tear in the cop's voice. "I suspect he woke up just long enough to make a couple of wild swings before he punched his ticket to Valhalla." Phil turns back to the press. "I'll be in and let you know when I'm through."

Monday
3:06 p.m.

The special edition of the Chronicle hits the streets at six minutes past three. I print six thousand copies, then print a thousand more. They are gone in fifteen minutes. We hand them out and give them away until there's nobody left in town.

It's not much of a newspaper.

Single sheet.

Printed on one side.

Large type. Probably made Mister Holland mad. I used 128-point type for the headline.

It's simple. It's to the point.

*WHO'S THE BASTARD WHO KILLED MY FRIEND?*

My story is just as simple.

*Neal Holland.*

*Age 86.*

*Dead.*

*Murdered.*

*Maybe shot.*

*Maybe stabbed.*

*Scissors made an ugly hole.*

*Found lying on the press he loved.*

*The press has printed the biography of Magnolia Bluff.*

*Day after day.*

*Week after week.*

*One story after another.*

*It printed this story.*

*May Twenty Third.*

*Did the killer strike again?*

*Someone sure as hell did.*

*Nine times a killer has come into our midst.*

*Nine times a prominent citizen has died.*

*Never the same way.*

*But always the same date.*

*May Twenty Third.*

*Neal Holland once swore to me he would find the killer if it was the last thing he ever did.*

*It was.*

*The killer remains at large.*

*Only two people know who he is.*

*Neal Holland was true to his word.*

*He knows.*

*He identified the killer.*

*If only for a moment.*

*It was the last thing he ever did.*

*A final Eulogy to Neal Holland.*

*In black.*

*And white.*

*Magnolia Bluff was the only family he had.*

*Funeral services pending.*

*Rest in Peace.*

# 23

**Monday**
**5:18 p.m.**

The clock on the wall above the front door tells me it's way past my time to go home. The day is ending, and the gray outline of crippled shadows has begun its daily afternoon journey across the street. On normal days, I would be sitting alone on the porch of the boarding house, sipping a jigger of Balcones Texas Blue Corn Bourbon and watching the sky turn a pale bird's egg blue before splashes of sunlight torch the clouds with a raging wildfire of gold and pink and crimson flames. Waiting for night. Waiting to crawl back into a black hole. Hoping the blue corn bourbon holds my senses together long enough to see the dawning of another day.

But this has not been a normal day. A good man is dead. I knew when I awoke this morning that the death angel could well be walking the sidewalks of Magnolia Bluff. I just didn't know he was on his way to visit Mister Neal Holland. I just didn't know that the old newspaper publisher would miss the biggest story of his lifetime. I did what I could, but it was not nearly good enough. He deserved better, and I don't know how to write better. I'm drained and can feel the loose threads of anger rubbing my nerve endings raw. Darkness is hovering over the town like a herd of vultures.

I'm sitting in Mister Holland's chair.

It's awkward.

I don't belong.

I wait for Rebecca to say something.

Anything.

She doesn't.

She is staring blankly at the front door as though she's waiting for someone.

No one's coming.

The town has closed down for the day.

The street is empty.

Store windows are dark.

The *Chronicle* office just may be the last building in town with its lights on.

The silence is so loud it's annoying.

We should leave and lock the door behind us.

But would anyone ever unlock it again?

I hear the faint whimper when Rebecca calls my name.

I glance toward her

Rebecca is slumped in her chair, her head lying on the desk, her eyes closed, her mascara a mess, her lipstick mostly chewed off.

It's the bitter end of a long and bitter day.

"What are you planning to do now?" she asks. I sense her words more than I hear them.

"Move on, I guess."

"Why?"

"I had no place to go when I got here," I tell her. "I have nothing to hold me here. I may as well find out what's waiting on down the road."

"What are you looking for?" Rebecca turns her face toward me.

"A reason to stay somewhere."

"And you didn't find it here?"

"I thought maybe I did. I found a good friend." My voice sounds hoarse. "Now I don't have him anymore."

Rebecca stands and walks to Mister Holland's old maple wood desk. It has seen better days. It won't see many more of them. She sits on the edge and crosses her legs. "What about me?"

She has a strange look in her eyes.

The suggestion of a smile.

The hint of regret.

I'm not sure what to say.

"You found my arms to be a comforting place to be the other night," she says. She places a hand on top of mine. It's soft. It's tender. It's seductive.

"You're a wonderful woman," I tell her.

"Please." She laughs. "You can turn me down. You can run me out of here," she says. "But surely, you can come up with a better line than that."

"It was a good night," which is the only thing that comes to mind.

"It could be the beginning of a beautiful friendship," she says.

The words worked in *Casablanca.*

I don't feel them working now

I shake my head. "I would only break your heart in the long run."

"Only if I give it to you."

"What?"

"My heart."

She has a mischievous smile playing across her face.

"I'm sure it's been broken before."

"But hearts heal."

"Some hearts do."

Rebecca crosses her arms. "How about yours?"

"It beats." I drum the top of the desk with my fingers. "That's about all."

She steps away from the desk and walks toward the percolator sitting on a table beside the Xerox machine in the back of the office

I'm sure the coffee's black.

I'm sure it's cold.

I'm sure it has the faint taste of battery acid.

But it might settle our nerves.

"Why did you come to Magnolia Bluff in the first place?" Rebecca asks.

"I had an errand to run."

"Did you run it?"

"I did."

"Can you tell me what it was?"

"Private matter."

"Involve anyone I know?"

"Doubt it."

"I know everybody in three counties."

"But you run in different circles."

"It didn't involve the sewing circle, the bridge club get together on Tuesday, The Crimson Hat Society, the Lions Club, Rotary Club, or Junior Service League?"

"Afraid not."

"The shit kickers out at LouEllen's shit-kicking lounge?"

I shake my head.

"A woman?"

I don't answer.

"An old flame?"

Still no answer.

"A coven of witches?"

Silence.

"Fishermen, deer slayers, or coon hunters?"

I smile.

Nothing else.

"A felony?"

"I've been around a couple," I tell her.

Rebecca sits a cup of coffee on the desk in front of me. I take a sip, and surprisingly, it's still hot. It's still strong. It doesn't taste anything like battery acid.

"Why did you stay?" she wants to know. "You could have been gone so long ago no one remembers your name."

"Had a job."

"You like sweeping floors?"

"It's a job."

Rebecca holds her cup with both hands. It's one of those fancy customized cups. The words on the side say: *The trouble with the rat race is that even if you win, you're still a rat.* She drinks slowly and lets the coffee slide luxuriously down her throat.

"Neal talked a lot about you," she says.

"Small town. Not much to talk about."

"He thought you had promise"

"As a broom pusher?"

"As a newspaperman."

I chuckle at the absurdity of it all. "Never been one," I say. "Never wanted to be one. Don't write well. Spell even worse. I'm not social. I'm not political. I don't know how to go along to get along. I'm blunt. Never learned to sugarcoat anything. Don't think I would even if I could. I can make people mad enough to spit nails just by walking into a room."

"Been to school?"

"In the military."

"What'd you study?"

"How to kill people."

Rebecca's face turns pale.

"That's what the army does," I say.

"And you?"

"I still see the faces of the dead."

"You kill any of them?"

"Sometimes."

"You have nightmares?"

"Sometimes."

Rebecca shivers. Her cheeks are flushed. "I would have nightmares all the time."

"It's better if you don't."

"How do you keep from having them?"

"I don't sleep much."

I wait for the color to work its way back into her face.

It takes a while.

"If you leave," she says at last, "what will happen to the *Chronicle*?"

"I'm sure Mister Holland's family inherits it."

"He has no family."

"I guess it'll die."

"We can't let that happen," Rebecca says. She is doodling on a page of copy paper with her ballpoint pen.

Don't know if she's drawing a triangle or a pyramid.

They all look alike to me.

"Nothing we can do about it."

She stands with her back leaning against the counter. "Sure there is."

"What is ricocheting around in that little mind of yours?" I ask.

"I've seen Neal's last will and testament. I typed it for him."

"What's it say?"

"He's leaving the *Chronicle* to anyone who's still working here when he dies."

She pauses. "That's me," she says.

Rebecca points to me. "And that's you."

I shake my head again.

"No," I say. "That's you. You're a writer and must be a damn good one. Everybody in town is on pins and needles waiting to see what you've got to say each week, and then they start quoting you as if they know the information first-hand."

"It's not news," Rebecca says, finishing one cup and heading back to fill up another. "It's gossip." She throws both arms in the air with exasperation. "I don't want to be a publisher. All I want to do is sell advertising and write gossip."

"Gossip sells."

"This paper needs a newsman."

"That's not me."

Rebecca sits down in my lap and puts an arm around my neck. "It could be."

She smells of lavender.

And jasmine.

With just a touch of honey thrown in.

"After all," she continues, "you published today's paper."

"It was just one page for God's sakes, and I used big type and filled up the whole damn page with less than two hundred words."

"People like the way you write." She has her fingers in my hair now. "I heard them talking around town after you wrote about the motel shooting last Wednesday. Short, concise, quick to read, easy to read. Just the facts. No bullshit. Besides, We only publish eight pages twice a week, and we have six days to fill up both of them." She winks. "I'll write half, and you'll write half. Nothing to it."

"Can't do it."

"Why not?"

"I'm leaving."

"Don't make any hasty decisions," Rebecca tells me. "You might regret it. Promise me you'll think about it before you make up your mind."

"You can hire an out-of-work reporter before I can get out of town."

Rebecca pouts. "But all I want is you," she says.

Monday
9:38 p.m.

Life is short and not nearly the mystery that most people think it is. Life only has a half dozen absolutes. Learn them early. Memorize them. Don't ever forget them. Rebecca pulls the covers back on her bed. A candle lights up the darkness. A pair of crystal glasses sit on the table beside her pillow. She brings a bottle of red wine, chilled, into the bedroom.

That's when the absolutes of life come back to me in a rush.

*Never negotiate with a beautiful woman.*

*Never negotiate with a long-legged woman.*

*Never negotiate with a woman who has the taste of wine on her lips.*

*Never negotiate with a woman whose stereo plays Rachmaninov.*

*Never negotiate with a naked woman.*

There's probably one more, but it slips my mind.

Somewhere around three o'clock, give or take a minute or two, she changes my mind.

I won't be leaving in the morning. I may not be leaving at all.

# 24

**Tuesday**
**8:12 a.m.**

The town is still in shock if you can gauge the psyche of Magnolia Bluff by the looks on the faces of those who walk its streets, work in its shops, and shop in its stores. It's a quiet Tuesday morning, and even the automobile tires passing me by seem to be whispering instead of grinding away at pavement streaked with cracks and packed with asphalt. Potholes dare them to go any faster. But drivers have learned to swing and sway and wind their way past them. Day begins on time. It ends on time. No need to hurry.

The Silver Spoon is still locked up as tight as Dick's hatband, whoever Dick is. Don't know when Lorraine may be coming back. Don't know if she's coming back. But I'll miss hearing the scalawags, reprobates, misfits, and great unwashed find a motive and solve Mister Holland's murder somewhere between their fourth biscuit and second mug of hot, leftover coffee. Sometimes tastes as if it was brewed in a crankcase, but nobody complains. It opens the eyelids and jump-starts the heart, and nothing else matters during those first calm and capricious moments after daylight wiggles its way into town.

I backtrack my way down the sidewalk to the Really Good Wood-Fired coffee shop. I'm already beginning to feel the sweat of a sultry morning roll down between my shoulder blades. Looks like a scorcher. Texans don't sweat until the temperature breaks the hundred-degree mark. But I'm a newcomer. I'm a Yankee. By the time I produce next week's newspaper, I'll probably be regarded as a Damn Yankee, and the folks who profile me just may be right.

I left Rebecca sleeping, her dark hair spread across the pillowcase, the sheet down around her waist, one bare leg lying on top of the pink and white duvet. She squirmed and whimpered as I walked out of the bedroom and left through the back door.

No one up.

No one out.

No one to see me.

No reason to give the ladies in the holy pack of the Crimson Hat Society any ammunition to use if they decide to defame Rebecca's reputation. Then again, I'm pretty sure she would be a hard target to bring down. She probably knows as much or more about them as they suspect about her. If they keep their thoughts, opinions, and accusations to themselves, then she'll keep their names and shenanigans out of her gossip column. I figure that's why type set on a small-town newspaper is the same color as dirt.

I feel like a pariah when I stroll into the Wood-Fired Coffee Shop. Everyone is watching me but pretending I'm not on the premises, and they don't know whether to hug me, kiss me, pay their condolences, bring me flowers, or decide to act if I'm nothing more than another stranger who won't be around come nightfall. Among certain social circles in Magnolia Bluff, if the ladies don't choose to speak to you or acknowledge your presence, then you have become the invisible man. Don't bother looking in a mirror. You're not in it.

*A large coffee.*

That's my order.

*No mocha.*

*No Frappuccino.*

*No cream.*

*No sugar.*

*Black.*

*No paper cup.*

*I want a porcelain mug.*

*Coffee tastes better when it's poured into porcelain.*

The interior décor is a little too sophisticated for my taste. Polished mahogany. Polished brass. Polished silver. Frankly, I prefer stained tablecloths, crumbs on the floor, and waitresses not opposed to lacing their sentences with a dash or two of profanity when the need arises, and it almost always does at the Silver Spoon.

But I will give Harry Thurgood credit. He does serve up a splendid mug of coffee. Thick. Rich. Black. Strong enough to deaden your throat and leave the remains of your esophagus begging for mercy. Damn expensive, too.

He smiles wistfully as he sets the mug on the tall-legged table in front of me, and then hurries off to leave me alone. Harry pretty much has my philosophy. When you don't know what to say, don't say anything.

*I guess he's feeling sorry for Mister Holland.*

*Then again, it may be guilt.*

*Or is he feeling sorry for me?*

*Why?*

*What does he know that I don't know?*

Harry and I were chiseled from the same rock, and it certainly wasn't a gemstone.

*Back story is a blank.*

*Where is he from?*

*Don't know.*

*Is Harry Thurgood his real name?*

*Don't know.*

*Who is he running from?*

*Or is he just hiding?*

*Don't know.*

*He's not saying, and I'm not asking.*

He has no reason to be in Magnolia Bluff.

It's just that one day he suddenly appeared.

Hasn't left.

Whoever is chasing him, provided anyone is chasing him, hasn't found Harry yet.

I feel a rush of hot wind and watch Judge Peacock come

swaggering through the front door. He looks around and frowns before heading straight toward my table. He seats himself without an invitation, removes a fishing cap that reads: *Even Jesus Had a Fish Story*, and hangs it on the back of his high-back chair.

"Sorry about Neal," he says.

"We lost a good one."

*Old.*

*Trite.*

*A cliché.*

*Can't help myself.*

"What do the police say?"

"They're working on it."

The judge shakes his head sadly. "They've been working on these murders through two mayors, a couple of bastard police chiefs, eight fishing tournaments, forty-eight marriages, fifty-two divorces, and a goat roping, and still they don't have a clue."

"Killer doesn't leave any clues."

"Hell, the killer could leave his name and address etched in cold, bold letters on the murder weapon, and Reece Sovern wouldn't be able to find him."

"You're the judge."

"I am."

"You're pretty hard on your lawmen."

Peacock nods. "I've been out on the lake since four o'clock," he says. "Didn't catch a fish. Didn't get a bite. I'm not in what you would call a good mood."

"Bad day."

"Getting worse."

"What's ahead of you in court today?"

"A convenience store robbery."

"Who's on trial?"

"My nephew."

"He guilty?"

The judge shrugs. "Guess we'll find out," he says. He blows away the smoke curling up from his coffee, and asks, "With Neal gone, what'll happen with the *Chronicle*?"

"It'll keep getting published."

"Be difficult without Neal at the rudder."

I grin. "Funny thing about newspapers," I tell him.

"What's that?"

"They just sort of publish themselves. Might have an editor. Might not."

"You staying on?"

"I think I'll give it a try."

The judge drains the last drop from his cup of coffee. "You'll do all right," he says, "Your kind of writing stirs folks up. Pricks their emotions a little. It reads like you're hammering every word straight into the damnation of their soul. Neal called it scattershot journalism."

"Don't think journalism has anything to do with it."

Peacock leans back, folds his arms across his chest, and asks, "You have any thoughts about Neal's death?"

"That's a question I should be asking you."

His grin is crooked, no wider than a quarter moon. "I'm a judge," he says. "I have no thoughts, no opinions, no assumptions, no theories, and no conclusions. Peacock shrugs. "I'm a truth seeker," he adds, "and truth is a damn sight harder to find than it used to be." The judge stands and slaps me on the back. "Son," he says somberly, "we live in a world full of fabrications, complications, prevarications, and condemnations. Nothing's black and nothing's white, and we manufacture the truth from the guilt of our own imaginations."

He walks across the coffee shop, gives Ember a hug and Harry a mock salute, and then he's out the door, leaving me to try and figure out what the hell he's been talking about.

# 25

**Tuesday**
**8:36 a.m.**

Reverend Ember Cole brings me a fresh mug of coffee although I'm finishing my second cup and already starting to feel my heart move from an easy gait to a hard gallop. The inside of my head feels numb, and my nerves are dancing a fox trot while my pulse is beating a waltz. I take the cup from her hand because she's awfully pretty to be a preacher, and I figure it would probably be a sin of either omission or commission to say so. She is smiling, but I can detect a deep sadness etched in her eyes.

"I feel terrible about Neal," she says.

"I'm sure the whole town does."

"We've got ourselves in quite a mess." Ember sits down beside me.

"Nine murders."

"They aren't random, you know." She presses the heat of her coffee mug against her lips. If Ember wasn't a preacher lady, the move would be downright sexy.

"But what's the connection between victim one and victim nine?"

"I'm sure they all knew each other," she says. "May have gone to church together, shopped together, sat through football games together, maybe even used the same doctors or dentists. This is a small town, after all. From what I've heard, they were more like passing acquaintances than friends. We all make somebody mad from time to time, but it's difficult to see how all nine people could make the same person mad enough to kill them."

"Any of the victims members of your church?"

"Victims three and four," Ember's voice softens. "But that was before I came to Magnolia Bluff, so I didn't know either of them. I think the first was Betty Gilmont. She was a retired schoolteacher. I think she had been high school principal for a time. And then there was Hank Dillard. Lorraine quit coming to church altogether when he was killed. Blames God. That happens a lot."

"Do you know how they died?"

She shakes her head. "I've heard rumors. That's all. Don't know the truth from the chaff. Betty's family moved closer to Nacogdoches, and Lorraine won't even talk about it." She stares at her coffee for a moment or two, probably deep in thought, then whispers, "It does worry me sometimes."

"What does?"

"Who's next?"

"I guess we'll find out in another year."

"Will you be here to write about it?"

"If I'm not the victim, I will."

"You won't be the victim."

"Why not?"

Ember stares at me, through me, and past me as her mind takes a brief journey from one side of her brain to the other. "Whatever the root cause is behind the killings," she says, "it began a long time ago, long before you ever set foot in this town."

"Revenge?"

"Maybe." Ember brushes a loose strand of hair away from her eyes. "Maybe not."

"What are you thinking?" I want to know.

"It might be redemption."

"That's a strange supposition," I tell her, then ask, "Do you know something that I don't know, that no one else knows?"

She shakes her head.

"I see a lot of loose pieces," Ember says. "I keep trying to put them together, and none of the pieces fit. I woke up this morning after a terrible nightmare wondering if someone was trying to wash away their own sins with someone else's blood."

"Sounds Biblical."

Ember laughs softly. "It's not."

She waits a moment.

I can tell she's trying to work up enough courage to ask me something.

Finally, she blurts it out. "Has anyone thought about funeral arrangements for Neal?"

"I'm sure Rebecca has," I answer. "She's known him for a long time."

"I'll be happy to deliver the eulogy," she says. "Neal was not a member of my church, but he wouldn't be a stranger among our congregation."

"That's kind of you." I drain the mug and realize I had not tasted any of the coffee after the first sip. "But Neal told me he was Presbyterian."

"I didn't realize that."

"He kept it between himself and God."

Ember raises a questioning eyebrow.

"I'm not sure God wanted the word to get out," I tell her.

She laughs. "I wonder why Neal became a Presbyterian?"

"I think he was taking the easy way out."

Ember laughs again. Hard this time.

"The Reverend Billy Bob Baskin will do a wonderful job," she says. "He's a great speaker. Full of sound and fury. If he can't bring the angels down, then the angels must be on strike."

"I guess I'll have to break the news to Billy Bob," I say.

"About what?"

"I doubt if Billy Bob knew Neal was Presbyterian."

"Doesn't matter." Reverend Ember Cole stands from the chair to leave. "He's got a funeral sermon that fits every reprobate."

"Scalawags and misfits, too?"

She starts toward the door, then stops and looks back over her shoulder. "Especially the misfits," she says.

Ember sways seductively as she walks toward the front door.

Every man in the Real Good Wood-Fired Coffee Shop is watching her leave.

The thought strikes me.

And I feel a little uneasy.

I try to shove it aside.

It won't go.

It strikes me that if she would shorten that black skirt of hers about a foot, Ember Cole would fill up the Methodist Church every Sunday morning.

Some would come for a front row seat.

Some would stay for a second sermon.

Then again, the righteous Methodist women might all leave and become Presbyterian.

Tuesday
7:36 p.m.

I'm late today, but my mind has been preoccupied with death, love, regrets, desire, guilt, and at least half a dozen of the ten commandments, especially those I've broken, and I've broken a few of them more than once. Freddy's not concerned. He knew I would come see him before the day ended. His is a lonely existence. His friends have all died or moved on. I'm the only one left, and I've never met him.

I place the flowers on his grave, white lilies freshly cut. They look especially brilliant lying on a patch of drab gray sand and clay where the oak thicket is too shady for grass to ever grow. He doesn't say anything. Neither do I. It's not the kind of evening for small talk. He knows I have other things troubling me. Don't know how he knows, but I'm convinced he does.

*Freddy is just glad he hasn't been forgotten.*

*He didn't die in vain.*

*He's no longer an unknown soldier.*

I sit on the cool earth with my back against a Sabinal oak.

My mind is filled with questions.

My gut is filled with answers.

They don't match the questions.

*Why have nine people died in Magnolia Bluff?*

*One a year.*
*Nine straight years.*
*Murder.*
*Cold-blooded.*
*Same date.*
*May Twenty Third.*
*What do they have in common?*
*Or did the dead simply happen to be living in the same town?*
*Who wanted them dead?*
*What was the killer's reasoning?*
*Anger?*
*Revenge?*
*Payback?*
*A grudge?*
*A cheated heart?*
*A broken heart?*
*A bitter heart?*
*Redemption?*
*Only a preacher lady would think of redemption.*
*It doesn't make sense.*
*Nothing makes sense.*
*Did the killer leave a message?*
*No one's said.*
*Does anyone know?*
*Does anyone remember?*
*Did the killer stalk his victims?*
*Does he live in town?*
*Near town?*
*Or does he merely return one day a year?*
*One deadly day a year.*
*May Twenty Third.*
*Why May Twenty Third?*
*It's just another day.*
*But it means something to someone.*
*It meant something for nine people.*

*Did they know what it was?*

*Or did they die as confused, as frightened, as ignorant as the rest of us?*

I look at Freddy's tombstone.

The light is fading.

I can barely read his name.

If I wait here long enough, it won't be dark anymore.

# 26

**Wednesday**
**7:32 a.m.**

I make my way down to the city library before it opens and wait on an old wooden bench that was placed on the neatly manicured lawn in nineteen and fifty-four in memory of Frances Moran, who served as the town's first librarian. She began collecting works of fiction and nonfiction both during the 1930s, during the Great Depression, and loaning them out to people who wanted to read but could not afford to buy books. During the next fifteen years, the residents of Magnolia Bluff borrowed more than three thousand of her books, and all but four were returned to her. One was lost in a house fire. One was stolen by a traveling medicine show peddler. One was buried with Miss Moran's father, a rancher. And one was given to six-year-old Carl Finebaum who grew up to become the town's sixth mayor. That's what the historical marker says. That's about all I have to read before the house containing thousands of books to read is unlocked.

I'm not quite sure what I'm doing, but I've walked through minefields before.

*Afraid to take the next step.*
*Afraid it might be my last step.*
*Moving quietly toward the great unknown.*
*Would I get lucky this time?*
*Would I feel the blast?*
*Or would the world go suddenly black?*

*Don't know.*

*Only one thing is for certain.*

*I will sleep that night.*

*Only time will tell if I wake up again.*

Here I am trying to dig out the truth buried in a story both old and new.

Not for sure what I'm doing.

Not for sure how to do it.

Have no idea what to do next.

But I know I have to start nine years ago.

I have to start on May Twenty Third of that year.

As far as I know, only one person in town can help me.

She archives history.

She has all of the old newspapers on file.

They might contain a few lies, a few opinions, a little gossip that no one can prove, but they do have all the facts, at least more of the facts than I know now. I doubt if Reece Sovern will let me see his police file. I wonder if Reece Sovern even remembers where he ditched his file, or does he have nine files scattered among various letters of the alphabet.

Let's see now.

*Are they under D for death?*

*M for murder?*

*K for killings?*

*U for unsolved?*

*Or S for shit if I know?*

*Or have they been filed under the victim's first name?*

*Last name?*

*Occupation?*

The librarian is my only hope, and here she is, Caroline McCluskey, coming down the sidewalk on emerald-green high heels, a giant leather purse dangling on her shoulder, her arms filled with books. I check the clock above the library's front door. In two minutes, it will be nine o'clock. Caroline McCluskey is always prompt. She's never late. She arrives wearing tan slacks, a green-and-purple striped shirt, and her blonde hair has been pulled back into a ponytail. It bounces on her shoulder as she walks. Her smile is warm enough to melt a block of ice or a bronc buster's heart.

She loses the smile as soon as she sees me.

Her dark eyes turn molten.

"I know," I say standing as she walks up to the bench.

"What?"

"You're sorry about Mister Holland."

Her face reddens.

Her chuckle is unexpected.

"I guess you've been hearing that a lot," she says.

I nod. "It's been mentioned."

"It's still a frightening day."

She hands me an armload of books and fumbles through her purse for a ring with enough keys to unlock every door in fourteen counties. She finds the right key – which looks as if it belongs to a treasure chest – and unlocks the door.

Inside, the musty aroma of old books, old paper, dried ink take me back to my childhood. My view of the world, near and far, came from books such as these. I learned as many truths from fiction as I did nonfiction. The words of writers long since dead opened up a secret door that led me beyond a forbidden veil into the dark space, dark towers, and dark alleys of fantasy and mystery and sin, cleverly disguised as romance.

I place Caroline's armful of books on the counter as she flips on the light switch behind a photograph of George Washington Crossing the Brazos River. I guess it was a gift from some local artist who failed to realize that Valley Forge was not a forge in a Blacksmith's Shop.

"How can I help you?" she asks.

"I understand you have copies of old newspapers," I tell her.

"Since August second, nineteen thirty-four."

"Long before our time."

She smiles. "Not before my time."

"You're not that old."

"No," Caroline says, "but I've lived every year of Magnolia Bluff since August second, nineteen thirty-four through the pages of those newspapers. I've celebrated weddings and births, grieved at funerals, cheered when the bad guys went to jail, held my breath during every election, and prayed the price of feed would go down and the price of beef would go up. Every year I turn the page, I begin to get those feelings all over again." She pauses a moment and a dark frown shadows her face. "I guess you think I'm a little crazy, don't you?"

"No," I answer, "I think you're a librarian. You're as comfortable living in the past as you are the present."

"There's a difference," Caroline says jauntily as she leads me down a narrow flight of stairs to the basement.

"What's that?"

"In the past, I know what happens. Don't always like it. But I know what it is."

"And in the now?"

"I don't. If I did, some bastard, as I believed you called him on the front page of the *Chronicle*, would be behind bars this morning." Caroline stops beside the library's microfilm reader and begins to wipe away dust sprinkled on the lens. "Do you know how to use one of these?

I nod.

"We have the rolls of film in those filing cabinets against the wall. The box with each roll is clearly marked with the months of the year." Her smile is comforting. "I don't think you'll have any trouble. What year do you want first?"

"Twenty fourteen," I tell her.

Her shoulders stiffen.

Her eyes darken,

Her perky little smile is gone.

"The month of May, I presume?"

"The days just before and after May Twenty Third."

Caroline takes a deep breath. "I should I have known," she says.

She hands me a roll of film, turns briskly, and heads back toward the stairs. "I hope you find it." Her voice quavers.

"Find what?"

"What nobody else has been able to find."

She leaves me in a room filled with the ghosts of the past, page after page recording their good deeds, their bad deeds, their comings, their goings, days filled with hope, nights filled with disappointments, lives begun, lives ended, and names no one has heard or remembered for a long, long time.

I go straight to May.

I'm trusting the words of a dead man.

*What can Mister Holland tell me?*

*What do his stories say?*

*What did he know?*

*What did he write in the Chronicle?*

*What did he leave out?*

The stories aren't long.

The headlines aren't big.

Not at first anyway.

I jot down scribbled notes I hope I can read later.

May, 2014

The first to die is a police officer, Charles Wegman, age forty-six.

Shot wearing his badge and uniform.

Shot in a back room of the police department.

Shot just before midnight.

Should have been off duty.

Should have already gone home.

Shot by an escaping prisoner.

That's what the justice of the peace ruled anyway.

Who's the prisoner?

No one knows.

Was there any prisoner?

No prisoner had been booked.

Shot twice.

Both eyes shot out.

His last report had been filed at three thirty-six in the afternoon.

An incident at LouEllen's Lounge.

Didn't say what it was.

*Must not have figured it was important.*

*A fight?*

*A drunken brawl?*

*A cowgirl with one too many cowboys?*

*Could have cost him his life?*

MAY, 2015.

Victim number two is Master Sergeant David Blankenship.

A life-long military man.

A Vietnam veteran.

Stationed in Saigon.

Stationed in the rice paddies.

Wounded.

Sent home.

Received the Purple Heart.

Walked with a limp the rest of his life.

Became a recruiting officer for the U.S. Army

Born storyteller.

The boys loved him.

Said he could tell stories so well even cowards wanted to go fight.

Retired for six years.

Found hanging from the rafters of an abandoned building a block west of the Courthouse.

Neck broken.

Hands dangling loose at his side.

Purple heart wrapped around his fingers.

Purple heart bought at a pawnshop.

Or stolen.

Probably stolen.

Ruled a suicide.

Justice of the Peace took the quick and easy way out.

*So many of the boys who came home from Vietnam were simply tired of living.*

*Gone through a living hell in war.*

*Came home to a living hell.*

*Enemy shot at them.*

*Friends spit on them.*

*Suicide killed as many as the Viet Cong did.*

*Couldn't escape the nightmares.*

*Found a way to end them.*

## MAY, 2016

The death of Betty Gilmont is the first to arouse any suspicion.

Graduated from Magnolia Bluff High School.

Taught English at Magnolia Bluff High School

Named teacher of the year a dozen times in a forty-two-year career.

Left the classroom.

Said it was the saddest day of her life.

Loved the kids.

Hated the parents.

Became principal of Magnolia Bluff High School.

Retired.

The town held a Betty Gilmont Day in her honor.

She served meals on wheels.

She taught Sunday School.

She mentored students at the Boys and Girls Club.

She drowned in a small cove at Burnet Reservoir.

*Nothing unusual about someone drowning.*

*Deep water can be treacherous.*

*Happens to drunks quite regularly.*

Betty Gilmont didn't drink.

She had baling wire wrapped around her neck.

It was tied to a concrete block.

Medical Examiner said she was alive when her head went below the water.

*I can almost hear her screaming.*

*I can almost feel the sense of dread in her chest.*

*What must she be thinking?*

*This is it.*

*This is all there is.*

*There is no tomorrow.*

*Goodbye.*

*And no goodbyes were ever said.*

Her body was found trapped in the brush on May Twenty

Eighth.

Medical Examiner said she had been murdered five days earlier.

May Twenty Third.

She was seventy-one years old.

That's when Mister Holland made the connection.

Three deaths.

Three violent deaths.

All on May Twenty Third.

"Is Magnolia Bluff cursed?" he wrote in a front-page editorial. "Why does death always come to town on May Twenty Third? Will death make a return visit next year?"

It did.

## MAY 2017

Some believed a killer was lying in wait.

Waiting for May Twenty Third.

Some laughed it off.

Some believed in coincidences.

There was no longer any doubt.

The death of Hank Dillard struck fear in the hardest of hearts.

Restaurant owner.

Had seen hope flickering in an abandoned downtown mercantile store.

Bought it.

Turned it into the Silver Spoon.

Home cooking.

Chicken fried steaks.

Turnip greens.

Okra gumbo.

Hank had his own recipes.

Had been president of the Chamber of Commerce.

Had been president of the Downtown Promotion Committee.

Never had a child.

Didn't matter.

Elected five times as President of the Magnolia Bluff School

Board.

Had one known vice.

Poker.

Missed one game in twenty-two years.

It was the night he died.

He went missing.

Someone brought him home.

Someone sat him in a rocking chair on the front porch.

Someone poured poison down his throat.

Rat poison.

A lot of it.

Someone removed both feet with a handsaw.

Police found the saw down in Shoal Creek.

Never found his feet.

## MAY, 2018

Robert Baker's family, generations ago, had come to the Hill Country long before there was a Magnolia Bluff.

Daddy was a rancher.

Brother raised goats.

Sold mohair.

Robert was a big man.

Liked to throw his weight around.

His face was scarred.

His knuckles were callused.

Robert kept the peace at LouEllen's Lounge.

She called him her director of security.

Sounded good.

Sounded important.

But everyone knew what Robert was.

He was a bouncer.

Get drunk?

Get in a fight?

Irritate the wrong woman?

Throw beer bottles at the band?

You had to deal with Robert.

Couldn't whip him.

Couldn't hurt him.

Don't make him mad.

You'd have a better chance against a rolling ball of switchblade knives.

Nobody called him Bobby.

He was Robert.

Always Robert.

And sometimes Mister Robert.

Wore a black suit.

Wore a black tie.

Called it his 9-1-1 tie.

If he took it off?

Call 9-1-1.

Had a little farm back toward Bandera.

Raised a handful of cattle.

A couple of horses.

Worked the auction barns.

Looked for cheap horses.

Fatten them up.

Sell them.

Didn't make a lot of money.

Stayed busy.

He was a man of the earth.

Bought a backhoe to irrigate a garden he had planned for the spring.

*Saw early spring.*

*Late spring escaped him.*

Didn't come to work one day.

Didn't come to work for a week.

LouEllen was worried.

Patrolman checked behind Robert's barn.

Someone had been digging.

Looked like a grave.

Found Robert Baker at the bottom of it.

Not a scratch on him.

But his mouth was filled with dirt.

So was his nose.

Robert had been buried alive.

Law looked for the backhoe.

Couldn't find it anywhere in Burnet County.

Hard to hide a backhoe.

Mister Holland quoted Barron Schiff down at the funeral home.

*Killer must have been a magician,* he said.

Mister Holland was pretty harsh on Robert Baker.

Didn't matter, he said.

Certainly didn't demean the man.

Certainly didn't reveal any secrets.

Everything he wrote, he said, was already common knowledge.

I have sat too long in a dim room staring into the reflections of a blinding light. The words are running together. The pages have become blurred. My eyes feel as though someone has raked the vines of a blackberry bush across them. The thorns remained behind. I'm dizzy when I stand and roll off the last pages of May 2017.

I don't want to quit. I still have four years to go.

Four murders to go.

But my mind has become too lethargic to look at another page. I'm in a library.

I'm surrounded by books. I'm ambushed by books.

I feel literary. I quote Scarlet O'Hara as I walk toward the stairs.

*Tomorrow is another day.*

# 27

**Thursday**
**9:18 a.m.**

Tomorrow isn't just another day. Don't know why I'd think it would be. For as long as I can remember, I've been drifting up one side of the country and down the other, taking every crossroad I could find to see if it would come out and was always a little disappointed when it did. The clock and I were strangers. Time was measured in light or dark. The sun was either up or it wasn't. Didn't worry about time. Didn't worry about distance. Wasn't concerned with either deadlines or consequences if I missed them. Fry cook in Roswell. Don't remember if it was New Mexico or Georgia. Used car salesman in Lake Charles. I sold one. Sold a 2002 Altima to myself but the sale didn't go through. My credit rating was on the downside of single digits. Pizza delivery in Chattanooga, Convenience Store cashier in Council Grove. A taxi driver in Jasper. Don't remember if it was Alabama or Texas. Would still be driving a cab still but had one phone call in three nights. It was a wrong number. And now I find that it is my responsibility to publish a newspaper, which might be easier if I had ever read one before last night at the library. Comes with a deadline. I know why it's called a deadline. Miss it and you're dead. That's what Rebecca tells me. She's not smiling.

She's already seated behind her desk when I wander in on the downside of a morning with waves of heat already rising from the sidewalks. She looks like summer in a pale teal sundress. Maybe it's foam green. Could be the color of the sea.

She smells of suntan lotion and a cologne that must have come from some Caribbean isle. It surely didn't come from one of those buy-one-and-get-one-free aisles down at the drugstore. Rebecca is all business.

"It's Thursday," she says.

"Came pretty fast this week."

"Comes pretty fast every week."

I slump down in Mister Holland's chair and stack my notes on his desk. It will always be his desk. It's just on loan to me. I may be here next month. I may be in Blue Eye, Missouri. Mostly depends on which fine citizen I make mad and how deep the mad runs. I've been shot at a time or two and would have been hit if I had stopped running.

The computer and I stare at each other. It looks at me like the kid on your first day at a new school, and you know immediately he will do his best to rearrange your face before the day comes to a dreadful end. That's why my nose looks left. It used to look right.

"What you got for the afternoon paper?" I ask Rebecca.

"Methodist Church has an ice cream social on Saturday night," she says. "The Crimson Hat Society has named its three candidates for Magnolia Bluff Woman of the Year. By the way, I'm not one of them. The Chamber of Commerce is beginning a new membership drive. Pastor Billy Bob Baskin caught the largest bass pulled this year from Burnet Reservoir. We have a picture. The downtown promotion committee is planning its annual Persimmon Festival, and I'm printing the speeches from the Valedictorian and Salutatorian at Magnolia Bluff High School." She grins wryly. "And we have three lovely couples who have filed for divorce, two more who are planning June weddings, and the usual bi-monthly break-in last night at Ciarra Doyle's Garage. I think they got two wrenches, a can of second-hand oil, four soda pops, and the back fender from a nineteen and ninety-three Buick. I can make it sound like a Brink's robbery."

"How do you find out all of that stuff?" I ask.

Rebecca shrugs apologetically. "I just walk around town," she says, "and my kind of news just sort of jumps into my purse."

"We got room for Mister Holland's murder?"

"The whole front page."

"I'll handle the story," I tell her.

"I've written the obituary."

"Planning to tell what a great man he was?"

"If Reverend Baskin can't get him preached into heaven, my obituary will certainly kick the Pearly Gates open. I told the Piggly Wiggly to order more Kleenex. Be lots of tears shed around town when the paper comes out." She chuckles.

"You have a photo of Mister Holland?"

"An old one. Back when he was honored by the Jaycees." A sad frown slides across her face. "He didn't like to have his picture taken."

"He was a nice-looking man."

"Thought he looked old."

I shake my head, and the words spill out before I can filter them. "He won't ever have to worry about looking old anymore."

I expect a severe rebuke from Rebecca.

I deserve one.

But she apparently understands.

She's probably had the same thought.

She starts typing as if I haven't said anything at all.

I grab a notebook and two ballpoint pens and head toward the door. "See you after lunch."

"We need to be on the press by five-thirty."

"Big story's mostly written."

"How many words?"

"Maybe a hundred."

"Won't take up a lot of space."

"Use big type," I say.

Rebecca sighs. "It's gonna be one of those kinds of days," she says.

"It is indeed."

I step onto the sidewalk and notice immediately that the parade of passersby outside the newspaper office is a lot thicker than usual. Some nod. Some wave. Some are taking pictures with their phones. They keep their thoughts to themselves. They are the reverent and the solemn and the curious who are drawn to a crime scene like moths to a flame. I shudder and wonder how long I've had that cliché stuck in my subconscious. Maybe the flame will burn the damn moths, and I won't think about it again.

**Thursday**
**10:04 a.m.**

Detective Reece Sovern is seated with his legs propped up on his desk and a cold cup of coffee in his hand as I wander into the back room of the police station. Rebecca calls it the dungeon. It's aptly named. Blinds drawn. Paint peeling. Overhead lightbulb giving off a ghastly, or maybe it's a ghostly, yellow glow. I presume the coffee's cold. It has stopped smoking. His white shirt is stained. Gravy. Coffee. Blood. Meatloaf. Hard to tell one from the other. And his dark trousers look as if they were washed in a bathtub and hung out to dry in a lint storm. He's frowning as he slides the phone back in its cradle. He's not happy to see me. Reece Sovern is never happy to see anyone, living or dead.

"What do you know now that you didn't know Monday morning?" I ask and take a seat on the side of his desk.

"Just hung up with the medical examiner."

"He finish with Mister Holland?"

"It's like we expected," Reece says.

"How's that?"

"Neal's dead."

He waits for me to laugh.

I don't.

He laughs loudly for both of us.

"What killed him?" I want to know.

"Stabbed with a pair of scissors."

"But I suspect it was the bullet that killed him," I say.

The detective's eyes narrow. "How did you know about the bullet?"

"Your shadow told me."

"Phil?"

I nod.

"Neal died about four in the morning," Reece tells me.

"He fight back?"

"Tried to." Reece takes a sip of his coffee and throws the rest in a trash can. "Hard to fight back with your heart is pumping blood through a hole in your chest."

"Killer leave anything behind?"

"A dead man."

I act as if I don't hear him. "Any clues?"

"None I can tell you about."

"DNA?"

"Won't know for months," Reece says.

"Anything that ties Mister Holland's murder to the other killings that take place every May Twenty Third?" I ask.

"One."

"What's that?"

"A dead man."

Reece laughs again.

"You're just what every town needs," I tell him.

"What's that?"

"A homicide detective with a sense of humor."

He shrugs a pair of thick shoulders. His shirt tightens around his neck. He wears his green and white striped tie loose. Thinks it makes him look like Sam Spade.

"I am what I am," he says.

*Give the man a can of spinach.*

"How long have you been working the May Twenty Third murders?" I want to know.

"Worked the first one when I was a traffic cop," he says. "Lost one of our own that night. Charles Wegman. He was working late, working overtime. Good man. Good family man. Charles taught me the ropes. I miss him."

For a minute, I think Reece Sovern may have a heart after all.

"Leave a family?"

"A wife."

"She still in town?"

"She's still around."

"I may want to talk to her."

"I wouldn't advise it."

"Why not?"

"I married her," he says. "Good looking little bitch, too." He winks.

*My mistake.*

*Forget it.*

*Reece might have had a heart once.*

*Not anymore.*

*Long gone.*

*Rolled away like a rolling stone.*

"Any suspects?" I ask.

I know the answer.

I'm needling him now.

"None I can tell you about."

"Why the murders?" I want to know.

"A lot of people made somebody mad," he says.

"Why May Twenty Third?"

"One day is as good as the next," he says.

"You have any idea about a motive?"

"Nothing concrete."

"When will you tell me?"

"When the cement dries."

Reece picks up the phone.

He's through with me.

He was through with me when I walked into his office.

# 28

**Thursday**
**10:38 a.m.**

The old man has found himself a seat on the iron bench in front of the library. He's dressed in a summer seersucker suit with a starched white shirt and red power tie. His hair is thick, white, slicked back, and hanging down over his collar. He looks like a Mississippi congressman from two or three decades ago, and his smile is warm and generous. A hand-carved and expensive walking cane lies across his lap. He beckons me to sit down beside him.

"I'm Buford McAllister," he tells me, his voice deep, resonant, and strong.

"Graham Huston," I say, shaking his hand.

His eyes are clear, his hands trembling.

"Attorney-at-law," he says.

"Newspaperman." It's the first time I've used that term in connection with my name, and it sounds like a word from a dead or dying language possibly spit out by a prevaricator of the truth.

"I know what you're looking for," Buford tells me.

I nod and wait.

His cobalt blue eyes are looking past me.

His smile has not wavered.

"You want to learn the name of the gentleman who has left it up to the good people of Magnolia Bluff to bury nine of its finest citizens."

"And you know who it is?"

"I do."

"Is the killer a client of yours?"

"Not at the moment."

"A friend?"

"Not anymore."

"But you know the killer?"

"I do."

"Tell me," I say, opening my notebook, ready to start scribbling, "how is it possible that you know the name of the killer, but no one at the police department does?"

"They're stupid," he says. "They're investigating the usual suspects, and there are no usual suspects this time."

I'm not quite ready to second that comment or attempt to second guess it. But it's obvious that Mister Buford McAllister is no stranger to the stark realities of law enforcement within the unpredictable confines of Magnolia Bluff.

"What is your interest in the murders?" I want to know.

"Personal."

"Care to explain?"

The smile darkens.

His chin quivers slightly.

"My son was murdered."

"When?"

"Middle of the night."

"And what was your son's name?" I ask.

"Carson," he says. "Carson McAllister."

Doesn't sound familiar. I have not run across an obituary for any poor soul named Carson McAllister yet. But I'm still crawling through names and victims and other tragedies connected to May Twenty Third. I have no reason to doubt the old man.

"How did your son die?" I ask as gently as I can.

"Hit and run." The old man gazes up at the sky, and I'm sure his mind is reliving a hot and bitter night when his world ended. The death of a son can do that. "One block south of his office," he continues. "Coming home. Walking. Didn't live far from home. Had a green light, he did. Jeep hit him and did not slow down. Carson died where he fell. One second, he's got the world by the tail. Next instant, he's left the world." Buford snaps his fingers. "Just like that."

"You sure it wasn't an accident?"

"Not if you read this note."

He pulls a wrinkled sheet of paper out of his coat pocket and hands it to me. Note was cleanly typed. Short. To the point. Not a letter out of place. It was six lines long.

*Today's the day.*

*Another one lies.*

*Another one dies.*

*Blindsided.*

*He failed.*

*He sinned.*

*He didn't care.*

"Came through the mail," Buford says. "Morning of Carson's funeral."

"The police see it?"

"Police said it was a prank. Some kind of sick prank."

I read the note again.

Clear.

Concise.

Confusing as hell.

A prank?

Or a dagger to the heart?

"Know what it means?" I ask.

"Means somebody wanted to kill him."

"Who?"

"Just wander around town for a while." A tear moistens his right eye. "Keep a good lookout. Don't trust anybody. Don't believe anybody. This town will lie to you. This town is evil as hell. Only one way to find the man behind all of these killings."

"What's that?"

"Find the meanest snake walking the streets of Magnolia Bluff." Buford stands and steadies himself with his cane. "I know. I've seen his eyes. Got death in them. God didn't make a pair of eyes like that. Devil did. Devil killed my boy. Was the work of the devil himself. I know. I've seen him. I could smell the scent of brimstone on his breath."

"Can you give me a name?"

"Saw his eyes." Buford begins walking away. "Didn't see his face. Doesn't have a face. Doesn't have a name."

The old man suddenly stops.

His head jerks around.

The smile has returned.

"Yes, he does," Buford tells me. "He does have a name."

"What is it?" I ask.

"Lucifer," he says. "Used to be an archangel." He shudders. "Not anymore, he isn't. Killed my boy. God kicked him out."

His eyes are bright.

They are still looking past me.

Buford starts laughing softly. "Baptists don't want him. Methodists can't tame him. Church of Christ locks the door whenever he's around."

The old man shuffles down the street.

"Drives a Jeep," he yells over his shoulder.

*So does most everyone else in town.*

Buford McAllister turns the corner and is out of sight.

I glance down at the pages of my notebook.

There's not a word on them.

**Thursday**
**11:16 a.m.**

Rebecca is typing frantically as I walk back into the office. She has a ballpoint pen stuck firmly between her teeth. She stops, takes a deep breath, and looks up at me.

"Learn anything?" she asks.

"Reece Sovern doesn't have a clue."

"Never did." She removes the pen from between her teeth.

I sit down heavily in my chair. "I met the strangest little man," I tell her. "He says he knows who the killer is."

A grin slowly weaves its way across Rebecca's face. "Well now, you must have met Buford McAllister," he says. "Comes out of the woodwork every May Twenty Third or the day after. Who's the culprit behind the killings this time?"

"Says it's the devil."

"He may be right," Rebecca says. "Last year, he claimed the killer was a one-armed fly fisherman who could strike the sky with lightning every time he cast his bait, and he said the sky would roll with thunder every time the bait hit the water. And the year before, it was the ghost of Elvis Presley driving a pink Cadillac."

"Are you saying I shouldn't consider Buford a reliable source?"

"He's crazy as a left-handed screwdriver."

"Was his son killed?"

"He was." Rebecca's voice grows softer. "At one time, Buford McAllister was one of the finest defense attorneys between Austin and Wichita Falls. He handled the high-dollar cases. The city fathers were always trying to convince him to run for district attorney. Wanted him to send the ne'er-do-wells to prison instead of putting them back on the streets. He would have made a fine DA. But when his son died, Mister Buford's mind snapped. Grief, I guess it was. He roamed the streets day and night, searching for the killer. He lost his practice. He lost his law license. He's a sweet old man, but no one pays him any mind anymore."

"Well," I say as I throw my arms in the air, "there goes my lead story."

"Print it, and you'll be run out of town."

"It's just a matter of time," I tell her.

"Until what?"

"Until I'm run out of town."

**Thursday**
**6:44 p.m.**

The Chronicle hits the streets on time, and a crowd is waiting out front to latch onto the newspapers as soon as they roll off the press.

I give them the facts.

Nothing else.

Neal Holland is dead.

The May Twenty Third killer strikes again.

No one knows why he strikes.

He's still on the loose.

No suspects.

No evidence.

Nothing.

Might as well be a tick in a sandstorm.

There's only one new piece of information to add.

Scissors didn't kill Neal Holland.

Bullet did.

Rebecca is true to her word.

Her obituary catches the town by its throat.

*You only thought Neal Holland was a newspaperman.*

*He wasn't.*

That's what she writes.

*You only thought Neal Holland was your conscience in print.*

*He wasn't.*

*Neal Holland was more than that.*

Rebecca knew.

She had sat beside him and watched him for years.

*He taught me about truth, the whole truth, and nothing but the truth.*

*He taught me to believe in myself and my town and in those who walked our streets.*

*He taught me that you can only show love when you give a stray dog your last steak, give a lost cat a warm bed on a cold night, give a child the only candy bar in your pocket, give a damn when your neighbor is in trouble.*

*Never strike a man when he's down.*

*Help him up so he can stand proud again.*

*Always smile at a stranger.*

*You never know what battle he or she may be fighting.*

*You can't change the man on the street.*

*But you can change the way you think about the man on the street.*

*And always believe in Magnolia Bluff even if you are the last one in town.*

*Don't ever turn out the lights.*
*The blood of us all ran through Neal Holland's veins.*
*We didn't have to worry.*
*He worried for us.*
*We didn't have to fight.*
*He fought our battles for us.*
*We didn't have to defend our town.*
*He was our first and our last line of defense.*
*We might shed a tear.*
*He was there to wipe it away for us.*
*But not tonight.*
*We reach for him.*
*We need him.*
*He's not there anymore.*
Neal Holland, in the words of Rebecca Wilson, was a saint.
Pass the Kleenex, please.
There wouldn't be a dry eye in Magnolia Bluff tonight.

# 29

**Friday**
**9:04 a.m.**

The library is already open by the time I climb the steps and walk into the cool darkness of Caroline McClusky's inner sanctum of books – great works of literature sharing the same shelves with cookbooks and self-help books and family memoirs, most of them based on the lies they have heard around the Christmas table for the past six generations. Doesn't bother me. If a dastardly lie is a good story, then tell it, and see if you can make it a little better next year. Until now, I've never worried about the truth, and now I wonder if anyone would recognize the truth if it walked up in a seersucker suit and sat down beside them. I wouldn't.

Caroline's smile is sincere. She's perched high on a chair behind the counter where she has stacked an Atlas, two dictionaries, and a thesaurus. None of them look promising to me. I don't use words unless I know what they mean and how to spell them. I use short words. My idea of a multi-syllable word begins and ends with *Magnolia.* And I don't plan to travel any farther west than Sonora if I ever decide to leave town. Never been there. Like the name.

She has her blonde hair pulled back in a bun on the back of her head. I prefer the ponytail. Guess she's going for the sophisticated look, especially with the black trousers, white lace shirt, and sharp high heels long enough to double as a lethal weapon.

"Rebecca has a nice piece about Neal in the paper," she says.

"She's good with words," I tell her.

"You don't use a lot of them."

"What?"

"Words."

"Don't need to." I glance out the front window. Slow traffic day. Wait until tomorrow, I'm thinking. Wait 'til the funeral. "I have something to say," I continue, "I say it. I quit."

"Maybe as a reader, I want to know more."

"Easy solution."

"What's that?"

"Wait 'til next week."

She laughs, and I figure Caroline is just being polite. "You going back down in the hole today?" she wants to know.

"For a couple of hours anyway."

"Learning anything?"

"It's easy to learn a lot when you don't know a thing," I tell her.

"Neal kept a really good record."

"Of the murders?"

"Of the life and times of Magnolia Bluff." She sighs. "He printed the good side of our faces as well as the bad. He glorified our accomplishments. He magnified our warts and justified our flaws, and small towns have plenty of flaws."

"You've read all of his May Twenty Third stories, I assume."

"More than once."

"You have an opinion?"

"Neal did."

"He tell you what it was?"

"No." She grows quiet. She's speaking in a whisper. "But I will tell you this."

I lean against the counter to hear her better. "I'm listening."

"Neal had better files on the murders than the police did."

"You ever see them?"

"He said they were confidential."

"Any idea where he kept them?"

"He never said."

"I'll see if I can find the files," I tell her.

"Don't look where you think they should be," Caroline says.

"Neal had a filing system that not even the Intelligence Agency could decode."

"A secret system?" I'm intrigued.

"No." Caroline laughs. "He simply threw junk into every nook and cranny he had in the office. Neal once told me the CIA could waterboard him, and he wouldn't be able to remember where he had anything stored."

"Might be a problem," I say.

"Might be a treasure," she tells me.

I wait for her to wink.

Caroline is dead solid serious.

I head for the stairs.

Her words stop me. "You once told me you swept the office."

"I am indeed the broom man."

"Be careful," she says.

"Why?"

"The next piece of paper you sweep out may be the one you want to keep."

May 2019

The old man was right.

His son, Carson McAllister, was indeed a victim.

Dark of the moon.

Vehicle hit him.

A Jeep?

Don't know.

Could have been a car.

Could have been a truck.

*Story doesn't say.*

*No witnesses.*

*No broken glass.*

*Just a corpse in the middle of the street.*

Justice of the Peace ruled accidental death.

Town didn't think so.

Mister Holland interviewed a dozen of its finest residents.

Nine men.

Three women.

They swore it was murder.

First-degree.

None saw the hit and run.

But Daisy Littlefield and Roger Heitmuhler did mention they were thinking about moving to some other town in some other state.

Don't know if they did.

Don't know if they didn't.

Roger called the town creepy.

Daisy said her old heart wasn't strong enough to let her stay around long enough to see another May Twenty Third.

Carson McAllister was a lawyer.

Same as his dad.

*Dad didn't mention that.*

Texas Law School.

Good education.

Good bloodlines.

Had begun as a public defender.

Worked in the District Attorney's office.

Decent record.

Some of the scoundrels went to prison.

Some still walking the streets.

"Don't worry," Carson was once quoted as saying. "They beat me once. Won't beat me twice."

*Who hit him?*

*Who killed him?*

*Maybe somebody did it after all.*

*Maybe somebody beat him twice.*

Unmarried.

No children.

In sixteen days, he would have been forty-eight years old.

May 2020

Bobby "Bulldog" Jenkins, age fifty-eight was once a professional football player.

Linebacker.

Mean.

Tough.

Played to win.

Knocked out teeth.

Gouged eyes.

Made as many tackles with his elbows as his arms.

*Another time.*

*Another game.*

In Magnolia Bluff, he was beloved.

Revered.

He took young men and turned them into champions.

A high school football coach.

A father to those who had no father.

Seven district titles.

Never won a state championship.

But he got Magnolia Bluff to the final game once.

The town had a parade in his honor.

The school changed the name of the team to bulldogs.

Forever, the Magnolia Bluff Bulldogs.

Retired.

Basking in the memories of the glory years.

Wasn't as fast as he had been.

But he ran the high school track every morning before sunup.

It circled the football field.

He had reached the fifty-yard line.

One more lap.

One more lap to go.

A shotgun blast caught him in the back of the head.

He was fifty yards from the end zone.

He never made it.

Didn't have any enemies.

Had his own personal table at the Silver Spoon.

Danced with his wife at LouEllen's every Saturday night.

A deacon at the Baptist Church.

*Must not have been a Baptist on Saturday night.*

Murder, the justice of the peace ruled.

No one questioned it.

But no one knew who killed Bulldog Jenkins.

Not even Bulldog himself.

The Reverend Chris Hayes preached his funeral on the football field

Big stadium.

Packed.

No church in town had enough seats to hold the two thousand and twenty-four grieving souls who came to mourn Bulldog's passing.

His casket was rolled to the twenty-yard line.

On the visitor's side.

*Red Zone.*

He was moving to score again.

**MAY 2121**

I study a photograph of Judge Amos Fitzsimmons on the front page of the *Chronicle.*

A man of distinction.

Might have been royalty.

Tall.

Stately.

Silver mane.

Silver goatee.

Black mustache.

Said it was natural.

Magnolia Bluff placed the judge on his own pedestal.

The innocent loved him.

The guilty loathed him.

Everyone feared him.

He spoke softly.

In a courtroom, his tongue was sharp as a scalpel.

Could cut out your heart with a half dozen words.

Mostly, it took less.

*Those were Mister Holland's words.*

He had served on the bench of Burnet County for thirty-two years.

Gave second chances.

Found homes for the homeless.

Forget to pay alimony?

He let it slide.

Forget to pay child support?

He had a special cell for you.

*Mister Holland's words again.*

Believed in justice.

Believed in self-defense.

Believed in justifiable homicide.

Sent scalawags to death row eight times during four different decades.

Had compassion for the guilty.

Loved to prosecute lawyers.

Especially big-city lawyers from Austin or Dallas or Houston.

*There's a big river between here and there,* he would tell them. *Don't cross it.*

*They may have walked across.*

*Needed a boat to get back.*

*Boat leaked.*

Had been retired for an even dozen years.

A pillar of the community.

Served as a lay preacher in the Baptist Church.

Hell was the hottest when he preached it.

That's what he did one Sunday morning.

He never left the sanctuary.

Pastor Chris Hayes found him before service that night.

In the baptismal tank.

Filled with water.

Judge might have drowned.

But he had a bullet in his forehead.

Fired by a military Sig Sauer M17.

He was holding the semi-automatic pistol in his hand.

He hadn't pulled the trigger.

He was seventy-four years old.

I rub my eyes and turn off the microfilm reader. The glare is gone. The room is dark. I glance down at my notes. Hard to read. I blink. It doesn't help. I reach over and turn on the overhead light. Still hard to read.

What do I have?

What did I miss?

What did I overlook?

What did the police overlook?

Mister Holland knew more.

That's what Caroline told me.

But what did he hide?

And where did he hide it?

And was he slowly connecting the dots?

That's all anybody had.

Dots.

And deaths.

That's the eight, I tell myself.

That's the eight who were murdered.

Then came number nine.

Then came Mister Holland.

May Twenty Third is no longer an urban legend.

For me, it's now real.

Now, it's personal.

Now, it hurts.

# 30

**Friday**
**12:48 p.m.**

The aroma of chicken fried steak reaches me while I'm still a good block away from the Silver Spoon. Lorraine's back. Lorraine's back in business. She smiles at me as I squeeze my way through the front door. Crowd's thick. Nobody's talking. Nobody's laughing. They don't want to upset Lorraine. Bad memories. Haunting memories. They're silent out of respect. Lorraine is cool, calm, and collected as if nothing tragic has ever happened to her. She has a cheerful lilt in her voice. Her smile is sincere and endearing. She's having to take care of us at a time like this. We don't know how to take care of her.

"How long a wait?" I ask softly.

"Got your table waiting," she says.

"How did you know I'd be here?"

"Easy enough."

"How do you figure that?"

"I'm here. Door's open."

She winks.

Lorraine walks me toward a booth near the window. It is already occupied.

Rebecca looks up and waves when she sees me heading her way. White dress shows off her tan. Short hemline shows off her legs. She's kicked off her heels. Her dark eyes are always probing, always prying. She's obsessed with the desire to know the forbidden secrets of everybody in town. She doesn't know mine. I don't remember mine. Not all of them.

"If you didn't show up," Lorraine tells me, "I got four old boys out in the lobby who'll tip me right handsomely if I let them sit with a pretty woman."

She waits for me to grin.

She doesn't wait long.

"Does that mean I'm supposed to tip you?" I ask.

"Just leave what you think it's worth on the table," she says, slapping down a menu before walking away.

Rebecca squeezes my hand as I slide into the booth. "I wondered when you'd get hungry," she says.

"Been here long?"

"Two cups of coffee, three glasses of tea, a half dozen fried pickles, four cheese sticks with barbecue sauce, and a chicken fried chicken sandwich, that's all." She pushes an empty plate away and leans forward with her elbows on the table.

"Tell me." My eyes are skimming the menu. Mostly they are on her.

"What?"

"Do you buy lunch by the dish or by the pound?"

"It's cheaper by the pound."

Rebecca waits until I lay the menu aside, then asks, "You been out playing newspaperman this morning?"

"Library."

"So you spent the morning with the lovely Caroline McCluskey?"

"She doesn't appeal to me."

"Why not?"

"She doesn't smell like fried pickles."

"I'm not worried," Rebecca says.

"Why not?"

"I'm afraid you're not Caroline's kind of man."

"Who is?"

"Some dude named Dior."

"They would make a right handsome couple," I say.

"Yeah," Rebecca mutters, "Caroline and a magazine cover."

"Vanity Fair?"

"It's not Popular Mechanics."

I'm trying to sound chipper.

I don't feel chipper.

Blue skies outside.

Dark clouds inside, mostly shadows drifting through my mind.

I watch the streets of Magnolia Bluff, at least the block that runs past the Silver Spoon. It troubles me that we live in a society too busy to remember and too quick to forget. When I was a boy, the past stayed with me for a long time. I wanted to hide away in yesterday. I knew what happened yesterday. Yesterday was safe. I had survived it. But I was nervous about waking up on a new morning. The dawn was peaceful enough. I slept through it. But I had no idea what the day might have in store for me, and I was more than just a little frightened about tomorrow. It was the great unknown, a black hole that swallowed people whole and seldom spit them back out. But time and space have changed us all.

In five days I had witnessed shock.

Sadness.

Regret.

Suspicion.

Curiosity.

Tomorrow, the town would be in mourning.

*We'll miss you, Neal.*

*We'll never forget you, Neal.*

*Whatever happened to Neal?*

*Who's Neal?*

*And when did he leave?*

One day, they would remember.

One day, it would all come back to them.

One day was enough.

May Twenty Third.

Rebecca's words interrupted my thoughts. "Where did you just go, Huston?"

"Not so far I couldn't get back before lunch."

"I didn't know if you were coming back or gone for good."

Silence.

I study the menu on the table beside me.

I don't read a word.

I ask her, "How long have you been with the newspaper?"

"Since I dropped out of college at the end of my junior year and bought a book entitled *So You Want to Be a Writer.*"

"And that's what you wanted to do?"

"More than anything." Rebecca shrugs. "Well, I didn't care that much about writing, although I had a little talent for telling stories. But I wanted to know what was going on inside the lives of everyone in town. Find out their secrets. Print them on the front page. That's what I wanted to do. Scandal was fine. Libel wasn't. The thin line between them? I learned how to walk it like a tightwire without a net. I wanted to walk down the street and have women whisper to each other, 'There goes Rebecca Wilson. She knows everything. She knows more about you than you do. Be careful. Don't make her mad. If you do, she'll tell your husband and your husband's boss's wife. And you know what? She might be right.'"

"The black widow of the news business."

Rebecca grew serious. "I hate to tell you, but sooner or later you will find out the truth."

"About what?"

"Neal wrote the cold, hard news," she says. "Read it today, and tomorrow it winds up at the bottom of somebody's birdcage. Women carefully clip out my columns. They save them. They collect them. They keep them pressed between the pages of the family Bible."

"Why?"

"Ammunition." Rebecca laughs softly. "Women fight. But women don't fight fair. Don't use guns. They use words. And words just may be the deadliest weapons of all. 'Don't you dare say anything bad about me. I know something worse I can tell about you. And what I have to say is true. You can't escape it. I have the facts. I know. Rebecca Wilson told me what they are and says she's planning to write them.'"

Rebecca is a purveyor of the elusive truth.

Listen.

Read.

What'd she say?

If you believe it, it's true.

Facts don't mean a thing.

Facts just muddy the water.

Magnolia Bluff has a lot of muddy water.

I change the subject. "So you worked with Mister Holland for a long time."

Rebecca nods.

"You probably knew him better than anyone."

"I'm sure I did." She glances out the window, and I can almost hear the gears meshing in her mind. "Neal had a lot of friends. He went to a lot of civic clubs. He attended a lot of banquets and a lot of shindigs out in the park beside the reservoir. He was on a first-name basis with just about every living soul in five counties. He had mastered the art of small talk, and he was a brilliant storyteller. But he kept the real Neal Holland buried deep inside him. He didn't have a family. I guess he confided in me more than anyone else simply because I was the only one around."

"Did he ever mention having a secret file?"

Rebecca looks at me strangely. "I don't know what you mean."

"Caroline told me Mister Holland had better files on the May Twenty Third murders than the police did."

Rebecca laughs out loud. "He could have written everything he knew about the mysteries surrounding May Twenty Third on the back of a bubblegum wrapper and still had better files than Reece Sovern and the boys down at the police station."

She spits out two words as if they had a bad taste.

Reece.

And Sovern.

I wonder why.

I don't ask.

"This is different," I say.

"How different?"

"Caroline said he kept his files buried so deep that not even the Central Intelligence Agency could decode their whereabouts."

Rebecca shakes her head. "That's news to me," she says. "How in the world would Caroline know something like that?"

"Maybe that's the one secret in town you haven't uncovered yet."

Rebecca doesn't see the humor in what I've just told her.

Her eyes are dark.

If they were darts, I would be seriously wounded.

I suspect I know what she's thinking.

*How could a librarian know something I don't?*

Lorraine breaks the awkward silence when she drops the plate in front of me.

Chicken fried steak.

Gravy on the side.

Green chilies in the gravy.

"I haven't ordered yet," I tell her.

"Don't have to." She winks. "I know what you like."

"What if I'd wanted a roast pork loin."

"You'd have gone somewhere else."

"Why?"

"I don't roast my pork loin." She frowns and looks down at me over the top of her glasses. "I smoke it."

She splashes iced tea on my jeans before setting the glass down.

I figure it's on purpose.

Lorraine turns to Rebecca. It's woman to woman. I'm out of the equation. "How can you date a wandering, vagabond, road hustler like this one?"

"This is not a date." Rebecca is adamant.

"How was I supposed to know that?"

Rebecca leans forward and props her elbows on the table. "If it was a date, I'd have ordered fried jalapenos."

"Certainly make you hot," Lorraine tells her.

"That's the general idea," Rebecca says.

Lorraine throws back her head in a sudden burst of laughter and cackles all the way back to the cash register.

**Friday**
**7:46 p.m.**

Shortly after sundown, I amble into the kitchen, pour two

fingers of Texas Blue Corn Bourbon, turn the burner on the stove to high, and begin deep-frying a handful of jalapeno peppers.

Probably a waste of time. But you never know. Rebecca didn't promise to drop by. Not for sure I even asked her. That has been man's downfall since the beginning of time. We take things for granted. We expect things that never happen.

We spend a lot of time alone.

I wait for a knock at the door. By ten-thirty, I figure it's not coming.

Another Friday night.

Me.

The bourbon.

And a jalapeno pepper.

One soothes the pain. One's hot enough to take the top of my head off. I finish the Texas Blue Corn. I throw the peppers away. Soak them in water first. Don't want to start a fire.

I hear the faint cry of a siren whining in the distance. Just one siren. That's all. Probably a disturbance of some kind. Nothing important. I've learned to read them. Two sirens are a wreck. Three are a fatality. Four means it's serious. Five means Buck Blanton is on the way. Sheriff likes to knock heads together and see what falls out.

I walk to the window and look out on the night.

Town's dead.

Town's as dead as I feel.

# 31

**Saturday**
**5:44 a.m.**

Don't expect to learn much this morning from the holy circle of scalawags, reprobates, misfits, and the great unwashed who have gathered at the Silver Spoon. Still dark. Day has not broken. Hope it's not an omen, the bad kind. It is a subdued band of merry men who solemnly drink their coffee and haven't yet bothered to order their pancakes, three-egg-ham-and-cheese omelets, sawmill gravy, or grits, heavily peppered and sprinkled with bacon bits. Somewhere between May Twenty Third and these early morning hours, they have lost their appetites.

Barron Schiff brings Lorraine a vase of roses, as I'm told he does every year, and we all sign a card expressing our condolences. It's old news, but the hurt never heals. She hugs his neck and wipes her eyes. Not sure there are a lot of tears involved. But she knows what's expected of her, and she performs well, considering a few years have passed since the murder of her husband.

Mister Holland's empty chair at the head of the table is the one no one mentions but the one hanging heavy on everyone's mind. Eyes dart toward the chair, then back. His was always the softest voice in the room, but his words carried the most weight. He'd take any side of an argument and win or at least give you a reason to consider some off-the-wall angle you had probably never thought about before.

Judge Peacock looks sternly at Michael Kurelek. "You have

a working acquaintance with the psychology of the mind, don't you, doctor?"

The professor opens one eye slowly. "I teach it down at the college." He slurs his words.

"What kind of kook are we looking at?"

"I assume you mean the killer." The professor's tongue slips off two of the words.

"The one that won't leave us alone." The judge drags out his words.

Xander Littleton pipes up. "Don't ask Kurelek."

Judge Peacock narrows his eyes until they are dark slits beneath the brows. "He has more experience with these kinds of behaviors than any of the rest of us," he says.

"Not this morning, he doesn't." Xander slowly wipes his mouth with the back of his hand. His napkin has fallen to the floor.

"Why the hell not?" Jack Rice wants to know.

"Well," Xander says, crossing both arms across his chest, "the professor may be spitting out words, but it's old Johnny Walker Red that's doing the talking."

Kurelek hammers the table hard with his fist. "I'll have you know," he says, "I'm as sober as any sonuvabitch at the table."

Xander Littleton chortles. "I rest my case," he says.

The professor blinks twice, drains his cup of coffee, and is suddenly all business. "Let me tell you a thing or two about the frightening and tormented mind of a serial killer," he says.

"Please do." Again, it's the judge.

*He's cruel to animals.*

That's what the professor says.

*He's obsessed with setting fires.*

*He's a bed wetter.*

"Leaves me out," Jack Rice says loudly.

"What do you mean?" Kurelek asks.

"Got a prostate the size of a grapefruit," Jack says. "Haven't wet anything of importance in three years."

Judge Peacock snaps his fingers, letting Lorraine know his coffee cup has run dry, then says, "I've got a question, Doctor."

"Go ahead."

"I'm a squirrel hunter," he says. "I shoot the little rascals, bag them, and leave them on the poor side of town for mamas to cook with collard greens."

"You must be a real and unusually thoughtful man, Judge," Kurelek says, fighting to keep his eyes from crossing as the red is slowly leaking out his pupils. Liquor may be wearing off, but it's still working on his mind as if it's a crossword puzzle.

"So does that mean I'm cruel to animals?"

"Squirrels suffer?"

"Not if I shoot them."

"Doesn't sound cruel to me," Xander says, loading down a piece of dry toast with butter and strawberry preserves.

Jack Rice chimes in. "I kill rats," he says.

"Use a trap?"

"I hung two," he says with a crooked grin. "Used a shotgun on the rest of the little buggers."

Dr. Kurelek leans back in his chair. He is losing the interest of the crowd, and he knows it. He makes one final stab at continuing his learned and scholarly discussion. "A serial killer might have a rough face, one that's hard as flint, and then again, his face might not be threatening at all. He may have kind eyes and a gentle touch. That's what's so frightening about serial killers. They're just like you and me. May work hard. May have a nice family. May coach little league baseball. But somewhere up there, his thought processes can take a sharp turn before anybody recognizes it. I'll leave you with one thought. If you happen to look into the eyes of a human being, you may be looking into the eyes of a killer."

"So that means any one of us might be the May Twenty Third killer," Xander says.

"Could be."

"So he doesn't need a motive." Phineas is uneasy.

"He doesn't."

"Doesn't need to be mad at anybody." Phineas is groping for answers.

"May not even know them."

"He just goes out and kills the first stranger he sees."

Kurelek shrugs. "Might just kill the first friend he sees."

"Doesn't need a reason." Phineas shudders.

"He simply kills for the sake of killing."

Xander pushes his chair away from the table. "You think that's what happens here every May Twenty Third?"

"No," the professor says, "I think our killer spends all year choosing a victim and deciding just how he wants the victim to die. It's all carefully staged. It's not unlike a drama in a theatre. He rehearses that crucial moment of dying in his mind day after day, time after time until he has it down perfect. He waits until every character is in place. The planning brings him as much pleasure as the killing. But you know what provides him the greatest thrill of all?"

We wait.

No one speaks.

"Nobody in town knows what he's planning to do until he does it," Kurelek says. "And after he strikes, nobody in town knows who done it."

"But what if we have a copycat killer or two in Magnolia Bluff?" The question comes from Phineas.

"Don't think we do," Sheriff Blanton says.

Xander places his elbows on the table and cradles his chin in his hands. "Why not?"

"Copycats get caught."

"And serial killers," Kurelek says, "can live in the shadows for a long time."

"How will we know if someone has decided to kill us?" Phineas wants to know.

Buck Blanton stands. "Chances are," he says, "you won't know until you're dead." He throws two dollars on the table and turns for the door. Morning's dying in the heat waves spiraling up from the sidewalk. It's time for him to go. There may be a speeder uncaught or a donut uneaten out in the cruel world.

Jack Rice rolls his wheelchair closer to the table. "I hope the damn serial killer's got good teeth," he says.

"How's that?" I ask.

He reaches in his pocket, removes a black Glock 9mm pistol, and slams it on top of the table. "Sonuvabitch will have a mouthful of lead to chew for dinner."

Blanton stops and looks back over his shoulder. "You got a permit to carry that, Jack?"

Jack uses the barrel to scratch his chin. "You got a permit to take it away from me, Buck?"

The sheriff grins.

"Not today," he says.

He is out the door.

For all intents and purposes, the meeting is adjourned.

**Saturday**
**7:32 a.m.**

I can sense something is terribly wrong by the time I walk into the *Chronicle* office. Rebecca is in her chair, and she's been crying. Mascara is running down her face like stitches at the end of a somewhat friendly knife fight. Won't leave scars but will temporarily change your looks for a while. Mister Holland's filing cabinet is overturned, the drawers ripped out with folders, letters, invoices, and copy paper scattered all over the floor. Rebecca's desk has been ransacked as well. The only thing left untouched is a box of Kleenex, and she's already emptied most of it. A wad of damp Kleenex is stacked atop the lid of her closed computer. The printer has been stripped down.

Detective Reece Sovern, as dapper and disheveled as usual, walks through the door from the press room and heads toward me. "I guess you're wondering what the hell happened here last night," he says.

"Looks like somebody was looking for something," I answer him.

"Know what they were looking for?"

"Don't have any idea."

"Huston." It's Rebecca's voice, barely audible, sounding as if it is coming from someplace far, far away. "I've already told him."

I nod.

*Caught.*

*Red-handed.*

*Guilty.*

"Know where Neal may have hidden his personal notes on the murders?" Reece asks.

"Don't have a clue."

"You looked for them yet?"

"Didn't learn about them until yesterday."

Reece Sovern slumps down into Mister Holland's chair and props his feet on the desk. "I don't think the thief found anything," he says.

"What makes you think that?"

"I think you've already found them, Mister Huston." The detective has spilled a well-oiled smile across his face. "I think you've hidden them again. I don't think you want us to see them. I think you like to keep your dirty little secrets to yourself."

"Why would I want to keep Mister Holland's notes a secret?" I'm telling the truth, but I don't even sound convincing to myself.

"That's what piques my curiosity." Reece lights a cigarette, a Marlboro I think it is. He blows a smoke ring and watches it fade away before reaching the ceiling. "Maybe Mister Holland knew something about you that the rest of us don't know. Maybe you don't want us to find out. You see, Mister Huston, we know most everybody else in town, knew their mamas and knew their daddies, went to school with them, dated the girls, skirmished with the boys, and know them real well. You are the odd man out."

"If I found the notes," I tell him, "and if I've secreted them away, why would I tear the place upside down?"

"Easy, Mister Huston. All you would have to do is report them stolen, and we'd spend the rest of our lives chasing wild geese and never know what Mister Holland knew. You think it may well be the perfect crime. We may be small-town police in your eyes, but we've had you figured out for months." Reece strikes another match but doesn't light another cigarette. He watches the flame burn slowly down to his fingers.

"That's where you're wrong," I tell him.

Reece looks startled. "What do you mean?"

"Let's say I have Mister Holland's notes." My grin is as crooked as his. "I don't. But let's say I do. There would never be a reason for you to chase a wild goose or look under a rotting tree root or even dig around inside a dead man's coffin to find them."

"Why the hell not?"

I lean close enough to Reece Sovern for him to smell coffee on my breath. I know I smell the onions on his. "Because I would print the damn things," I say. "That's what I do, Mister Sovern. I print things. I spill a few secrets, and, hell, look at Rebecca. She spills the rest of them."

His eyes shift to Rebecca, then dart back to me.

He stands and drops a little notebook into his shirt pocket.

"We'll be keeping an eye on you," he says as he strolls toward the door.

"Won't make me feel any safer."

"It shouldn't."

"I want you to do something for me," I say, following Reece out onto the sidewalk.

"What's that?"

"Before you go to bed tonight, think about this little morsel of truth." I hear the train whistle in the distance. Train is right on time for a change. "I've been in town for one murder. You've been here for nine. So who's the odd man out now?"

He opens his mouth to speak.

I slam the door shut before he can get a word out.

**Friday**
**8:28 p.m.**

A newspaper office is a lonely place to be when night falls and darkens the streets, and time keeps passing, but the ticks on the clock mean very little to anybody unless you work the midnight shift and can't wait to get home. I'm alone and leaning against Mister Hollands's desk, my eyes trying hard to find any nooks or crannies where the old editor might have hidden his personal notes about the murders. Just me and the ghosts. We're the only ones around. I'm the interloper. The ghosts have been around a long time. There's one more tonight. I feel his presence, but he's still intent on keeping his secrets to himself.

Rebecca picked up the loose folders, stuffed the scattered pieces of copy paper back inside, and stacked them neatly on Mister Holland's desk. I've worked my way through them twice, found nothing, and am skimming through them one more time. Still nothing. The office is as spare and stoic as Mister Holland had been in life. Nothing on the walls, not even photographs of famous politicians visiting Magnolia Bluff nor any newspaper awards. Nothing prestigious or pretentious on his desk. Nothing on the counter. Nothing on top of a small bookcase stuffed back beside the door to the pressroom. The world's full of that. There's more nothing scattered around us than trash.

The books are what I would expect Mister Holland to have. How to write. How to edit. *The Associated Press Stylebook. The Chicago Book of Style.* William Strunk's *The Elements of Style. Best Sports Stories* from 1990 to 2020. *Ethics in Journalism.* Doubt if it was ever opened. On the bottom shelf are his literary works, the ones he discussed on our journeys around town and across the country. *Old Man and the Sea. Of Mice and Men. You Can't Go Home Again. The Web and the Rock. For Whom the Bell Tolls. Red Badge of Courage. The Sound and the Fury. Sandburg's The War Years.*

My eyes stop.

A thought strikes me.

Out of the blue.

That's where most of my thoughts come from anyway.

I lean over and pull *For Whom the Bell Tolls* off the shelf.

Maybe it's inspiration.

Maybe I'm just tired.

But in Magnolia Bluff, the bell has tolled for nine people.

I open the book, and beginning on the Twenty Third page, I find seven notes all left behind by the killer, one for each victim.

The police hadn't found them.

Mister Holland had.

Or did the killer send him the notes?

I read them silently in chronological order. Mister Holland had scratched initials in the upper left side of each note.

C.W. for Charles Wegman:
*Out of place.*
*Out of touch.*
*Out of time.*
*Never stray.*
*Should have stayed.*
D.B. for David Blankenship.
*Who's here?*
*Who's gone?*
*Who's all alone?*
*A death.*
*A den.*
*Twists in the wind.*
B.G. for Betty Gilmont
*Time to weep.*
*In too deep.*
*Time to leave.*
*No time to breathe.*
H.D. for Hank Dillard
*Look away.*
*Fly away.*
*Walk away.*
*Won't walk away.*
*Again.*
R.B. for Robert Baker
*Ashes to ashes.*
*Dust to dust.*
*Dirt to dirt.*
*Only one way.*
*One way to die.*
B.J. for Bulldog Jenkins
*Try to win.*
*Win again.*
*Roll the dice.*

*What's the price?*

*Of sacrifice?*

A.F. for Abner Fitzsimmons

*Tough love.*

*Tough shove.*

*No sign of grace.*

*A tiny place.*

*To suffocate.*

One note was missing. Wonder if Mister Holland ever wondered what happened to it. Wonder if he ever saw it. Wonder if he ever knew it existed.

I have it.

I take it from my shirt pocket and place it with the others.

I read them all.

Again.

And a third time.

From the front forward.

From the back backward.

The mystery deepens.

The notes mean something to someone.

They mean nothing to me.

Back again to where I began.

Nothing plus nothing equals nothing.

Only one thing is clear.

The killer is not a poet.

# 32

**Saturday**
**2:04 p.m.**

They came to a small knoll on the west side of the cemetery to lay Neal Holland away, and they came by the hundreds in cars and pickup trucks, one pulling a boat, a couple of RVs, and a Fifth Wheel. They were his friends. Neal Holland had no acquaintances. You met him. You knew him immediately. He didn't let you leave until he let you know you had found a friend for life. Sometimes, it took no longer than a handshake. These were his subscribers, his advertisers. Sell two dominicker chickens, a hound dog, and weed killer for Johnson grass in his Wanted section, and you might be invited to his home for Thanksgiving dinner. Mister Holland had no children and no wife anybody ever knew about. He and the town, both blue-bloods and rednecks, feuded and sometimes fought with him, but everyone knew he loved them, and so he did.

Neal Holland was the heartbeat of Magnolia Bluff. He wasn't always totally accurate in his coverage of the news. Everything was slanted in the town's favor. Football team never lost. Even when the boys didn't win, they didn't lose. Fish were always biting down at the reservoir. The mayor didn't get caught embezzling a few thousand from city funds. He was simply a few years too late paying back the loan. The Silver Spoon never burned a steak. No official was ever guilty, not even if he crawled out of town in the dead of night with an arrest warrant hanging over his head. He was simply the victim of a misunderstanding that would, no doubt, be cleared if they ever found the missing concrete truck, two fire wagons, one ambulance, or a squad car dumped in Burnet Reservoir.

The burnt heat of August is waiting for us when we reach the cemetery and stays with us to the bitter end. It is a short sleeve kind of day. Only the preacher is dressed for a formal occasion, and he's wearing a robe, sweat dripping profusely from his face, his eyes the color of spent embers.

No need to mention hell.

We're standing in the midst of it.

The Reverend Billy Bob Baskin does not preach Mister Holland into Heaven, but he gets him as far as the Pearly Gates. May take a while to go any farther. It doesn't matter as long as his shoes aren't smoking. I figure Angels are having a few problems with the Book of Life. Mister Holland has already snuck in a couple of edits.

Don't think God is ready for the old editor to set foot inside. Doesn't want anybody telling him what to do and how to do it. God has been running things just fine until now.

Reverend Baskin calls Mister Holland's funeral a Celebration of His Resurrection. Every eye goes skyward. If Mister Holland has been resurrected, no one sees him go.

There are tears.

Some real.

Some imagined.

Rebecca Wilson tells of Mister Holland's good points, which are a good ten minutes longer than the sermon. Most of what I'm saying is coming straight from her notes. She is stoic. She is talking to us but staring above us. I glance around and watch the sky with her in case it parts like the Red Sea to welcome a good brother home. A couple of clouds shift gently from north to east, but that's about it. I'm sure she could tell stories all afternoon, but, thank the Good Lord and the sweat rolling down our legs, she doesn't.

Members of the Crimson Hat Society sing the closing hymn.

Glad it doesn't have any high notes.

Just scratchy ones.

Professor Michael Kurelek offers the final prayer.

Glad there is no lightning in the sky.

Sky crackles, but it must be the heat.

We all say *Amen* and go home, everybody, that is, except Neal Holland.

**Saturday**
**6:12 p.m.**

The log cabin where Jack Rice resides looks exactly the way I expect. Small. Compact. Sits back on the edge of town beneath the gnarled limbs of an oak thicket. A creek cuts through rocks at the bottom of the hill. His truck was parked in the shade about ten o'clock this morning. Shade's long gone. The fender's too hot to touch. His front yard looks like the rest of the hillside, except the weeds are trimmed, and broken limbs have been stacked for firewood, provided winter is cold enough for him to need them, and February usually is. I expect to see chickens scratching in the flowerbed, but there are no flowers, and a chicken hawk circles high overhead in the wind. The heat sizzles around me. It wasn't a long walk, but in August in Texas, all walks seem longer than they should.

Jack rolls his wheelchair out his front door to meet me. I don't see the Glock. But I know it's probably close. He's carrying a glass with two fingers of whiskey. There may have once been three fingers, maybe even four, but that was several swallows ago.

"Get you a drink?" he asks.

"Don't think it's five o'clock yet."

"What time is it?"

"Fifteen minutes after one."

"Hell," Jack says, "It's been five o'clock for more than eight hours."

"Bourbon," I tell him.

His grin tells me I've made a good choice.

I hand him a copy of the Saturday afternoon newspaper.

Ink's not yet dry.

Four pages.

Mostly advertising.

"It's kind of thin, isn't it?" Jack scans the front page.

"I wrote a memory piece," I say.

"What's that?"

"A retread of all nine murders. Keeps people up to date. "

Jack sadly shakes his head. "Neal did that every year. Thought it might shake somebody's memory loose, cause somebody to remember some little nugget of information that might help Sovern break the case wide open."

"Never did?"

"Waste of time, ink, and paper."

"I guess I'm guilty, too."

"You're forgiven this time."

"Why?"

"You've got no more business running a newspaper than I do."

"What would you have printed?" I ask him.

Jack shrugs his thick shoulders. "The price of hogs."

I raise an eyebrow. "Who cares about the price of hogs?"

Jack winks. "The hogs," he says.

I follow him back into the front room of the cabin. It's cool. It's dark. A single lamp is burning on a small table beside an easy chair. Wooden shelves from floor to ceiling are filled with books mostly dealing with hunting, fishing, boating, firearms, and geology, beginning with the day man left his first footprint on the earth. He does have a small collection of novels written by Raymond Chandler and Dashiell Hammett, so he's all right as far as I'm concerned. A half-empty bottle of Jack Daniels Black sits on a silver platter atop his coffee table. He picks it up and pours enough to last me a week.

"Water?" he asks.

"Straight."

"I knew I liked you for some reason."

"You'd need a good reason to like me," I tell him.

"I've been told that before."

His laughter comes off as a little too harsh. Jack may not be a spiteful or bitter man, but in his condition, I know I would be insufferable and impossible to get along with, too.

*Ignore friends.*

*Wary of strangers.*

*A solitary existence.*

*A loner.*

*Pretty much the way I already am.*

Jack hands me the glass of bourbon, then rolls back to the table where a thin light is casting shadows the size of razor blades across his face. "What do you have on your mind, Huston. I know you didn't come all the way out there to discuss the mating habits of bluegill catfish or the nightly travel habits of flying squirrels."

The Jack Daniels cleanses my throat on the way down. "Jack," I begin, "I know you like to come off as a backward, iconoclastic, old maverick who doesn't give a damn about himself or anyone around him, but I think that just happens to be the character you invented for yourself. You like to fool people." I pause to let him think about it a moment, then tell him, "But I think you're a smart man, Jack. I think you may be the smartest sonuvabitch in the whole damn town."

He scratches the stubble of whiskers on his chin. "You may have me figured all wrong," he says. "I may be as uncouth and as unschooled as everybody believes I am."

"You forget," I tell him.

"Forget what?"

"I have a computer."

"So?"

"I did a little checking, and I know the degrees you have and the colleges that gave you those degrees."

Jack laughs.

This time, it is genuine.

"You come here to blackmail me?" he wonders.

I shake my head.

"You want to know why a crippled old man with a fistful of degrees has chosen to come out into the woods and live pretty much like a damn hermit?

"Don't care."

"So what is it that you want?"

I lean forward, Jack Daniels in my hand, and tell him, "All I want to do is pick your brain."

"Be slim pickings."

"That poor little old me attitude won't work anymore, Jack."

He raises his chin in defiance. "Pick away," he says. "My brain is at your service."

I nod. "I want to know what your thoughts are about these killings that rock Magnolia Bluff every May Twenty Third."

Jack closes his eyes. I can almost hear him rummaging around inside his brain, shoving old ideas away like yesterday's newspaper, pilfering through a garbage dump of forgotten memories, digging through the mud, hoping to find a diamond and winding up with a pocketful of river rocks. He slumps his shoulders. His hands are no longer knotted into fists. His face is stoic. He opens his eyes. They are bright and clear. He looks as if he has just walked into a classroom to deliver a morning lecture.

"I've given the murders a lot of thought," he says.

"I figured you had."

"I've broken it down the best I could."

"What have you found?"

His glass is empty. He no longer needs the bourbon for support. "I looked at the victims first," he tells me. "Why did they have to die? Why were they chosen? Put two people in a room. One is murdered. One isn't. Fill up a room. One is murdered. Everybody else walks out. Why did that one person draw the black bean when nobody else had any beans? Gives me a headache if I think about it too long."

"Find any link between the victims?"

"Three were in education," he says. A coach, a principal, and a school board president. So I figured we might be looking for a disgruntled student who carried a grudge and settled it with violence. But what about the others who died? Where do they fit in? We have three in law enforcement, more or less. A police officer, an attorney, and a judge. So it crossed my mind that we might be facing some demented outlaw who holds a grudge against the policeman who arrested him, the lawyer who defended him, the judge who sentenced him."

"Either scenario makes some sense," I say. The bourbon no longer burns on the way down. It has lost its taste. I may as well be drinking water.

"But how do you fit in a bouncer from LouEllen's Lounge?" Jack asks. "He's an outlier and doesn't belong with either the educators or the legal system."

"Neither does an old newspaper publisher getting ready to retire." I'm thinking out loud.

"I've twisted it every which way and then the other," Jack tells me, "and I can't find a common denominator. What scares me is that the professor may be right. Maybe there is no common denominator. Maybe the killing is random. Maybe the guy just picks a name from a hat and watches the poor sucker twist in the wind for a year before he strikes."

"Makes you wonder why anybody would want to settle down in Magnolia Bluff."

"I hear some folks are packing up and leaving."

"I understand those rumors fly around every year about this time." I shrug. "But I haven't seen any moving vans backing up to anybody's house just yet." I pour myself another finger of bourbon. "Why do you hang around?"

"It's home."

"You weren't born or raised here."

"Home is a place where everybody leaves you alone."

"You like being alone."

"Just me and Jack," he says raising the bottle. "Just Jack and Jack."

Jack doesn't say it, but I know he's ready for me to leave.

I sense it.

I can see it in his eyes.

I stand and lean over to shake his hand. "I appreciate the time," I tell him. It's as sincere as I've been in some time.

"Learn anything?"

"I think I did."

"What?" He sounds incredulous.

"Maybe we've been looking in all the wrong places."

"Where else is there to look?"

"Let's say you have a bag of gold," I say. "Where would you hide it? In the cabinet? Under the bed? In a kitchen jar? In a shoebox in the closet? Don't think so. That's where everybody goes to start looking."

"Where do you think I'd hide it?"

"I think you'd go outside to the biggest oak in the forest, take thirteen steps toward the setting sun, dig a hole the size of a small chest, bury the bag, cover the little grave with rocks to throw everybody off, then take the gold to the one man in town who won't lose it."

"Why won't he lose it?"

"He doesn't know he has it."

"Who would that be?"

"You tell me."

Jack ponders the question and a slow smile works its way across his face. "Well, it sure as hell wouldn't be the funeral director," he says. "But there's not a chance in hell he would let anyone steal my gold."

"Why not?"

"The sonuvabitch would wait until I was dead, then steal it himself."

"We go back to the beginning," I say.

"Twenty-fourteen?"

"No." I shake my head. "That may be when the first death happened, but I think the reason for this bloodletting began a long time before that."

"How long."

"Only one man knows."

"Who?"

"He's dead now."

"When did he die?"

"Monday."

"Neal Holland?"

I nod.

"Did he know he knew?"

"Maybe." I pause and look down at the wrinkled newspaper Jack has thrown on the sofa. "But I doubt it."

"So he took his secret to the grave?"

"No," I say. "He printed it in the newspaper."

"When?"

"Damned if I know."

I'm through the door and on my way down the road. I've left

jack behind scratching the whiskers on his chin.
The evening star almost touches the toe of the moon.
A soft light filters down through the thicket.
The night has packed away the heat.
Won't turn it loose until early morning.
My mind has changed gears.
It's working hard now.
Needs new oil.
The squeals are all rust.
I have it all figured out, and I have nothing figured out.
Jack Daniels solved the mystery.
Just a moment ago, he did.
By morning, he won't remember what the mystery was.

# 33

**Sunday**
**5:48 a.m.**

It was a restless night. Rebecca was waiting for me when I crawled into bed. Well, that's more or less a lie. Rebecca was asleep, her dark hair flayed out on the pillowcase, her face framed by a splinter of moonlight falling past the curtain. I should have let her sleep. I kissed her lightly on the cheek, and she rolled into my arms.

"What time is it?" she asked. Sleep was heavy in her voice.

"A little after two."

"Where have you been?"

"Walking."

"Any place in particular?"

"Just walking."

"Lost?"

"Usually."

She sat up and touched my face with the tips of her fingers. "You're still lost, aren't you?"

"Probably."

"Where are you right now?"

"I don't know, but I've been here before."

"What do you see?"

"A wall, maybe brick, maybe stone. Can't go any farther."

"Then come back here to where I am." Rebecca giggles. "I'll make you glad you did."

"I want to see what's on the other side."

"What do you expect to find?"

"I'm not sure."

"Maybe it's nothing."

"I won't know until I look."

"Then take me with you," she whispers.

"Why?"

"Maybe I can find the door."

I was still staring at the wall when Rebecca yawned twice and went back to sleep.

So much for romance.

I wait for dawn. It's slow this morning. I guess I'll try to go find it. I'd have as much luck fighting windmills. Don Quixote told me I was a fool once, and Donny boy should know. He had a losing record against windmills, even the simple ones.

Rebecca is still sleeping as I walk out the door.

I make three stops.

I pick up the vase of flowers Florence has left for me outside her shop. Looks a lot like carnations. Some pink. Some white.

I make my morning walk to the cemetery. Maybe Freddy knows something. I talk to him until an hour past sunup. He's as much in the dark as I am. I'm hoping he may have heard the whispers of the dead. They know things we don't even suspect. I hear them sometimes. If Freddy does, he doesn't say.

I save one carnation.

White.

I drop it on top of Mister Holland's grave and bow my head in prayer.

I wait a few minutes.

Nothing comes.

I'm like Freddy.

I have nothing to say.

**Sunday:**
**8:13 a.m.**

I wander back down the gravel path to the Wood-Fired Coffee Shop. The coffee is a little rich for my blood, but the beautiful people in town, the socially elite, prefer to spend their mornings with Harry instead of the cowboys and kickers over at the Silver

Spoon. He's smooth, could have probably been a movie star, and has the ability to make every woman, young or old, believe she's the one. Harry serves a café latte. The Silver Spoon has Folger's drip, heavy on the cream, poured from a milk carton. It's basically the difference between Texas Blue Corn Bourbon and a jar of good old Alabama kerosene.

The Wood-Fired Coffee Shop is the kind of place Caroline McCluskey would come early on a Sunday morning, no doubt on her way to hear the Reverend Billy Bob Baskin preach the Presbyterian version of the gospel. Should be good this morning. I'm sure the preacher's still on a high from his command performance beside Mister Holland's grave yesterday. It was a good day for Billy Bob.

Didn't save any souls.

Didn't lose any either.

I have nothing better to do.

I sip, sit, and wait.

Maybe she comes.

Maybe she doesn't.

I nurse a forty-cent cup of dark roast.

Harry charged me three dollars and a dime.

"You're a crook," I tell him.

"Just trying to keep the doors open," he says.

He flashes a smile.

He winks.

He's no longer looking at me.

The lovely Caroline McCluskey has just walked through the door, clad in a sundress the color of butternut cream – looks a lot like a root beer float with the sun behind her back – wearing pearls around her neck, and clutching a King James Bible firmly against her breast. The six-inch heels make her look as if she has the legs of a runner, tanned and tight. Her smile is always bright enough to keep the sun brooding outside.

I wait until Harry places a mocha on the table in front of her.

She doesn't have to order.

Harry already knows what she wants.

Caroline doesn't drink out of a paper cup.

Harry keeps those for derelicts like me.

Caroline drinks from a crystal mug.

As soon as she takes her first dainty little sip, I drop down into the chair beside her. Her smile doesn't fade or even flicker, and as near as I can figure it, that's always a good sign.

"Very good wrap-up story on the murders," she says.

Her voice is a harmony of words.

Her eyes are heavy metal.

"Don't think anybody read it," I say.

"Why not?"

"I understand Neal's done it before."

"Neal went into great detail with precise facts about each victim," Caroline says. "You fired every word like a pistol shot."

"No need to waste words," I say.

"You ever work on a newspaper before?"

"Can't say that I have."

"Then what makes you an authority?"

"Common sense."

"Care to explain yourself?"

"You ever see a harvest moon?" I ask.

She laughs nervously. "Sure. Plenty of times."

"I don't have to describe it, do I?"

She frowns. "What are you getting to?"

"All I need to say is *harvest moon*, and you know immediately what the moon looks like and how pretty it is lying low like a fading gold nugget over the top of the hills."

Caroline cocks her head to one side. "I never thought of it like that. But you're right. If you use the correct word, then one word is enough, or, in the case of *harvest moon*, two words."

She glances at her watch.

She hurriedly drains her crystal mug.

Expensive coffee.

Doubted if she tasted it.

"I'm running late," she says.

"Didn't think Billy Bob started preaching until eleven."

"Choir practice."

As she stands, I know I'm running out of time so I blurt out, "I have a favor to ask."

"What would that be?"

"I need to spend some more time in the library."

"When?"

"Now."

"We're closed Sunday."

"That's why I need a favor."

She looks flustered, and Caroline McCluskey never looks flustered. "I can't just give you my keys to the library."

"I'll lock the door behind me."

"We're open tomorrow, Huston." She appears aggravated. "Come by then."

"Can't wait until then."

"What's so all-fired important?" She is rocking from one foot to the next like a sprinter waiting for the starter's gunshot. I expect her to start running at any moment.

"I think I have a way to find the reason behind these killings."

"Neal thought the same thing."

"I think he was looking in the wrong place."

Caroline hurriedly glances from her watch to the splintered rays of sunlight blasting their way through the front window to her empty mug and back to her watch again. She's wrestling with a decision, and when I'm in the middle of the match, I hardly ever win.

"I'll make a deal with you," she says.

"All right."

"We'll trade keys." The perky little smile has returned. "I'll give you the keys to the library, and you give me your car keys. That way, I know I'll get my keys back."

"Can't," I tell her.

"Why not?"

"Don't have a car."

Now she looks exasperated.

"But I'll let you take the key to my apartment." I begin digging around in my pocket.

"Don't bother," she says.

"Why not?'

"Sounds like an invitation."

The grin happens before I can stop it. "What's wrong with that?"

Caroline slings her purse over her shoulder. It looks sexy the way she does it. "Why would a lady want to walk into a gentleman's apartment and find Rebecca Wilson already there?"

I know my face reddens.

It feels like fever.

She has a satisfied look on her face, the kind women get when they know they've shoved a dagger into a man's chest and hit the heart.

"What do you think you know about Rebecca Wilson and me?" I ask.

"Nothing that everybody else in town doesn't already know," she says. Caroline pitches the keys to the library toward me as she turns toward the door. "I expect you to be waiting outside promptly at nine o'clock tomorrow morning when I get to the front door."

I'm a step behind her.

She turns left.

I go right.

She's looking for salvation.

I'm looking for a killer.

She believes in redemption.

I'm going for retribution.

My friend is dead, and he shouldn't have died.

# 34

**Sunday**
**11:04 a.m.**

I think i know, but I'm not quite sure of what I think I know. It made a lot of sense last night, but last night, I had Jack Daniels whispering in one ear and Rebecca whispering in the other, and somewhere between those conversations, the thread I was clutching began to unravel, and a single strand of truth got lost in the maze running from premonition to suspicion. I have a feeling I'm right. I suspect I'm wrong. And so it goes.

I often feel, on those nights I choose to walk the streets, sidewalks, and back alleys of town that a strange presence of evil slithers like a snake behind me, separating the town, leaving one side in the light and one in the dark. My heart beats a little quicker, and I am reminded that I was born solely for the sake of dying, and I take each breath for granted knowing that on some morning, maybe as early as tomorrow I'll beg for another breath, but whoever is counting them on the far side of darkness will decide that I've had enough and probably one more than I deserve. The evil has no face and no name, and I wonder if it is hiding as an anonymous source somewhere between the ink-stained pages of a small-town newspaper.

I look at the stack of microfilm rolls that holds the life and times, the lies and assumptions, the dirt and glamour, the contentment and deep malignity of Magnolia Bluff in black and white, never in living color. A small town lives and dies in eight-point type and usually with the comma out of place.

*Don't start in 2014.*

That's what I tell myself.

*Don't start when the first murder struck Magnolia Bluff.*

That's not the beginning.

Go back to the beginning.

*Why did the killings start?*

But where is the beginning?

I sit at the microfilm reader, partly in light, mostly in the dark, trapped in a repository of forgotten words, and go back five more years to 2009.

No reason.

Don't even have a hunch.

It's as if I've tied a rope around my waist and lowered myself down into the recent past.

I find the May issue.

I read every headline on every page.

First one year.

And then the next.

And then the year after that one.

It's slow going.

I fear I'll miss something.

A tiny fragment.

A fleeting memory.

Might seem trivial.

But something triggered the mind of a killer.

Did he even know he was a killer?

Or did the mind suddenly snap?

And once unleashed, he couldn't stop.

There was no one to stop him.

Part of him was all smiles and handshakes.

Another part hid in the shadows among the headstones.

Waiting.

Counting the months.

Counting the days.

And then it was time to kill again.

No one knew.

He had the last laugh.

He was still laughing.

I have no idea what the missing link between life and death might be.

From year to year, hardly anything ever changes in Magnolia Bluff.

Not even the names.

*School's coming to a close.*

*Graduation's right around the corner.*

*High School.*

*College.*

Find the road out of town.

Any place better than Magnolia Bluff?

Don't know.

I'd like to find out.

*Births.*

*Deaths.*

Nothing out of the ordinary.

*Old age.*

*Car wrecks.*

*Carly Mooney shot while deer hunting.*

Nothing suspicious.

Shot himself.

Expected to live.

Didn't.

*Twin brothers marry twin sisters.*

There's a honeymoon made in Heaven.

*Chamber of Commerce changes Presidents.*

Every year.

Why would anyone want the job?

Read some time ago that any town large enough to have a Chamber of Commerce is beyond all hope.

Don't remember where.

Lot of truth to it.

*Recipes.*

*Carnival comes to town.*

*Strange folks walking the streets.*

How could anyone tell?.

*Three rapes.*

*Eighteen robberies.*

*Seven criminal assaults.*

*Two dozen domestic disturbances.*

Reece Sovern can't solve any of them.

Too busy posing for front-page pictures.

Always has a new clue to report.

Never has a new arrest.

Every year, he loses a little more hair.

*Big Box Store coming.*

*Hundreds are out front protesting.*

*Big Box Store opens.*

*Hundreds are out front, waiting to shop.*

Discounts.

Cheap prices.

All is forgiven.

For four years, nothing.

My eyes are beginning to itch.

I'm allergic to dust.

I'm allergic to boredom.

But wait.

On May Twenty Third, in the year of our Lord 2013, a small story, only three paragraphs long, appears down on the bottom of page eight, the last page.

It's almost an afterthought.

It's a story I never expected to see.

For a moment, I forget all about the murders.

My breath leaves me.

My heart aches.

*Word was received today from the United States Army concerning the official declaration of death for former Magnolia Bluff resident and high school star running back Harley Spooner.*

*He was declared missing in action during August of 2004 after intense fighting in northern Afghanistan. For years it was believed Spooner might have been captured as a prisoner of war by the Taliban.*

*He was nineteen years old.*

That's all.

He died a hero's death.

And all Magnolia Bluff afforded him was sixty-four words.

No quote from his mother.

No mention of his mother.

Poor boy.

Wrong side of town.

His life didn't count.

Neither did his death.

What was the lead story that day?

I roll back seven pages.

*Mary Lou Fight Named Woman of the Year.*

I feel the anger churning inside my gut come to a slow boil.

I want to scream.

I want to walk up one side of the street and down the other cursing the whole damn town.

A rain could come tonight and wash it away.

I wouldn't care.

It could wash me away as well.

Still wouldn't care.

May God have mercy on us all.

I snap off the machine.

The basement grows dark.

A splinter of light is leaking down the stairs from a window up above.

Too bad it doesn't have a switch.

I would turn it off.

I sit alone until dark, and by then, I know what I have to do. It is a last measure of regret and redemption. We don't come waltzing into this chaotic and unpredictable world with a reason or a purpose, but if we're fortunate enough, we stumble across it along the way. Harley Spooner still lies beneath the rocks on a mountain pass. I'm sure nobody ever went back to bring his bones back down. He left his footprints on the streets of Magnolia Bluff, and now his name is little more than a whisper in the wind. He breathed this air, walked these streets, heard the trains that came whistling past, ate chicken fried steak at the Silver Spoon, and carried the football on Friday nights he thought would never end. He marched away out of everyone's minds and into that dark, deadly mist of oblivion.

I will tell his story in big type the way it should have been told years ago, a story of hardship and sacrifice, bravery and honor.

He was a proud son of Magnolia Bluff.

No one will ever ignore him or forget his name again.

Harley Spooner will get his front page photograph.

The Army will send me one with Harley dressed in full uniform.

As he was.

Not as he is.

That's the only promise of death.

Harley will forever be young.

Full of vitality.

Full of hope.

Full of duty.

Honor.

And sacrifice.

I know.

I marched with him.

Always in front of him.

Then one day I didn't. One day I fell behind. I should have stayed where I was.

If I had, Harley would be home tonight.

Harley would never be home again.

# 35

**Monday**
**6:42 a.m.**

I'm sitting on a wooden bench outside the Silver Spoon Café when Buck Blanton wanders out, adjusts his gray felt Stetson, glances in the big plate glass window to make sure it's on straight, and begins ambling down the street. He's carrying a Styrofoam cup of hot coffee and whistling a tune that doesn't have much of a melody, his broad shoulders dancing as he walks along. He tips his hat at a passing Cadillac. Mary Lou Fight is driving. She looks his way but doesn't smile. She's the queen, the queen of dirt, the queen dowager of the Crimson Hat Society. Buck's the hired help. She knows it. I wonder if he's figured that out yet.

He drops heavily into his black Dodge Pursuit patrol car, and I slide into the front seat beside him. "Got a minute?" I want to know. "I'd like to ask you a couple of questions."

"Mama told me not to talk to strangers," he says.

He's grinning.

Buck is always grinning.

Now he's laughing out loud.

"Won't take long," I tell him.

"Want to take a ride?" Buck asks. "You can ask away while I drive. Need to check on a little burgling job up by the marina."

"Beats walking."

"Then tell me, Huston, why don't you have a car?"

"Rather ride with you, Buck."

"I might forget my manners and arrest your sorry ass."

"Be your first arrest this year."

"That hurts, Huston. You forget that just last week I picked up a handful of migrants sleeping down on a sandbar beside the east shore of Shoal Creek."

"You didn't charge them with anything."

"What's the charge, Huston? I forget now. Is sleeping a felony or a misdemeanor?"

"How about trespassing?"

"It's not trespassing if you go fishing."

"They weren't fishing."

"How do you know?"

"Did you find any bait?"

"They ate it for supper the night before."

"They tell you that?"

"They did, for sure."

"And you believed them?"

"I sure as hell didn't pump their stomachs to find out."

Crime in Magnolia Bluff hardly ever amounts to anything if you don't count murder. "You just let all five of them go?"

"Fed the boys breakfast before I did."

"You're a real saint, Buck."

"Beans and tortillas don't cost much."

His laughter rises from deep in his belly. "What do you want to talk to me about, Huston?" Between one swallow of coffee and the next, Buck has switched to his, deep, baritone, down-to-business voice.

"You've been in Magnolia Bluff a long time, haven't you?"

"All my life. Joined the police department in nineteen and ninety-eight and been driving up and down these streets ever since."

"Do you remember a boy named Harley Spooner? He grew up here."

Buck stares hard at the windshield, wrinkles forming across his forehead. "Harley Spooner. I haven't thought about that boy for a long time."

"He left about twenty years ago."

"That boy sure could run with the football." Buck slowly shakes his head. "He was fast and lightning quick. I think he could have outrun a jackrabbit in a fair footrace. Harley, he joined the army if I remember correctly. Could have gone to college. Had himself a scholarship. But those middle eastern boys rammed the Twin Towers in New York with their airplanes, and Harley ran off to one of those places I didn't even know existed."

"Afghanistan."

"That's the place."

"He died there."

Buck turns left onto Burnet Reservoir Road and heads toward the Marina. "If I remember correctly, we all thought he was missing in action for a long time. Then one day, a letter shows up that declares him dead. That's just like the army. Harley may have been in one of those prison camps for years. May still be there for all we know. Can't trust anything the army tells you."

"Harley's dead."

"For sure?"

"I watched him die."

Silence.

Buck drives into marina parking lot. He doesn't climb out of the car. He just sits there. "You knew Harley?" His voice is soft, reverent.

"He was my best friend."

"Is that why you're in Magnolia Bluff?"

"I came to visit his mother." I take a deep breath. "I thought she would want to know the truth about her son, where Harley was, what he was doing, and how he spent his last day. Maybe her nightmares wouldn't be so bad anymore."

"Sylvia have nightmares?"

"I do."

"And you were there?"

"As close as I am to you."

"Must have been scared."

"One more step and I wouldn't have been anything."

"You surely are a man of secrets,' he says. "I thought you were just a drifter trying to change your luck."

"You may be right."

Buck opens the car door. "I'll talk to you some more about Harley," he says. "But in the meantime, you might want to pay a visit to Lily Greenly."

"The lady who runs the Flower Bed and Breakfast?"

"Been here a long time. Knows anybody and everybody who ever lived in Magnolia Bluff. She used to hire Harley to do some odd jobs for her. He'd pull weeds out of her flower garden, and I remember he painted her gazebo one summer. She kept him fed when his mama couldn't."

I nod my thanks. "How about his old football coach?"

"Can't talk to him."

"Why not?"

"He's dead."

"That's a shame. He probably knew Harley better than anybody."

"Probably did." The Sheriff slams his door shut. He adjusts his pistol on his hip. "Sorry to walk away on you like this. But right now, I have to talk to man about a busted garage door and stolen lawnmower."

"Think you'll find the thief?"

"I will if he rides the lawnmower down Main Street."

"Make an arrest?"

Buck laughs. "I'll file a report," he says. "We don't catch many bad guys, but we do help our good folks collect their insurance money." He pauses, then asks, "Need a ride back to town?"

"I'm sure you'll be here a while."

"Probably grab a boat and drift around the coastline for an hour or two." He starts rolling up his sleeves. "I hear the crappie are biting real good up around Minnie's Cove."

"Who's Minnie?"

"She was Magnolia Bluff's Woman of the Year in nineteen forty eight." He grins. "But that was before they found her making moonshine whiskey in a ravine back of the cove."

"She still in business?"

"Her son is."

"You gonna stop him?"

"I'm gonna gather up some evidence."

I turn toward town. It's not a long walk, the day is overcast, the morning's cool, and with any luck, I'll be back long before nine o'clock. Don't want to keep a lady waiting.

Pretty.

Or otherwise.

And Caroline McCluskey is certainly not otherwise.

**Monday**
**8:54 a.m.**

Caroline does not look surprised to see me leaning against the front door of the library as she strides with a certain amount of sophistication up the sidewalk. Dressed in a shade of red that wasn't used to paint a barn, blouse and skirt alike, she looks like the personification of spring. Her blonde hair has been pulled back into a ponytail, and her gold earrings dance on her shoulders.

I don't speak. I simply dangle the keys to the library in front of her.

She nods her approval. "You're a man of your word, Huston," she says.

"I may need them again sometime."

"Find what you were looking for?"

"I didn't really know what I was looking for."

"Solve the mystery?"

"Found a new one."

Caroline unlocks the big front door, opens it, and I follow her inside to the dark cool inner sanctum of the library. "What's the new mystery?"

"I ran across a story about a friend of mine." I lean against the counter as Caroline begins checking in books stacked up from the day before.

"Who was that?"

"Harley Spooner." I shrug. "I doubt if you've ever heard of him."

"He was the soldier boy," she says.

I raise an eyebrow. Hers is an answer I don't expect. "Know anything about him?"

"I know his mother." Caroline replaces one stack of books with another. "She's a member of our Wednesday night reading club. Quiet lady. I asked her a couple of times about Harley, but she only smiles sadly and tells me her son doesn't live here anymore. I don't know if she will ever accept his death. Sometimes it helps if you talk about the loss of a loved one, but Sylvia simply buries it inside her and doesn't talk at all." Caroline chuckles. "She prefers books instead. I guess she'd rather lose herself in someone else's misery than her own."

"I understand Harley went to school in Magnolia Bluff."

"He did but didn't graduate," she answers. "I think he joined the army instead."

"That's where I knew him."

"I was wondering how you two were connected."

"Same outfit," I tell her. "Same unit. Same squad."

Caroline looks up abruptly and studies my face, her eyes tracing every scar. "Were you a prisoner of war, too?" she asks.

"Neither one of us was captured."

"That's the prevalent rumor in town," she says. "I know he was missing in action for a long time. Then came word of his death."

I nod. I don't bother to correct her. It's no longer important.

"Did you come here looking for Harley?" Caroline asks.

I shake my head. "He died in my arms."

She instinctively reaches out and touches my shoulder, an act of compassion, nothing more. "I'm sorry." It's a whisper.

"His death didn't cause a lot of fanfare in Magnolia Bluff," I tell her. "It should have. He was a hometown boy. He went off to fight for his country. He died a hero. And all he's worth is three little paragraphs at the bottom of a page nobody reads."

"His body never came home." Her voice is soft and sincere. "No funeral. No eulogy. No Taps. No twenty-one-gun salute. It had been ten or eleven years since he left. At least that's what Neal told me once. Years deaden the pain. Years make us all forget."

"Years erase a boy's name."

"I'm afraid so."

"It's like yesterday's newspaper. Nobody remembers." I start toward the door, then stop and turn around. "I want to make sure they have one more chance to remember."

"You writing his story?"

"He has one. It deserves to be read." I pause and turn my head slowly from left to right, taking in all of the books that are stacked from floor to ceiling.

A lot of lives.

A lot of mysteries.

A lot of loves.

A lot of heartbreaks.

And if no one reads them, the characters never lived at all.

Well, once upon a time in Magnolia Bluff, Harley Spooner lived. At least for one day, if no more, he, like Neal Holland, will be remembered in 128-point type.

# 36

**Monday**
**1:30 p.m.**

I had called Lily Greenly at the Flower Bed and Breakfast, and in a feisty voice, she told me she could give me thirty minutes of her time but only if I was knocking on her door promptly at one-thirty that afternoon and only if I brought a dozen tea cakes. She was hosting a game of Mah Jongg at two o'clock, and if I was interested in filling up the newspaper with gossip and rumors and heavy doses of juicy hearsay scuttlebutt, then I could sit beside them at an empty card table and take notes.

I was prompt.

So was Lily.

She is opening the door before I have a chance to knock. She takes the box of teacakes before I offer them and welcomes me inside with the wave of her arm. Lily is a small woman, probably nearing sixty, and her hair is jet black. I was not aware they concocted dye that dark, but there is a lot about women I don't know and am afraid to know.

She is trim and takes long, confident strides when she walks. She looks at you with the smile of an angel and the eyes of a skeptic. She is the kind of woman who lives on different sides of her own personality. She loves everyone and trusts no one, especially not a newspaper writer coming to her door with questions and gifts.

"I hope they're plain," she says.

"They are."

"How did you know?"

"I told Noonan Brown down at the bakery they were for you."

This time, the smile touches her eyes.

"I have my own special icing for them," she says. "Care for a cup of tea?"

"Please." I pause, then take a chance. "With cream, if you have it."

"Like the English," she says.

"The English know their tea."

"I'm English," she says.

It figures.

I sit on a Victorian settee in the sunroom. Lily takes the chair next to me. "Fire away," she says. She glances at the clock on the wall. "You have twenty-six minutes and eighteen seconds."

"It may not take that long."

"Good." Her smile broadens.

I lean forward with both elbows on my knees. "I understand that maybe twenty or so years ago, you hired a young man named Harley Spooner to do some work around the Bed and Breakfast for you."

"I did, and he was a delight. Pleasant young man. Didn't talk a lot. Appreciated the small amount I paid him. Never asked for a raise. Came early and stayed late." She cocks her head to one side. "Why do you want to know about Harley?"

"He and I were in the army together."

"I'm sure he was a spit and shine soldier."

"He was."

"It was terrible about what happened to him."

"I was with him when he died."

"Oh, I'm not talking about that," she says. "Harley got himself into a little trouble at school during his senior year."

"What kind of trouble."

"It didn't amount to much, not the way I saw it." Lily's eyes were afire. "All I know is that the principal suspended him. He couldn't play football his senior year. And he left town to join the army. I missed him something terrible. Sometimes when I think about little Harley, I still do." Her smile returns. "He was a big, strapping boy by then," she says. "But I always remember him as a little boy."

"Do you know his mother?"

"Sylvia is a fine lady, a church-going kind of lady. Her husband left her when Harley was a baby, and as far as I know, she never saw him again." Lily shudders. "She had a hard life. Was barely able to scrape by. That's why I hired Harley to clean the Bed and Breakfast and keep the sheets washed and dried, the garden weeded, and the lawn mowed. And, of course, little Harley walked home with a pocketful of nickels and dimes I paid him for his little jobs. I had to look hard to keep him busy."

"Sylvia ever work for you?"

"For a couple of years, she cooked the breakfasts we serve in the morning. But when she got word that Harley was dead, she became an invisible woman. I think she blamed the town for sending her son off to war to get killed." Lily lingers over a long sip of tea. "I took her some chicken soup about two years ago when I heard she was ailing. She didn't even come to the door. I left the soup on her top step. Two days later, I found it washed and dried on my front porch. I guess it's been a good seven or eight years since I've seen her. Sylvia mostly wants to be left alone, and I honor her privacy."

The clock says it's five minutes 'til two.

I stand.

"Don't worry," she says, "the clock's a little fast."

But I can hear women's voices coming up the sidewalk.

"I have only one more question," I tell her. "Can you give me the name of the school principal who suspended Harley?"

"That would be Betty Gilmont."

Name sounds familiar. I'm positive I've heard it before.

"She still live in Magnolia Bluff." I ask.

"No." I can barely hear her. A mist frosts Lily's eyes.

"She retired? Move somewhere else?"

"I'm afraid there's no way you can talk to Betty," she says.

"Why not?"

"She was murdered." I hear a tear creep into Lily's voice. "Somebody tied a concrete block around her neck and threw the poor thing into the river."

"May Twenty Third," I whisper.

"It's a dastardly day," she says.

A dastardly day to die.

**Monday**
**4:43 p.m.**

I'm no stranger to being alone. But within the past hour or so, I have begun to feel as alone as if I'm locked away, on the inside looking out, and the faces staring back at me are faces I've never seen before, and some are solemn, and some are laughing, and I can't hear any of them, not even those whose faces are pressed against the big front window and shouting while I have been misplaced inside a wall of silence. Part of me thinks I know what has been going on for the past nine years in Magnolia Bluff, and the rest of me doesn't have a clue about what's been going on or why it has spread the wings of a deadly shadow across a little town where the just walk side by side with the unjust, and it's often difficult to tell the wicked from the righteous, or maybe there's no difference at all.

The door is jerked open, and the honorable Sheriff Buck Blanton sticks his head inside the newsroom. "Had any supper yet, Huston?"

"Haven't had lunch either."

"Grab your notebook and come with me," he says. "I'll feed you some barbecue, the likes of which you've never had before and may never have again because Jumbo won't let you darken his doorway if I'm not there to treat him right."

"Beef or pork?"

"Might be roadkill, but you won't care a lick."

"Who's paying?" I ask.

"I get you in." Buck grins loudly. "You pay the bill." The grin suddenly fades. "You got cash? Jumbo, he doesn't take plastic. Thinks it's the money of the devil."

"He may be right."

"Cash?"

"Got it."

Buck drives out of town, then winds his way down one dirt road onto a gravel road that becomes a pair of ruts cut into the open prairie. When the ruts play out, we're among the battered second-hand Fords, Chevrolets, and Plymouths that crowed around Jumbo Jim's barbecue pit. Piles of rust on four wheels, some running, some not. The weather-boarded cabin is not quite good enough to be a café and not quite bad enough to be a juke joint.

"See that front door," Buck says. .

I nod.

"That's the imaginary threshold that separates good and evil." Buck climbs out of the car and straightens his hat. "The bad guys may be out here, but when they walk through that door, they receive redemption until they leave. You'll usually see a handful of petty thieves, a burglar or two, a couple of armed robbers, and maybe a car hijacker inside. As long as they are inside, they are safe from the law. However, If I happen to catch them on this side of the door, then they belong to me."

"Who made those rules?"

"Jumbo."

"And you simply accept them?"

"Jumbo's my daddy." Buck shrugs. "If my daddy says it, then it's the law."

"Voters care?"

The grin is back. "Look inside," he says. "They're all voters."

"And they all vote for you."

Buck slaps me on the back. "I wouldn't have it any other way," he says.

Jumbo is the image of age. Ragged face. Shaggy white hair. Slumped shoulders. Plastic-rimmed glasses. And, dripping wet, he might weigh a hundred and twenty pounds. You wouldn't have to tell me he's Buck's daddy. They both have the same grin, and their teeth are always shining. I have the only white face in the room, but no one seems to care. I'm with Buck Blanton. I'm with the lord of dispensation. If he approves of me, I might as well be black.

We find a table at the back of the room. We don't order. We eat what Jumbo brings us. A pile of ribs, stacked high, dripping with sauce that's been stirred with brimstone. When we finish, the platter will look like a boneyard, washed white by sun and time and a random hailstorm.

"I did a little digging for you," Buck says. He leans back and places his Stetson on the table beside him.

"About Harley?"

He nods. "Seems the boy ran into a little trouble his senior year of high school. Caught him smuggling whiskey. Bottles and bottles of whiskey. Officer stopped him from speeding not too far from LouEllen's Lounge. The whole trunk of his car was filled with whiskey, which, as you can imagine is unlawful for an eighteen-year-old to be hauling around in the dead of night. Officer didn't want to, but he didn't have a choice. He arrested Harley, and the boy spent a month in jail."

"That's a long time to serve for a little bootleg whiskey," I tell him.

"Judge was a strict disciplinarian," Buck says. "Make a believer out of a boy, and you might be able to straighten him out and make a good citizen out of him before he passes that point of no return, if you know what I mean."

"How much time do most of your petty criminals stay in jail?" I want to know.

"Most of them are out by morning."

"And Harley spent a whole month?"

"Couldn't make bail, I guess." Buck shrugs wearily. "Mama didn't have any money."

"So they let Harley rot."

"Judge said he'd let the boy out on one condition. He had to join the army. A good drill sergeant is sometimes more effective than a warden."

"Harley didn't have a choice."

"Harley wanted out." Buck shrugs again. "Being in the army is better than being a poor boy in Magnolia Bluff," he says.

"Judge still on the bench?"

"I'm afraid we lost the judge."

"He leave Magnolia Bluff?"

"More or less. He was shot in the head one Sunday afternoon. We found him floating in the church baptizing tank." Buck finishes his last rib. "For a long time, we thought he killed himself. The medical examiner even ruled suicide."

"But it wasn't."

"Judge had a bad case of rheumatism. If he pulled the trigger, somebody sure as hell helped him do it."

I stared into the flames dancing in the barbecue pit. The place was hot and getting hotter. Gray wisps of smoke curled around a pair of lanterns hanging from the ceiling. The door was open. So were the windows. But the breeze didn't bother to come inside.

"I have a question," I tell him.

"Shoot."

"Was the arresting officer named Charles Wegman?"

Buck sits up straight, a look of surprise splashed across his face. He wipes his mouth with a red napkin. "How did you know?" he asks.

I finish my last two ribs.

Sauce spills on my shirt.

I won't wash it.

I'll throw it away.

I have the bitter taste of bile in my mouth.

Sour.

Unsavory.

It has nothing to do with the barbecue.

# 37

**Monday**
**9:24 p.m.**

The dark and I are old friends. It's when daylight comes that I feel like a stranger. Daylight exposes our flaws, our fears, our failures, who we are and who we try to be, and we are always trying to be somebody we aren't and hoping that nobody finds out until we're on the road to someplace else, leaving before I make the mistake of spilling my secrets out in the open where the curious public can realize I'm nobody at all, just another wayfarer who has nothing worthwhile to offer and won't be missed when he's gone.

I've come to sit a spell with Freddy. He's not used to me being around this time of night, but he has not yet complained, and he listens when I'm thinking out loud. Freddy could have been a psychologist, a counselor, or a bartender. He passes no judgment on my shortcomings, but on a few occasions, I think I've heard him snicker, but I can't be sure it's not the wind rustling through the newborn leaves.

I have never been a good solver of puzzles. I wound up as a foot soldier in the mountains of Afghanistan for one solitary reason. I did not have a good track record of diving deep into the abstractions of military riddles. War is black and white. It boils down to a singular and simple phrase. Kill before you are killed. The only ones not worried about surviving are sitting back in plush offices continents away from the battlefront, playing war games with pawns on a chessboard, solving riddles filled with anticipations and expectations, and usually solving them wrong. There was no rationale for us to be on a narrow footpath through a mountain pass on the day Harley Spooner died. But some fool with bars or stars on his shoulder tried to add two and two and came up with six, which was fine because he had been looking for six all morning. We died. He lived. And they gave him another puzzle. *Be more careful this time,* they said. Too late for Harley.

It all comes back to Harley.

*Fear.*

*And death.*

*And May Twenty Third.*

*They all come back to the days before Harley left town.*

*Someone cared deeply for him.*

*His mother?*

*Probably.*

*Someone has suffered in silence.*

*Someone is bitter.*

*Someone wants revenge.*

*Someone is exacting revenge.*

*I have no answers.*

*I have no solutions.*

*I don't know who.*

*But now I know why.*

*It's so clear when you take the ragged pieces and start fitting them back together.*

*I wonder why no one else has figured it out.*

*Maybe no one tried.*

*A boy is missing.*

*A boy dies.*

*Anybody important?*

*No.*

*Just a kid down the street.*

*Have a rich daddy?*

*No.*

*Doesn't have a daddy.*

*Got a tear?*

*Shed it.*

*The town moves on.*

*But on May Twenty Third, someone remembers.*

*Someone else pays a debt.*

*It's a large debt.*

*Someone collects every year.*

I have a theory, but it is still full of holes.

Black holes, every one of them as deep as a grave.

It is confounded by a few loose ends.

Loose ends tied to a puppet.

Loose ends tied to May Twenty Third.

I stand and wait for a muscle cramp to ease, lay a dandelion growing wild on the headstone of Freddy's grave, and walk softly out of the cemetery.

Don't want to wake him. His is the eternal sleep.

**Tuesday**
**5:04 a.m.**

I am standing on the porch of the Silver Spoon when Lorraine unlocks the front door. The Southern winds are gently blowing a few loose strands of gray in her hair, and a blue and white checked gingham dress fits loosely over her thin frame. I had never noticed before, but Lorraine obviously does not eat enough of her own chicken fried steak, gravy on the side.

A smile jumps on her face. "You're up early, Huston," she says.

"I need a cup of your coffee."

"Can you wait until I brew up a fresh batch?"

"If you let me ask you a couple of questions while the coffee perks."

"We don't perk it these days."

"I'm old-fashioned," I say.

The smile still hangs on her face, but the sincerity is gone. Her eyes grow wary. "Depends on what you want to know."

"Tell me what you know about Harley Spooner."

Lorraine relaxes her shoulders. "That's a name from long ago," she says.

"Almost twenty years."

"Harley was a fixture around town," she tells me. "Working anywhere he could to help out his mother. Waited tables for Hank and me one summer. Pleasant. Polite." She pauses and I can see her probing the backside of her memories. "Left town while he was still in school. No. I think he dropped out of school. Never saw him again."

"Hank know him pretty well?"

"Not as well as I did. I spent a lot of my time hiring kids to work during the summer. Hank was tied up with his school business."

"What kind of business?"

"For several years, Hank served as president of the school board."

"Was that when Harley was in school?"

Lorraine frowns and taps the ends of her fingers on the countertop. "Probably was. He was elected to the board in two thousand and one and served four terms. But he grew tired of all the red tape and forms he had to fill out every week. He ran for the board to help the kids. But he said education was changing, and he didn't want any part of it."

The coffee pot rings a bell. The red light pops on.

"You drinking here?" Lorraine asks.

"Need a to go cup."

As Lorraine pours, she asks, "Why did you want to know about Harley?"

"I knew him once."

"Ever know what happened to him?"

I nod, take my Styrofoam cup of coffee, drop two dollars on the counter, and head toward the front door.

"I hope I could help you," she calls out.

She did.

One more missing part had slid into place.

"Thanks," I answer as an afterthought and hope she hears me before the door closes. A car horn is honking, and the Southern Pacific Train comes rattling past town. If I were smart, I would grab a brass railing on the caboose and ride out of town with it.

**Tuesday**
**9:12 a.m.**

I stop by the courthouse. It's not unusual. I make a regular run to the county clerk's office two or three times a week to check out the court docket. Who's on trial? Who isn't? Who's out on bail? Who's been paroled? Who's skipped town? Edna doesn't mind when I interrupt her. She likes to show off her new digital records system.

"Used to take a week and sometimes a month to track down old records," she's told me more than once. "Now it only takes a minute or two – five minutes if I hit the wrong key."

Miss Edna should have retired ten years ago.

But she likes working in the courthouse.

She likes knowing the dirt that goes with it.

Miss Edna looks up when I sit down beside her. Almost seventy years old. Gray hair fresh from the Head Case Beauty Salon. Wrinkles smoothed by some kind of cream or ointment or snake oil. Not criticizing. It works. I may need to find out where she buys it. She's wearing a short-sleeve emerald green dress and tiny diamond earrings.

"What do you need today, Mister Huston?" she asks.

"An old file, Miss Edna," I tell her.

She is into formality.

I don't mind playing along.

I drop a box of cream-filled doughnuts on her desk.

"Trying to bribe me again?"

"I am."

"It works." She turns to her computer. "What's the date?"

"Two thousand and three."

"Only take a minute," she says. "Used to take a week."

I nod.

"It's a court date," I tell her.

"Got a month?"

"I don't."

"Got a name?"

"Harley Spooner."

I can tell by the look in her eyes. The name doesn't register with her.

"Here it is," she says a minute or two later.

"Looks here like he had been charged with bootlegging a little whiskey," she says. "Never went to trial. Case dismissed. What else did you want to know about him?"

"Who was his attorney?"

She spins the computer screen around for me to see.

I read the name.

I expected the name. I had to make sure.

I kiss Miss Edna on the cheek.

She blushes.

I'm out the door.

Everything fits exactly the way it's supposed to fit. But there is one outlier, one name, one death on May Twenty Third that doesn't make sense.

*Who the hell was Robert Baker and why did someone want to kill him?*

# 38

**Tuesday**
**2:04 p.m.**

What role did Robert Baker play? Is he the missing link, or did he just get in the way and wind up dead? I don't think the killer made a mistake. Each death was well calculated and well-orchestrated by an ingenious but diabolical mind. Or was Robert Baker the wild card? Maybe he died to throw everyone off. Maybe the killer was afraid someone might awaken in the middle of the night and decipher a very predictable pattern. Maybe Baker was murdered to break the pattern. Send everyone back to square one. I am often convinced that life begins and ends at square one. We never leave it. We are afraid to venture too far past square one. It is our comfort zone.

Robert Baker is a name no one has mentioned, not even Buck Blanton, and the Sheriff has long held all of the loose ends. He just keeps them in a bag and never takes the time to tie them back together. Then again, maybe he did, didn't like what he found, and began throwing the loose ends away as if they were quarters in the deep end of a lonely heart's wishing well. Well, there is also one more name, Master Sergeant David Blankenship, but it doesn't take Sherlock Holmes to figure out his part in the drama.

I don't spend a lot of time congregating with the boot-scooting cowboys and damsels in distress who find their way nightly to the whiskey-stained and knife-scarred ballroom known as LouEllen's Lounge. The damsels hardly ever know they are in distress until they sober up and realize that the cowboy kicker who told her he loved her and would love her forever suddenly ran out of love somewhere between midnight and two o'clock on a cold, dark morning. I don't like to pay seven dollars for a jigger of watered-down bourbon. Don't like jukeboxes. Don't like fiddles. Don't like country music. Don't like dancing. Don't think there's been a song worth remembering since Tom T. Hall sang about old dogs and children and watermelon wine. It's a far piece to walk from town to the lounge. Besides, I'm too old to be a kicker and too young to waltz.

This afternoon, I make the walk.

Don't have a choice.

The lounge has two front doors, one fashioned from weathered barn wood and one gilded with gold painted wrought iron. LouEllen knows how to drag in paying customers from both sides of town, both sides of the tracks. I come through the door that, by late on Saturday night, smells like sweat, beer, and cattle dung scraped from the bottom of boots. On the far side, you can find a genuine, first-class, high-dollar, and respectable bar where waiters in white shirts and ties will bring you Martinis, dry or otherwise, fifty-dollar-a-bottle wines, and Long Island Iced Tea. Ladies are always dressed for Sunday church or better, and men wear jackets, Hawaiian shirts, and spit-shined leather shoes. I never go to that side. Don't like wine. Don't like cocktails mixed with assorted flavors of ice cream. Don't like the aroma of perfume that costs more than the wine. Don't like Champagne music. Don't like Lawrence Welk.

The country lounge opens promptly at two o'clock in the afternoon in case you want to get a head start on the night. Inside, it's cool and dark, and the lights have not yet begun glittering like stars on a giant mirrored ball hanging above the dance floor.

The bartender is washing glasses.

It's a chore that never ends.

Don't recognize him.

Of course, it could be that I've never seen him in the dark before.

A heavy-set man dressed in a blue suit, his tie loose around his neck, sits alone at the bar, nursing a glass of beer. Probably a salesman. Been on the road. Hasn't sold a lot. Been rejected too many times in business and in love. Likes to hide out in a bar where night comes early and he doesn't have a lot of trouble concealing three or four beers on his expense account. The lounge cleverly offers businessmen credit card receipts from The Pedernales Cove Steakhouse, either for a Porterhouse, T-Bone, or a filet mignon, depending entirely on how much liquor the customer has poured into his gullet.

Other than the lovely and striking LouEllen Mueller, I'm the only one else around. She's sitting at a back table, squinting in the dim light, reading through a stack of papers, no doubt her daily financial reports. From what I hear, she has the best financial statements in six counties. She learned a long time ago that if you sell fifty cents worth of liquor for seven dollars, you stand a better than average chance of breaking even.

Her dress is artwork of stitchery and sequins, a pale turquoise trimmed with white lace. She has a strong face but with delicate features. Blonde curls are piled high on her head. She has a beauty mark beneath her left eye. It may change before the week is out. Her lipstick is a little too red, but it works fine in the dimly lit room. And her eyes are not unlike melted hot chocolate. She wears a squash blossom necklace of white turquoise around her neck. It rests gently on a bosom large enough to make her cleavage look similar to the Continental Divide.

She raises her head as I make my way to her table. "Looking for something?" she asks.

"You," I answer.

"Well, you've found me. Now, what are you going to do about it?"

Her eyes twinkle.

LouEllen's a widow.

A wealthy widow.

She can have any man she wants at any time she wants him.

But she likes to make every man audition.

That's what Harry Thurgood told me.

He auditioned.

He got a call back.

"I'm Graham Huston. I work at the *Chronicle* now."

Her smile is broad and genuine. "I thought I recognized you," she says. "You're the man who tries to use the fewest words possible to tell the biggest story in town."

"Guilty."

"Sit down." She pauses a moment, then says, "You know this is a bar."

"I do."

"I don't talk to anyone who isn't drinking."

"I'll take bourbon."

"What brand?"

"As long as it's brown, it'll do fine," I tell her.

She snaps her fingers twice, and the bartender splashes bourbon into a glass of ice and brings it to the table.

I fish around in my pocket, find a ten-dollar bill, and lay it on the table.

"The bourbon's on the house," LouEllen says. "But Andy appreciates the tip."

The ten dollars vanish.

The room grows quieter than before.

Have no idea how it happened.

"I'd like to know what you can tell me about Robert Baker," I say.

A look of surprise crawls from one eye to the other. "Why in the world do you want to know about Bobby?" she asks.

"I read where nobody called him Bobby."

"I wrote his paycheck," she says. "I called him whatever I wanted to." She sighs deeply. Maybe a pain from the past.

Beautiful woman.

Big, strong bouncer.

Maybe nothing happened.

"Bobby worked for Jacob and me for a long time," she says. "He was a big man, maybe six inches taller than six feet, probably weighed a good two hundred and fifty pounds. He had muscles like sacks of concrete. He kept the peace inside the lounge. Feeling stupid? Want to fight? Take one look at Bobby. The fight left you and crawled away like the coward it is. He was the son Jacob never had. But I'm afraid Bobby was a little wild. Not even Jacob was able to tame him."

"And you?"

"I didn't even try." She laughs. "But wild is not too bad sometimes."

She sighs again.

Long.

And heavy.

"Bobby's not here anymore."

"I know."

"He was killed."

I nod.

"For the longest time, I thought Jacob killed him."

"Jacob have a reason?"

"Jacob was good at manufacturing reasons."

I glance down at my notebook, read through my scribbling for a moment, then say, "I understand Bobby did a little bootlegging on the side."

Her eyes harden.

They become chipped flint.

"You can't call him Bobby," she says.

"I'm sorry." I begin again. "I understand Robert did a little bootlegging on the side."

"He would steal from us and sell the whiskey out of his barn," LouEllen says.

*Sold mostly to kids.*

*Didn't care if they were old enough.*

*Law didn't bother Bobby.*

*You had twenty dollars.*

*Bobby had a bottle.*

*Even if you wore a badge.*

"Jacob catch him stealing?"

"No. Bobby had quite a scheme. He'd take the whiskey out, a bottle at a time, throughout the day, stash it in a wheelbarrow. And he hired a kid to come pick them up about sundown and haul them out to his barn." LouEllen chuckles. "Bobby was always clean when he left the lounge. Jacob checked his car a dozen times or more. Never found a thing."

"Who did Robert hire to drive the whiskey away?"

"Don't remember, Huston. That was a long time ago." She shrugs. On her, it looks elegant. "Just some high school kid who wanted to make a few easy dollars."

"Was his name Harley Spooner?"

"Could have been," she says. "Name sounds familiar."

I stand to leave.

"You didn't finish your bourbon," LouEllen tells me.

I smile. "Not quite brown enough," I say as I walk away.

**Tuesday**
**3:26 p.m.**

It takes me almost an hour to walk from the lounge to Sylvia Spooner's house. I have the facts. I have the details. I sprinkle in a few assumptions. I've added them together. I've torn them apart. I've rearranged them. I've turned them upside down and inside out, and every time I draw the same conclusion. It's staring me in the face. Now, what am I going to do about it? I don't believe it. Can't believe it. Then again, I can't ignore it either. Every murder on May Twenty Third for the past nine years has been linked to the death of Harley Spooner.

I have no choice but to tell Sylvia what I know.

Be blunt.

Can't do it gently.

She has to know that I know.

She can't run anymore.

She can't escape the cold, sordid facts.

But how do you accuse a mother of murder, of multiple murders?

She's had every reason to commit them.

Part of me understands.

Part of me wants to forgive her.

I knock on the door.

My hand is trembling.

My stomach is churning.

My gut hurts.

My heart aches.

I should have left town when I was still mostly in the dark.

My timing is never any good.

"Who is it?" I hear Sylvia say.

Her voice is soft.

Angelic.

Not a note of bitterness in it.

"Graham Huston."

"Come in, Graham," she says. "Door's open."

The room is dark.

No lamp is lit.

I see shapes.

I see gray shadows.

I find Sylvia on the sofa.

I sit down beside her.

I take her by the hand and tell her what I know.

I give her every detail.

It's as though I'm giving my final summation to the jury.

Point by point.

By the numbers.

*A dot on top of every i.*

*A cross on every t.*

I finish.

My hand is still trembling.

Hers isn't.

We sit in silence.

I watch the gray in the shadows turn to black.

Sylvia suddenly breaks out laughing. She squeezes my hand. "Huston," she says, "do you honestly believe I committed those murders?"

"I'm sorry," I tell her, "the facts are all there, and they all lead here."

"Don't you know?" she asks.

I'm puzzled.

"Can't you tell?"

I have no idea what she's talking about.

"I couldn't have killed anyone nine years ago or yesterday. I wanted to, but I couldn't."

"Why?" I ask weakly.

"I'm legally blind," she says. "I haven't been able to see

anything since the day I received the letter telling me my son had died."

I'm stunned.

I'm at a loss.

I know she is always shuffling across the floor.

Her feet unsteady.

Her hands groping for the back of furniture to keep from falling.

She always has a blank stare.

Her eyes look like broken glass.

I've been blaming it on age.

How could I have been such a fool?

"What happened?" I ask.

"The doctor blamed it on stress," she says. "I had been sick with worry for years. Then when I heard that Harley had died, something snapped in my head. The shock suddenly disrupted the blood flow to my eyes and to my brain. I screamed. I passed out. When I awoke, the world was dark. It has been black ever since."

I have entered the same world.

I can see, perhaps.

But I can't see a thing for the dark.

I'm back where it all started.

I'm standing again on square one.

# 39

**Tuesday**
**4:42 p.m.**

I finally reach the library with only moments to spare before it locks up for the day. Two young women, probably college students; are hurrying out as I rush inside. Caroline McCluskey is walking toward the nonfiction section, a load of books under her arm when I spot her. She may be the nicest lady in Magnolia Bluff, but she's not particularly pleased to see me.

She doesn't smile.

She doesn't say *hello.*

She blurts out, "Huston, we close in seventeen minutes, and I was hoping to get away a little early for a change."

"One quick question," I say, taking the books from under her arm and following along behind her.

"The quicker, the better."

"You told me Sylvia Spooner is a member of your Wednesday Night Reading club."

"She is."

"Sylvia tells me she's blind."

"Blind as a bat."

"Then why is she coming to a reading club?"

Caroline stops and turns around with a deep, exasperated breath. "We have seven ladies in the county, eight when Aunt Emma comes, who love to read but are legally blind. We have a small van that goes out, picks them up, brings them to the library, and I read to them. During the past three years, we have finished a dozen books. And while they listen, they can smell the faint aroma of ink and paper. It takes them back to an earlier time in their lives."

I am still perplexed.

"You should have told me Sylvia was blind."

"I didn't have a reason."

"Why not?"

"You didn't ask."

I know Caroline will want to shoot me, but I ask anyway. "I need the keys to the library one more time."

"Do you ever sleep?"

"Not anymore."

She reaches in her pocket and hands me the keys. "It's a small price to pay if I can go home a little early for a change."

I lock the door behind her and head back down the stairs.

I look at the shelf filled with microfilm files.

Don't need them.

Already read them.

I sit and let my eyes drift across each shelf.

Old magazines.

Old diaries.

Old family histories.

Old reference books.

Old genealogies.

Old yearbooks.

Old school newspapers.

I stop.

My eyes dart back to the yearbooks.

They're out of order.

Nothing's ever easy.

I wonder if I can find anything about Harley in the annual from 2003.

Big man on campus.

Football star.

Friday night hero.

It's slow going.

The images are old.

They're fading.

Print job wasn't very good.

I go page by page.
The heat has warped most of them.
The dampness has taken its toll.
I feel the dust on the pages beneath my fingers.
Spiders have left the remains of their webs.
On page fifty-seven, I stop.
A single photograph.
Full page.
I stare at it for a long time.
I should feel something.
I don't.
I gently close the yearbook.
No reason to look at another page.

# 40

**Tuesday**
**9:18 p.m.**

When you walk down dark sidewalks at night, through aging neighborhoods with no street lamps to pierce the shadows, the night begins to wrap its cloak tightly around your mind, so tight you can feel your eyes bulge and your throat grow dry. Above, the sky is black velvet adorned by more stars than you could count in a lifetime. A full moon hangs above the downtown square. Sometimes white, sometimes alabaster, sometimes reflecting the splintered glow of the sun. My eyes shift across the milky way, from the evening star to the big dipper and on to the mysterious layout of Orion. Every star is in its right place. The arrangement of the planets is in perfect order. But down on the sidewalk where I happen to be walking, everything is confused, chaotic, missing, and out of place. Mankind has made an awful mess of the earth. It's a quagmire where the truth sounds like a lie, and we guard our lies as though they are golden, and virtue is merely a crutch we lean on when we can no longer outrun the lie.

I walk into my apartment and am surprised to see a small lamp burning beside the bed. I shouldn't be surprised. It's something I've come to expect, maybe even a comfort and convenience I've been taking for granted.

Rebecca is lying in my bed, reading.

Her slacks have been neatly draped across the back of a chair.

Her blouse is folded neatly on the edge of the sofa.

The sheet has fallen to her waist.

She smiles as she closes the book.

"Where were you last night?" she asks.

"In the library."

"With the lovely Caroline McCluskey?"

"Alone."

"That's depressing." Rebecca chuckles.

She makes no attempt to hide her nakedness with the sheet.

Modesty is no longer a necessity.

"What were you doing?" she asks.

"Reading through old newspapers."

"Enlightening?"

"Depressing."

"Sounds like a wasted night," she says.

I drop wearily onto the sofa, an old yearbook in my lap.

"I kept your bed warm for you," she says.

"I should have been here," I tell her. "I would have been a lot better off if I were here."

She brushes a strand of dark hair out of her eyes. "What makes you say that?"

"I prefer being in the dark."

"And you're not in the dark anymore?" Her voice weakens. Her eyes grow wary.

I watch her.

Soft.

Lovely.

Tempting.

Deadly.

"Why did you lie to me, Rebecca?"

"What do you mean?"

"You told me you hardly knew Harley Spooner." It is an accusation.

She shrugs. "We were in high school together," she says. "That was a long time ago. I don't think your question deserves a long-winded answer. I was in school with a lot of boys. He was one of them."

I toss the yearbook on the bed beside her.

She stares at it.

She makes no attempt to open it.

"Go to page fifty-seven," I say.

She shakes her head.

"I don't have to," Rebecca says. "I know the picture you want me to see."

"Magnolia Bluff sweethearts." I spit the words out. "That's what the caption says. In love today. In love forever. The caption says that, too."

Rebecca's shoulders stiffen.

The softness in her face slides away.

Still lovely.

But tough and bitter and angry.

Her words are as harsh as mine.

"We were engaged to be married," she says. "Harley had a big football scholarship to Southern Methodist University. I had been accepted to a modeling school in Dallas. It would be a wonderful life, then the bastards took it all away from us."

"Harley was arrested for bootlegging."

"He was taking every job he could and packing the money away so I could live in an apartment in Dallas. Nothing fancy. Nothing expensive. I had plenty of money but couldn't touch my inheritance until I was twenty-one. That's what the fine print in the will said. That's what the judge said. Besides, Harley felt it would be cheap to live off my inheritance. He wanted to be able to pay for it all, and I wasn't about to step on is pride. He was scraping together every nickel and dime he was able to earn."

"Got caught with whiskey in his car."

"This town has an imaginary line between the social side of town and the poor side of town. The police know where it is. The police are the ones who drew it. Come from a rich home, a cop slaps you on the back and warns you not to do it again. Harley came from the wrong side. He was thrown in jail."

"And Judge Amos Fitzsimmons wouldn't let him out."

"Judge Amos Fitzsimmons should have been horsewhipped."

"Or worse."

"He deserved what he got."

Rebecca's eyes are firing bullets.

"Let me tell you what I know." I drop the yearbook on the floor beside me.

She glares at me.

I give her the facts as I know them in chronological order.

*Robert Baker was a bouncer out at LouEllen's Lounge. He hires Harley to help him do a little bootlegging, make a few extra dollars. Pick up the whiskey. Drive it out to Robert's barn. Stash it, probably behind a hay bale. Takes ten minutes or less. Easy money. A boy from the wrong side of town won't dare turn it down. So you dig a hole and drop Robert Baker in it. What did you do, Rebecca? Seduce him. Put him to sleep with a pill or a hammer? Ashes to ashes. Dust to Dust. Only one way. One way to die.*

I pause.

I think she may say something.

Rebecca's expression doesn't change.

I've seen faces on statutes that weren't as hard.

*Patrolman Charles Wegman catches Harley one night and finds the boy has a trunk full of booze. Maybe it's stolen. Maybe not. Doesn't matter. Harley's underage. He's arrested. Sees the inside of a jail cell for the first time. I'm sure Harley's full of remorse and regret. Nobody cares outside of you and Sylvia. Wegman is shot in the police station. As you wrote: "Never stray. Should have stayed." If Charles had stayed in the station on that night years ago, Harley would have never been arrested.*

*The judge keeps Harley in jail and refuses to let him out. Judge likes his power. Likes to throw his weight around. Show off for the movers and shakers and power brokers in town. Prove how tough he is on lawbreakers. No mercy. No quarter. Not even for a seventeen-year-old boy. Might as well have been Al Capone. Judge keeps Harley in a tiny little cell. Judge dies in a tiny little baptizing tank. I believe you put it this way: "No sign of grace. A tiny place. To suffocate."*

Her eyes darken.

Her face remains calm.

I blink.

She doesn't.

*Harley doesn't have a lot of money. He can't hire an attorney, so he's given a public defender. Carson McAlister is young and naïve, right out of law school. He doesn't yet know his way around the courthouse or the jailhouse. Judge plays him like a puppet swinging on a string. Carson doesn't do anything. He leaves Harley high and dry to fend for himself. Justice blindsides Harley, and Carson leaves him at the mercy of Judge Fitzsimmons. So you blindside Carson with a car, maybe a Jeep, probably stolen, and leave him dead or dying in the middle of the street. Another one lies. Another one dies. Blindsided. He failed. He sinned. He didn't care.*

Her lips twitch.

She leans forward.

I wait for Rebecca to speak.

The silence deepens.

*The high and mighty high school Principal Betty Gilmont suspends Harley from school. Sure, he can run the football, but the boy will never amount to anything. That's what she thinks. Boys from Harley's side of town never amount to anything. Harley's mother appeals the decision, and you're probably helping her every step of the way. Time to weep. In too deep. Time to leave. No time to breathe. She chokes the life out of your dream. You leave her choking with baling wire around her neck in twenty feet of swamp water.*

Rebecca grimaces.

It becomes a smile.

A strange smile.

She's remembering the night and the moment.

She seems to be enjoying every second of the memory.

*But School Board President Hank Dillard backs his principal and upholds the suspension. He's not involved. He doesn't want to be involved. Harley is not a human being. He's not really a student. To Hank, he's just another name on a piece of paper. Hank walks out on Harley. Big mistake. You cut off Hank's feet the night you poured poison down his throat. Look Away. Fly away. Walk away. Hank Dillard won't ever walk out on anyone else again.*

Her body tightens.

Is it a shiver?

Maybe.

She watches a fly crawl across the ceiling.

She shrugs.

Fly's trapped.

So is she.

*Coach Bobby Jenkins has no choice but to throw Harley off the football team, which, I'm afraid, throws his scholarship to Southern Methodist in the dumpster. He'll miss Harley. Won't have much of an offense without the boy. But it doesn't matter. I know. I checked the newspaper. Football team wasn't going to the playoffs. Had a losing record. Just run out the string and go fishing. That's all Jenkins was thinking. You had me confused about the coach, Rebecca. Why did you use a shotgun? Then I read where Harley had scored eight touchdowns, running from the shotgun formation. Strange. Insane, maybe. But it fits the way your mind fits things together. Roll the dice. What's the price of sacrifice? For Jenkins it was a high price to pay.*

"Sorry," she whispers.

"You sorry for what happened."

"He was a sorry football coach."

Her words are hard like nails.

"Newspaper said he won championships."

"Boys won championships." Rebecca finally blinks. "Bulldog just drove the bus."

*Judge Fitzsimmons hears a few complaints around town about the way he's treating the boy. I'm sure you were stirring up everybody you could. Judge doesn't like criticism. He has an election coming up. So how can he keep everybody happy? He decides to show how sympathetic he is to a boy down on his luck, so he gives Harley a chance to take the road out town. Out of sight. Out of mind. He works with Master Sergeant David Blankenship, agreeing to release the boy from jail if Harley enlists in the army. I'm sure you're not happy. But Harley agrees. He's out of options. You see that wonderful life all fading away. In reality, Blankenship was just an innocent bystander. But you didn't see it that way. You believed he sent Harley into a den of death where bullets were always buzzing around our heads. You used a rope, a noose. A death. A den. You left the sergeant to twist in the wind. Poetic justice.*

Rebecca's eyes brighten.

They have a sheen.

Like glass in the moonlight.

Have I struck a nerve?

*I'm sure you waited like a faithful wife to be for your soldier boy to come home. Even when word came that Harley was missing in action, you had hope. The days turned to months, the months to years, and the memories of you and Harley and the life you planned together began to fade. But you held on. You held on to your dreams, and your expectations became little more than a pipe dream. And you died a little more each day.*

*Then came the letter.*

*Harley was dead.*

"He shouldn't have died," Rebecca whispers.

A tear glistens on her eyelashes.

"He shouldn't have gone to war," she whispers.

The tear slips down to her cheek.

"He should have been here with me," she says.

*What you didn't know, what the army didn't tell you, Harley had died ten years earlier.*

*I was there.*

*You would have been proud of him.*

*I don't know what might have snapped, Rebecca, but something did.*

*You blamed a bootlegger, a policeman, a judge, an attorney, a principal, a football coach, a school board president, and an army recruiter for your loss.*

*And they all had to die.*

*You wanted to cleanse your soul with their blood.*

I wait for Rebecca to respond.

I want her to tell me I'm crazy.

I want her to defend herself.

I want her to deny everything I've said.

I want her to prove me wrong.

She doesn't.

I wish I had a bourbon.

She's heartbroken.

I'm heartbroken.

Finally, she speaks. "Do you blame me?" she asks simply.

I don't.

She says, "What are you going to do now, Huston?"

I look into her eyes.

I don't recognize them anymore.

They're as fractured as her dreams.

"You're a beautiful woman," I answer softly. "You're smart. You're ambitious. You're a great society editor and even better at selling advertising. You and I could publish the *Chronicle* side by side for the rest of our lives, probably turn it into an outstanding newspaper. Who knows? We might even fall in love, might even get married, and you would probably wind up as Woman of the Year."

She doesn't blink.

Her smile is gone.

I don't think it's coming back.

"But you murdered nine people, Rebecca. There's a price to pay for that."

"I have no regrets." She's speaking in a tiny, faraway voice I've never heard before.

"One question."

She waits.

"Why Mister Holland? He treated you like a daughter."

She curls her lips into a sneer. "I was desperate. I went to Neal and begged him to write an editorial asking the judge to turn Harley loose, to give Harley a second chance. Harley had never been in trouble. He had never even been given a ticket for speeding. He deserved a second chance."

"Neal didn't help you, did he?"

"Turned a deaf ear. Said Harley wasn't worth the trouble. Said he didn't want to upset the applecart. Those were his words. Well, to hell with his applecart. I probably hated Neal worse than any of them. I knew I couldn't count on anyone else. But I believed he would help me, maybe even turn out to be a crusading journalist. Might even pay Harley's bail. Might even lend me money to pay his bail. But he turned out to be as worthless as the rest of them."

Rebecca reaches under the pillow and pulls out a pistol. Looks like a 9mm Beretta. I'm sure the clip is full. The automatic is pointed squarely between my eyes. At least, from here, it sure looks that way.

Her hand is steady.

She's killed nine.

What's one more?

"I hope you don't think you can take me in," she says. She's out of bed now, pulling on her slacks, taking her own precious time to button her shirt, which isn't the easiest thing to do with a Beretta in your hand. She slides her feet into a pair of black heels. Beautiful shoes, I guess. Not much for running.

"Turning you over to the police was never my intention," I tell her.

"You're just going to let me walk out of here?"

"I've checked my choices." I smile. "That's the best one I've got."

She stops just long enough to kiss my cheek.

Then Rebecca is through the door and gone.

I sit in silence and wait.

I expect to hear a gunshot.

Maybe more than one.

I don't.

I guess Buck Blanton has taken her into custody without incident.

He's been waiting at the end of the block since nine o'clock unless, of course, he grew tired and went home.

He didn't.

# 41

**Wednesday**
**5:34 a.m.**

I have the special edition of the *Chronicle* printed and stacked on a bench outside the office by the time Magnolia Bluff wakes up at daybreak.

One page.

Printed on one side.

No advertising.

Losing money on this one.

Don't care.

The story is simple and to the point.

The headline is 128-point type in all of its glory.

*IT'S OVER.*

That's all the headline says.

Here's the rest of the story.

*May we never fear May Twenty Third again.*

*The killing has ended.*

*The killer is in custody.*

*It's a sad tale.*

*A heartbroken woman.*

*A boy done wrong.*

*A town that forgot.*

*A town that didn't care.*

*Now it does.*

*But it doesn't have to worry anymore.*

*Rebecca Wilson charged with murder.*

*Taken into custody by Sheriff Buck Blanton.*

I use two photographs.

The face of a beautiful woman.

The black, burly face of a county sheriff.

Both are smiling.

One has a reason.

The other doesn't.

I spill out what I know over coffee at the Silver Spoon and leave Lorraine crying when I go. Maybe's she's sad, maybe just relieved to know the truth. I don't ask. I just pat her arm and walk out the door.

I decide the good folks of Magnolia Bluff can ferret out the details from the gossips and rumor mongers running loose with tongues wagging in beauty salons, coffee shops, a Bed and Breakfast, and on the downtown streets. It's a grand day for the Crimson Hat ladies. It'll keep Mary Lou Fight and her gang digging up dirt 'til autumn leaves hit the ground again. From a distance, the noise sounds like bumblebees trading stingers on a hornet's nest.

They'll do a better job with the rest of the story than I can.

# EPILOGUE

**Thursday**
**5:24 a.m.**

The three of us walk up the hill to the cemetery at daybreak.

Sylvia Spooner.

Father Lee Gorman.

And me.

Sylvia rests her hand on my shoulder, and I step slowly to make sure she doesn't lose her footing on the gravel, loose rocks, and dried twigs that litter the pathway. I can hear her muttering to herself. It's probably a prayer, a long one.

The morning's quiet.

The birds have quit singing. I believe they respect the reverence of the moment. Birds have an intuition and a compassion that the rest of us may seek but seldom find.

I had knocked on Father Lee's office door late yesterday. He and I had seen each other around town a time or two. We had not yet met.

I'm not Catholic.

He's not heathen.

We had nothing in common, did not hang out in the same places, and never had a lot of chances to cross paths.

He was young and looked to be right out of seminary, or wherever Catholics go to learn about homilies and preaching and singing in Latin. Dark hair. Fair complexion. He didn't spend a lot of time in the sun, and confessionals had never been a good source for tans. He was known for his charm and energy, and he could always see the lighter side of life, especially in time of crisis. But when it came to his religion, he was as devout as anyone in Magnolia Bluff, which obviously wasn't saying much.

"I have a rather unusual request," I told him.

He sat back in his chair and waited.

"Early tomorrow morning," I continued, "I would like for you to say a few words over the burial of a fallen soldier."

"A funeral?"

"More or less."

He frowned.

I'm sure he thought I was somewhat slightly off center.

Maybe even crazy.

Wouldn't blame him a bit.

"His name is Harley Spooner," I said.

"I don't recognize the name." Father Lee leaned forward, his brow filled with wrinkles, and placed both elbows on his desk.

"He was a good Catholic boy, a hometown boy."

"You knew him then?"

"He and I were together when he was shot."

"Where?"

"Afghanistan."

"When was that?"

"Eighteen years, six months, and twenty-one days ago."

Father Lee casually thumbed through a big leather-bound copy of the Bible while he tried to think of exactly the right words to say.

"Have they shipped Harley's body home?" he asked finally.

I shook my head.

"His body won't be shipped." I feel my voice waver. "His body was never found."

"This is highly unusual," he said.

"I said it would be."

"Do we need to reserve the chapel?" Father Lee asked, his voice slipping respectfully into a tone of reverence.

"The service will be in the cemetery."

"Graveside?"

I nodded.

"When?"

"As soon as the sun gets ready to show up for the day."

"Is it a memorial service?"

I shrug and take a deep breath. "It will be if you're there."

His voice became a whisper. "What are we burying?"

"A memory."

"Are we allowed to do what you're planning to do?" Still a whisper.

"Probably not."

"Good," he said, rubbing the palms of his hands together. "I'll meet you at the cemetery gate at five o'clock."

"I really appreciate it," I said.

"I wouldn't miss being there for the world."

I handed Father Lee a few words I had written about Harley, thanked him again, and walked out into the sunlight.

NOW IT IS dark. But we see a faint streak of gold filtering its way through the trees and crawling up the backside of the hill. Unlike the rest of us, the sun is almost always on time, even when it hides behind the rain.

I kneel upon a small barren patch of dirt and leaves beside Freddy's grave. I remove a small spade from my hip pocket and dig a hole about a foot deep and four inches wide.

Father Lee reads the twenty-third psalm.

He expresses a few words in Latin.

Don't know what he's saying.

Not important.

He's speaking to God.

God's listening.

I'm just eavesdropping.

I remove Harley Spooner's dog tags from around my neck, say a short and silent prayer, place them down in the hole, then wait a moment before I cover them with handfuls of dirt and rocks and rotting leaves.

Sylvia says briefly: "Harley was mine for a little while. I needed him more than anything on earth. God must need him more than I do."

She squeezes my hand tightly. Her words are sodden with grief.

Father Lee speaks gloriously of Harley as if he and Harley had been lifelong friends. He quotes briefly from the notes I had left him:

*Harley Spooner didn't walk with us for long, but he will walk through our hearts forever. He died because he loved his country. He died because it was his duty to defend his country. He died to keep us free. We will miss him and pray for him and often wonder if his death was in vain.*

*Amen.*

We are halfway down the hillside when I detect movement out of the corner of my eye and hear the deep, no-nonsense baritone voice of Sheriff Buck Blanton.

"I see what you did," he said.

"Freddy's not alone anymore," I say.

"Freddy always needed a friend."

"He and Harley have a lot to talk about."

"He and Harley know what we don't know yet."

"About dying?"

"About how precious life is."

I can see Buck grinning in the dim light.

"You know what you did is illegal as hell," he says. "I think they call it defacing the cemetery, maybe even conducting a burial without a plot. Probably constitutes theft if you don't own that little strip of ground."

"You planning to arrest me?"

"I could," Buck says. He winks. "I should. But I'm not here."

He slips back into the dark.

I take Sylvia's hand and place it on Father Lee's shoulder, then I wander back up the hill to sit for a while with Harley. He hasn't met Freddy yet and probably needs an introduction. They have a long time to spend together.

**Wednesday**
**10:06 p.m.**

WARS ARE FOUGHT.

Wars are won.

Wars are lost.

Wars never end.

We think they do, but they don't.

Too many times, the most difficult wars of all are fought across the landscape of our own psyche, a battlefield scarred by grief and angst, anger and sometimes retribution.

Never a truce.

Never a surrender.

Every night about ten, I'll lay down, close my eyes, and wait for the bullet meant for me.

I know it's coming.

Don't know when.

Harley won't be around to catch it this time, not like he was eighteen years, six months, and twenty-two days ago.

# SNEAK PREVIEW OF THE GREAT PEANUT BUTTER CONSPIRACY

## BY CINDY DAVIS

**Book 2 in the Magnolia Bluff Crime Chronicles**

## CHAPTER ONE

## BANK OF BAD HABITS

For almost four hundred miles I've been tooling along belting out the lyrics to my favorite Jimmy Buffett songs—well, one at a time, of course—any other way would be dumb. I no sooner bark *money don't mean nothin' to me* when my scooter shoots out a boisterous belching sound. I like that word: boisterous. It says so many things in just the proper number of syllables. Right now, it means the motor has stopped in a big way. One explosive belch and a horrific stench of manifold-seared oil, and the road comes to an abrupt halt.

I'm surrounded by a boisterous amount of greenery. The only thing breaking the expanse of lime-green, jade-green, pea-green, and emerald—you get the picture—is a mile-wide once-white billboard. Apparently my journey has ended in a place called Magnolia Bluff, Texas. Jeez-looweez. Really? An image forms in my head: a grove of giant sweet-smelling trees under which are seated an anthology of ancient people in rocking chairs, some crocheting and some puffing corncob pipes, forties music wafting on the breeze. Scratch that, there is NO breeze. Nada, zilch, zippo.

I stifle a shiver and rub down the goosebumps that pop up all the way to my toes. For whatever it's worth, and the fact that I seem to have no other options, I slide off the bike, pluck the wedgie from my cargo shorts, and start pushing, and reading: *Welcome to Magnolia Bluff, Texas. Home of Burnet Reservoir.*

Underneath is a list of the town's perks to sweeten a traveler's expectations, or perhaps to keep them from u-turning and heading back the way they came. The joke's on them right now, isn't it, because u-turning isn't an option for me.

Stretched from one telephone pole to another across the road is a giant banner.

**Magnolia Bluff**
**47th Annual Persimmon Festival**
**June 2–9**

I gotta start with a question. What the heck is a persimmon? Is it a sport? Can I sit on sun-heated bleachers and watch persimmons in different color uniforms duke it out on a grass-green field? I've heard of festivals featuring a particular kind of flower, bundles of them lined up on long tables and judged by the shape of the display and use of color. Can you arrange persimmons in a vase? I've heard of Seafood Festivals where all sorts of ocean-grown food is deep-fried and served in cardboard bowls dripping with grease. Is a persimmon a creature we can roll in breading and dunk in fry-oil? I get no answer for these meanderings, so I leave them for now and peruse the rest of the sign.

*Costumes*—Where does one get a persimmon costume? I mean, being that it's already the 4th of June, wouldn't the best costumes be taken already?

*Face painting contests*—I've never been to a festival before, so another question arises: how do you paint persimmons on a person's face. Or wait! Maybe they paint people's faces on the persimmons. Yes, that makes far more sense. Sort of like carving pumpkins.

*Parades and floats*—This conjures images of Rose Bowls and Macy's that keep people glued to the boob tube for hours. Where persimmons fit in…no idea.

*Rides*—Perhaps this could be more specific. Would rides be on camels, bicycles, or zero gravity cylinders? Personally I vote for the latter. But somehow I doubt that's what's available in a place called Magnolia Bluff.

*Crafts*—I conjure tables selling crocheted doilies, keychains, and bath bombs smelling like, um…persimmons, and stifle a shiver.

*Music and dancing*—Normally I'm all for any kind of music, except maybe rap and opera, and dancing is my most fave thing to do in the world, but I get a visual of oompah tunes being burped out by men wearing leather lederhosen. This is after all, German hill country, correct?

*Pie eating contests*—I'm growing more interested by the minute. Then I realize, it might just be pies made from persimmons. My stomach does a flip-flop.

*Food*—Now my attention is riveted. In response, and quite predictable under any circumstances—read that ANY circumstances—my stomach growls. Which makes sense since I haven't eaten since a bag of stale chips in my tent beside a babbling brook in East Hicksville, Louisiana. I know you're wondering if that was the town's actual name on the sign, and the answer is no; they probably didn't want to sour a traveler's anticipation.

I lose track of the rest of the promo for the festival's perks because a new scene is playing in my head: a ginormous pepperoni and jalapeno pizza being delivered by a tuba-toting centenarian wearing suspenders arched around a paunchy stomach. I shake off the shiver of dread. Hopefully, one person in this town of rocking chair jockeys has heard of the Italian delicacy called pizza. Revving my bike-pushing muscles, I move on.

My name is Bliss. That's it, just Bliss. Most of you folks have probably figured I'm between homes. Long story you don't need to hear right now. Maybe never, as it's not very interesting. Suffice to say, all that matters is where I am at this moment.

This morning I woke, as has happened every day since leaving home, with Jimmy Buffett lyrics playing on a loop in my head. I hummed along: *I'm nobody from nowhere you'd have ever heard of anyway. Ain't no city way down there…* Hmm. The message seems spot-on considering that billboard, but before I can think too much more about it, I spy another sign attached to the roof of a building. It's pretty beaten-up by weather: *Doyle's Garage.*

I squint but can't make out the smaller print until another hundred feet have passed. By now I'm sweating like the proverbial pig. If I sag to my knees and crawl toward the crusty once-red but now a corrupt shade of pink building, maybe someone will run out with a moisture-coated bottle of water to dislodge the mud clogging my throat. Seems like all it's done is rain since I crossed the Louisiana border. My wish doesn't manifest. What does happen: a car shoots by throwing up a tornado of mud-clumps…so many that the road grows invisible. I slog through the almost-solid barrier.

By now, sweat drips from every crevice, and I enter a wet t-shirt contest I'll lose even though I'm the only participant. Need I say more? Rivers trickle along the roots of my hair and down into my eyes. My vision is blurred, but it's easy to tell Doyle's garage is huge and the yard is crammed with cars of every description. Must be in the right place.

I nearly trip over a pair of Converse-clad feet protruding from under a Dodge Power Wagon about the same color as the garage. The feet twitch. A muffled voice calls, "I'll be right out."

"No hurry," I say because what else can you say at time like this? "Hurry, I'm about to pass out from heat exhaustion!" or "It's fine, you can find me prostrate against that rusted-out Pinto." I thought Pintos went out with the Pony Express. I chuckle at my dumb joke, glad no one's in my head to intercept it.

The heels dig into the tarmac; the stained denim-wrapped legs perform an elaborate shimmy, then the body rolls from under the truck. Inch by inch, a person encased in a baggy t-shirt bearing *I Am the Warranty* appears, and it's immediately apparent that her assets have been a lot more liberally applied than mine, and my ego takes a hit. Then I feel a little better noticing she is sweating too, and it's not a pretty sight. It forms circles under the arms and down the center of her chest; the curly brown hair looks oily and not all that feminine.

She hops from the dolly to her feet in one envy-inspiring motion, like a gymnast, rakes grungy fingers through her hair, and blinks at the intrusion of daylight in her deep brown eyes. I always wanted eyes that color. For a while I tried colored contact lenses but they kept falling out, so I settled for my pale blues staring back at me each morning.

A hand appears in my peripheral and I take hold of it. Then, a thought comes at me as to whether the grease will transfer to my flesh like an uninvited germ. Too late, so I give a hearty squeeze.

"I'm Ciara." She points to the sign high over us. "Ciara Doyle."

"Bliss." From her possessive tone, I make an assessment that might bring a snort of derision so I head-gesture in a generic direction meant to include the yard. "You own the place?"

No snort. Just an emphatic nod. "Sure do. And before you ask why a stunning creature like me spends my time swimming in grease and oil…let's just say it was the only course left at the technical school."

Behind her words is surely another story, but it's not coming out today. This is a-okay with me because I don't have time to get involved in people's backstories. Which is another joke because in reality I have all the time in the world. These days, I'm on a highway to nowhere. I laugh again because Magnolia Bluff appears to be just that—nowheresville.

Ciara points at my bike. "You got trouble?"

"Wow, you must be psychic." The words pop from the mouth before the brain can filter them. No surprise here. This happens a lot. To say the feature that came standard with this model has gotten me into trouble is probably clear enough.

Ciara doesn't miss a beat. "I've been told I'm good at deductive reasoning." She steps around me and crouches beside my new-to-me bike, her nose contracting and expanding in search of the odor that's pouring off it like month-old fish bait.

A big dog, the same color as the road-mud, shuffles from

the shade of the garage. He squints at the sunshine the same way his owner did, plants big shaggy feet, and shakes, nearly toppling over with the intensity. Mud balls pepper the air similar to the volley from the passing traffic. Traffic being a broad term since the only thing to pass was the one coating me in grime as I entered town. The dog finishes blinking. He spots the dripping wet stranger and saunters in my direction, tail beating a metronomic rhythm with his feet. He never makes it to me. Apparently the ten-foot distance is too much in this heat. Or maybe I didn't smell interesting enough. I chuckle internally. More likely he got the aroma all the way over there and decided up-close-and-personal was a bad idea. He swings around and retreats back into his cave. A huge part of me wants to follow.

As if reading our minds, Ciara says over her shoulder, "There's a fridge in the office. Help yourself to a water."

Not waiting for a second invitation, I track the dog's footsteps until he disappears under a black car perched on a lift. This girl is no dummy; no way the fridge is over there, so I locate it in a too-neat-for-words office. I mean, really, our maids didn't keep the bathrooms this clean. Stepping from my too-personal backstory, I suck down an entire bottle, crumple the empty and toss it in a pail with others in similar condition. I bring one out to Ciara who's standing beside my bike, hands on ample hips. She nods thanks and tips the bottle high. After she's screwed the top back on, she says, "I have to order some parts. You wanna know what's wrong with it?"

I give a light chuckle and a head-shake. She really must be psychic. Somehow she knows the information would tinkle around inside my brain then get lost in the void.

"Might take a couple-a days…"

I want to ask if I'll need to take out a loan, like that's even possible, but, worse-case-scenario I find a job to pay it off. Maybe Ciara needs someone—I shoot a glance around the place. No thanks, not even for big furry dog cuddles.

I shrug. "I got nothin' but time so long as there's a pizza place here, cuz, next to peanut butter, it's the best food on the planet."

She gestures left and then wiggles an index finger. I take

that to mean it's to the left then down a side street, and set off with a fake jaunty step to my overheated body. After all, there's a prize at the end.

Since I have no cell phone, I call over my shoulder, "How will you find me?"

She gives a hearty chuckle. "Our gossip hotline works faster than the speed of light. If I need you, you'll hear about it. The good news is that if the hotline is working on schedule, your pizza should be waiting on the table."

A few hundred feet along Main Street, using the Town Hall as a dividing point, the road separates around a grassy area called...Town Square. Unique, right? I move to the left side, which is East Main, and pass the expected stores: restaurant, pharmacy, hairdresser, coffee shop, etc. Lots more along West Main scream for further exploration, but the stomach buzzes in a boisterous way, so I stride past them all, ducking my head against the bright afternoon sun wishing I remembered my sunglasses on the bike.

Moments later, I have good news and bad news. Which do you want first? Okay, good news first...I find the pizza restaurant in record time. The bad news? Food is not waiting. This doesn't bode well for me hearing when my bike is fixed, but the aromas send my senses into full-out starvation mode.

I plant my butt in a yellow vinyl booth near the window so I can people-watch. A female server—when did they stop calling them waitresses—starts in my direction, but a customer keels over and she's got to stop or trip on her. She crouches beside the woman. When she doesn't pull out her pad to take the person's order, I realize something's wrong.

"Help," she calls, "does anyone know CPR?"

As a matter of fact...

I leap from the booth and race over. The woman's face is—I'll spare you the gory details. "Help me sit her up." I grab one upper arm and the server takes hold of the other. We quickly get the woman upright. Again, sparing the messy details...just know the food-clog shoots from her mouth and lands on the brand new looking shoes of her partner standing anxiously nearby. Nobody but me seems to notice. The woman gasps her first full breath in a while, straightens her spine, and glances over her shoulder into my face. I help her up. "Glad you're okay," I say and head back to my seat.

Menus are jammed into a holder that also corrals the condiments: red pepper flakes, grated cheese, and oregano. It's good to keep them contained so they can't get away. The server—my accomplice in Heimlich-land—arrives bearing a glass of water and a wide smile. Right behind her is a pudgy woman toting a similar toothy grin. Normally I'd return the tooth-show—my childhood orthodontics can compete with the best of them—but my attention is otherwise engaged by the most boisterously decorated pizza I've ever seen. She sets it on the table on a tin plate that takes up most all the space.

"I hope you like jalapenos and pepperoni." She slides in across from me.

Shock and awe take control of my body. Pepperoni is probably the most common topping for a pie, but jalapenos? How could she know I'd been drooling over this combination all afternoon? Now I wonder in all seriousness about the aforementioned gossip hotline. Or whether everyone in Magnolia Bluff is psychic.

I gesture toward the pizza. "Help me eat this?"

She smiles, showing a mouthful of white square teeth similar to the pudgy server—probably made that way by an expensive orthodontist when she was a gangly teen. Gangly she's not any more. But she gives off an air of class, like she would be comfortable in a room full of people.

"I'm Olivia. I own the place."

She head-points toward the middle of the room. The Heimlich-victim and her not-so-new-shoed-anymore partner have since departed for more heady entertainment—pun intended—but the significance of the gesture is clear. She provided the pizza as a thank you. I'm okay with this, but still in shock as to how she knew what toppings to add. I frown, thinking back. Did I mention anything to Ciara at the garage? It might be possible the supervisor of the gossip grapevine phoned ahead. But, no, pretty sure all I said was I craved pizza.

"I haven't seen you in Magnolia Bluff before," Olivia says,

thereby demonstrating her psychic ability. She smiles. "Sooner or later, everyone ends up here. We have the best pizza in town."

"Let me guess, you have the only pizza in town."

"There is that." She again motions toward the center of the room. "For that, you get pizza for life."

"Wow. Totally not necessary." She puckers her lips at me so I relent. We are, after all, talking about pizza. "Thanks."

Olivia helps herself to a slice, biting into the crust first, the same way I do. It's the best way to test the quality of someone's pizza-making skills. A snake of cheese comes loose and dangles from her upper lip. I wait while she winds it around her tongue and sucks it into her mouth. She folds the remainder of the monster piece and leans over it to ask, "Who does your hair? The blonde streaky look is amazing."

I point upward. "Mr. Sunshine. It's natural."

"They gotta bottle that. So, how long are you staying in our fair town?"

"Till my bike gets fixed."

"You leave it with Ciara?"

"Yeah."

"Good deal. I meant what I said about pizza for life."

No answer seems needed, especially since I'll be gone way before I can take advantage. She probably knows this—that's why she feels confident in her offer. I take another bite. Her attention aims at something out the window. I turn to see a dark blue uniform poured over a most impressive-shaped torso, and hair just long enough to twine fingers through. The word "whoa" slips from my lips before I can clamp them together. I cover by plucking a slice of pepperoni, topping it with a jalapeno, tipping my head back, and sliding them into my mouth.

Olivia laughs. "My thoughts exactly. That's Chief Tommy Jager. He's been on the force, for lack of a better word, for about two years. Transferred from a small town south of here."

How far south can you go from here? A truly unspeakable answer comes into my head. Before it can root itself someplace unmentionable, I shake it off and pose the original question out loud.

"Brownsville," she says. "It's on the Mexican border."

"That is south, for sure."

The chief isn't handsome in the sense of a blond California surfboard junkie. He's more like a cross between a young Clint Eastwood and Mark Wahlberg. He walks as if his pockets are full of gold coins—a kind of swagger. What I can't figure from here is whether it's natural or movie-fake. I will find out though.

Once the chief is out of sight, I spot a man and woman across the main street in front of the pharmacy. I don't know how, but I can actually see their anger. It's not the body language or the hand waving, there's an actual cloud around them. It's red, and yet not red—kind of like mud's mixed in—and not the mud from the road. I understand right off that I'm seeing an aura. Which person it belongs to, I'm not sure. Maybe it's both of them. I've never seen an aura before, and the only thing I know about them is they reflect a person's emotions. In this case, there's no doubt what I'm witnessing is anger.

"They're probably *discussing* the strip mall," Olivia explains. "It's the only thing that's gotten people riled in a long time. A long time."

I left-roll my eyes toward her.

"Long story short, Phineas Henry owns the pharmacy." She points diagonally to a tan building with cocoa-brown trim. "His brother-in-law, Merrick Doyle, rest his soul, owned Doyle's General Store a couple of blocks east. You probably passed it on your way here. Anyway, Merrick began stocking many of the items people once went out of their way to get at the pharmacy. This took business from Phineas, so, being the entrepreneurial guy he is, he decided to build a place a block back from the general store. This meant he had to purchase three separate lots of land. The trouble was, Merrick owned the final piece he needed to make the project work."

I see where this is going. "Merrick wouldn't sell."

"Right. And it divided the town."

"Until he died." I purse my lips as a thought occurs. "How did he die?"

"The coroner's report said natural causes due to nicotine poisoning."

Wait for it…

"I believe, somehow, someway, somebody close to all of us killed him."

# ABOUT THE AUTHOR

Caleb Pirtle III is an award-winning author who may live in the present, but he prefers the past. He is happiest when he digging down beneath mounds of antiquated newspapers, diaries, and other research materials to track down information that become part of his historical mysteries and historical thrillers. He believes that good fiction is always built on nuggets of truth.

Pirtle has been writing all of his life and has published more than 85 books, mostly nonfiction travel and historical books. He began working with newspapers, both large and small, including the Fort Worth Star-Telegram. He was hired to handle travel publicity for Texas when Governor John Connally created the Texas Tourist Development Agency and moved on to become the first travel editor for Southern Living Magazine. He later served as editorial director for a Dallas custom publisher and began writing fiction about ten years ago.

Pirtle's Boomtown Saga includes three novels about the discovery of oil in a mythical East Texas town during the Great Depression. Oil begat money. Money begat greed. And greed begat murder in *Back Side of a Blue Moon, Bad Side of a Wicked Moon,* and *Lost Side of an Orphan's Moon.*

His Ambrose Lincoln series follows the exploits of a government agent whose mind and memory were erased by electrical shocks during the beginning of World War II. If a man has no memory, he has no fear and will tackle missions go places where the sane would never venture. The thrillers include *Secrets of the Dead, Conspiracy of Lies, Night Side of Dark,* and *Place of Skulls.*

Pirtle's Man on the Run series features a rogue CIA agent who walked away from the agency and became a wanted man. His battles may be freelanced and unsanctioned but still need to be fought in *Lovely Night to Die, Rainy Night to Die,* and *Lonely Night to Die.*

Pirtle grew up in Kilgore, a small town that became a boomtown during the Great Depression. He majored in Journalism at The University of Texas and became the first student to ever with the National William Randolph Hearst Award for feature writing. Much of his life is covered in his memoir of sorts, *The Man Who Talks to Strangers,* and his travel writing can be found in *Confessions from the Road.* His *XIT: The American Cowboy* was produced with members of the Texas Artist Association and became the third best-selling art book of all time.

Pirtle presently lives with his life Linda, a cozy mystery author, in Fort Worth, Texas.

Contact Caleb at calebpirtle2@gmail.com. He would love to hear from you.

Visit their website at https://www.calebandlindapirtle.com to learn about some of the best books and writers in today's literary marketplace. Check out his other titles, available in eBook and print editions.

## THE BOOMTOWN SAGA

*Back Side of a Blue Moon*
*Bad Side of a Wicked Moon*
*Lost Side of an Orphan's Moon*

## AMBROSE LINCOLN SERIES

*Secrets of the Dead*
*Conspiracy of Lies*
*Night Side of Dark*
*Place of Skulls*

## MAN ON THE RUN SERIES

*Lovely Night to Die*
*Rainy Night to Die*
*Lonely Night to Die*

## THE MAGNOLIA BLUFF CRIME CHRONICLES

*Eulogy in Black and White*

## PSYCHOLOGICAL THRILLERS

Last Deadly Lie
Friday Nights Don't Last Forever

## WESTERNS

*The Gambler Series*
*Dead Man's Hand*
*Jokers Are Wild*

## MEMOIR

*The Man Who Talks to Strangers*
*Selected Works of Nonfiction*
*Gamble in the Devil's Chalk*
*Confessions from the Road*
*XIT: The American Cowboy*
*Fort Worth: The Civilized West*
*The Trail of Broken Promises*
*Dark Side of the Rainbow*

## SPORTS BOOKS

*No Experience Required*
*Never Afraid, Never a Doubt*
*The A Game: The Greatest Moments in the History of Alabama Football*

## TRAVEL BOOKS

*Texas: Its Lore and Its Lure*
*The Texas Outback*
*The Unending Season*
*The Grandest Day*
*Where the Stars Are Always Shining*
*Georgia Through the Looking Glass*
*Tennessee Through the Looking Glass*

## KILGORE HISTORICAL SERIES

*Echoes from Forgotten Streets*
*Visions of Forgotten Streets*
*The Unforgettable Streets of Kilgore*

CROSSROAD
PRESS

Made in the USA
Middletown, DE
26 September 2022

11134611R00170